JANIE FACE TO FACE

NOVELS BY CAROLINE B. COONEY

The Lost Songs
Three Black Swans
They Never Came Back
If the Witness Lied
Diamonds in the Shadow
A Friend at Midnight
Hit the Road
Code Orange
The Girl Who Invented Romance
Family Reunion
Goddess of Yesterday
The Ransom of Mercy Carter
Tune In Anytime
Burning Up
What Child Is This?
Driver's Ed
Twenty Pageants Later
Among Friends
The Time Travelers, Volumes I and II

THE JANIE BOOKS
The Face on the Milk Carton
Whatever Happened to Janie?
The Voice on the Radio
What Janie Found
What Janie Saw (an ebook original story)
Janie Face to Face

THE TIME TRAVEL QUARTET
Both Sides of Time
Out of Time
Prisoner of Time
For All Time

JANIE FACE TO FACE

caroline b. cooney

EMBER

Text copyright © 2013 by Caroline B. Cooney
Cover photographs copyright © 2013 by IZO/Shutterstock (frame) and Giorgio Fochesato/Getty Images (figures)

All rights reserved. Published in the United States by Ember, an imprint of Random House Children's Books, a division of Random House LLC, a Penguin Random House Company, New York. Originally published in hardcover in the United States by Delacorte Press, an imprint of Random House Children's Books, New York, in 2013.

Ember and the E colophon are registered trademarks of Random House LLC.

Visit us on the Web! randomhouse.com/teens
Educators and librarians, for a variety of teaching tools,
visit us at RHTeachersLibrarians.com

The Library of Congress has cataloged the hardcover edition of this work as follows:
Cooney, Caroline B.
Janie face to face / Caroline B. Cooney — 1st ed.
p. cm.
Summary: At college in New York City, Janie Johnson, aka Jennie Spring, seems to have successfully left behind her past as "The face on the milk carton," but soon she, her families, and friends are pursued by a true-crime writer who wants their help in telling her kidnapper's tale.
ISBN 978-0-385-74206-1 (trade hardcover) — ISBN 978-0-375-99039-7 (glb) — ISBN 978-0-375-97997-2 (ebk) — ISBN 978-0-385-37137-7 (intl. tr. pbk.)
[1. Kidnapping—Fiction. 2. Authorship—Fiction. 3. Universities and colleges—Fiction. 4. Love—Fiction. 5. Identity—Fiction. 6. Family life—New Jersey—Fiction. 7. Family life—Connecticut—Fiction. 8. New York (N.Y.)—Fiction.]
I. Title
PZ7.C7834Jan 2013
[Fic]—dc23
2012006145

ISBN 978-0-385-74207-8 (tr. pbk.)
RL: 5.3

Printed in the United States of America
10 9 8 7 6 5 4 3 2
First Ember Edition 2014

Random House Children's Books supports the First Amendment
and celebrates the right to read.

To my grandchildren
Elizabeth
Margaret
Maximus
Simon

THE FIRST PIECE OF THE KIDNAPPER'S PUZZLE

The woman who had once been Hannah barely remembered that day in New Jersey.

It was so many years ago, and anyway, it had been an accident.

It happened because she was driving east. There was no reason to head east. But when she stole the car and wanted to get out of the area quickly, she took the first interstate ramp she saw. It was eastbound.

She had never stolen a car before. It was as much fun as drugs. The excitement was so great that she had not needed sleep or rest or even meals.

Everybody else driving on the turnpike had experience and knew what they were doing. But although the woman once known as Hannah was thirty, she had done very little driving.

Back when she was a teenager and everybody else was learning to drive, her cruel parents had never bought her a car. They rarely let her drive the family car either. They said

1

she was immature. And in the group she joined, only the leaders had cars.

She found the group during her freshman year at college. She hated college. She hated being away from home and she hated her parents for making her go to college. Even more, she hated admitting defeat.

The group had embraced Hannah. Inside the group, she did not have to succeed or fail. There were no decisions and no worries. She did not have to choose one of those frightening things called a career. Her parents—those people from her past—had always been on her case about her future. Always demanding that she consider her skills and abilities.

Hannah did not want to consider things.

She wanted other people to consider.

While she was still useful to the group, earning money and getting new converts, she kept the name they had given her. But time passed and the group disbanded. Its members ended up on the street. She found herself homeless and helpless, and she needed another name. For a while she called herself Tiffany. Then she tried Trixie.

In the years that followed, she made use of stolen paperwork. She was pretty good at lifting the wallets of careless college kids in coffee shops. They had too much anyway. They needed to share.

After many hours on that turnpike in that stolen car, Hannah was amazed by a sign reading WELCOME TO NEW JERSEY. She had crossed the entire country. If the road kept going, it would bump into the Atlantic Ocean. She stopped for gas. Now the signs gave directions for the Jersey Shore.

During her childhood in Connecticut, her family used to go to the beach. She didn't mind the sand, but her parents always wanted her to learn how to swim. Swimming was scary, and she refused to try, but her parents were the kind of people who forced you to do scary things. She still hated them for it. The group had told her not to worry about her mother and father. Parents were nothing; the group was her family.

No. She would not go to the beach today, because it reminded her of things better forgotten.

She got back on the interstate. It was difficult to merge with traffic. She crept along the shoulder for a while until there was finally a space. She couldn't seem to drive fast enough. People kept honking at her.

It occurred to her that she had not eaten in a long time. A billboard advertised a mall. She took the exit.

The mall was disgusting, full of American excess. People were shopping too much, eating too much, talking too much.

Her parents had been like that. They loved things. They always bought her things. They spoiled her. It was their fault that she had struggled later on.

She decided she wanted ice cream. At the food court, she was shocked by how much they charged and had to take another turn around the mall to walk off her fury. How dare they ask that much! American society was so greedy.

She took the escalator to the second floor. She was an

excellent shoplifter, but she could not think of a way to shop-lift ice cream. She would have to pay for it. Like the gas! She had had to pay for the gas, too!

A toddler was standing just outside a shoe shop.

Hannah did not care for small children, who were sticky and whiny. But this one was cute enough, with ringlets of red-gold hair. Hannah reached down, taking hold of those warm little fingers. The toddler gave her a beautiful smile.

The grown-ups with this child were probably only a few feet away. But they were not watching at that split second, or they would have come over. Hannah had possession. It was a hot, surging feel. A taunt-on-the-playground feel. *I have something you don't have,* sang Hannah.

She and the little girl walked to the escalator. Hannah's pulse was so fast she could have leapt off the steps and flown to the food court. Stealing a car had been much more fun than stealing a credit card. But stealing a toddler! Hannah had never felt so excited.

"What about Mommy?" said the little girl.

"She'll be here in a minute," said Hannah. And if she does come, thought Hannah, I'll say I'm rescuing the kid. I'm the savior.

Hannah giggled to herself. She was the opposite of a savior.

At the ice cream kiosk, Hannah lifted the toddler onto a stool.

"How adorable your little girl is!" cried the server. "Daddy's a redhead, huh?"

The toddler beamed.

Hannah did not.

How typical of American society that even a stupid ice cream server cared more about pretty red hair on some kid than about the suffering soul of a woman in need. The server turned to a second worker behind the counter, a skinny young man whose apron was spotted with chocolate and marshmallow. They helped each other with orders and they seemed happy.

Hannah had had a life once where people helped each other and seemed happy. But that life was gone now. The leader had been arrested, and when the group melted away, Hannah stumbled around the country, following various members, hoping they would include her in their lives again.

But they wouldn't. Grow up, they said to her. Get a life.

Hannah could not seem to get a life. It was her parents' fault. She had known that when she was a teenager. She had known that when she was in her twenties. And now she was thirty, and what did she have to show for it?

Nothing!

A stupid ice cream server had more of a life than she did!

She hated the server.

"What about Mommy?" said the little girl again. She wasn't frightened, just puzzled.

Hannah hated the cute little girl now, with her cute little outfit and her cute little barrette in her cute curly red hair. She hated the way the little girl sat so happily among strangers, assuming everybody was a friend and life was good.

You're wrong, thought the woman once known as Hannah. Nobody is a friend and life is bad.

I'll prove it to you.

CHAPTER ONE

Janie Johnson wrote her college application essay.

PERSONAL STATEMENT
Please write an essay (750 words or fewer) that demonstrates your ability to develop and communicate your thoughts. Some ideas include: a person you admire; a life-changing experience; or your viewpoint on a particular current event. Please attach your response to the end of your application.

My legal name is Jennie Spring, but I am applying under my other name, Janie Johnson. My high school records and SAT scores will arrive under the name Janie Johnson. Janie Johnson is not my real name, but it is my real life.

A few years ago, in our high school cafeteria, I glanced down at a half-pint milk carton. The photograph of a missing child was printed on the side.

I recognized that photograph. I was the child. But that was impossible. I had wonderful parents, whom I loved.

I did not know what to do. If I told anybody that I suspected my parents were actually my kidnappers, my family would be destroyed by the courts and the media. But I loved my family. I could not hurt them. However, if I did not tell, what about that other family, apparently my birth family, still out there worrying?

What does a good person do when there is no good thing to do? It is a problem I have faced more than once.

I now have two sets of parents: my biological mother and father (Donna and Jonathan Spring) and my other mother and father (Miranda and Frank Johnson). The media refers to the Johnsons as "the kidnap parents." But the Johnsons did not kidnap me, and they did not know there had been a kidnapping.

Usually when people find out about my situation, they go online for details. I have friends who have kept scrapbooks about my life. Among the many reasons I hope to be accepted at your college is that I ache to escape the aftermath of my own kidnapping. It happened fifteen years ago, so it ought to be ancient history. But it isn't. People do not leave it or me alone. It is not that distant crime they keep alive. It is my agony as I try to be loyal. "Honor thy father and mother" is a Bible commandment I have tried to live by. But if I honor one mother and father, I dishonor the other.

If I am accepted at a college in New York City, I can easily visit both sets of parents—taking a train out of Penn Station to visit my Spring family in New Jersey or a train out of Grand Central to visit my Johnson family in Connecticut. I need my families, but I don't want to live at home, because then I would have to choose one over the other.

New York City is full of strangers. I don't want to be afraid of strangers anymore. I want to be surrounded by strangers and enjoy them. It is tempting to go to school in Massachusetts, because I have relatives and a boyfriend there. But I would lean on them, and I want to stand alone. I've never done that. It sounds scary. But it is time to try.

I know my grades are not high enough. My situation meant that I went back and forth between two high schools. At my high school in Connecticut, where I grew up and knew everybody, people were riveted by what was happening to me. They were kind, but they wanted to be part of it, as if I were a celebrity instead of somebody in a terrible position trying to find the way out. At my high school in New Jersey, my classmates had all grown up with my New Jersey brothers and sister, and they knew about the crime in a very different way, and sometimes acted as if I meant to damage my real family. As a result, I didn't study hard enough. I promise that I will study hard enough at college.

I am asking you to accept me as a freshman, but I

have something even more important to ask. Whether you accept me or not, will you please not talk about me with your faculty, your student body, or your city? Thank you.

She was accepted.

The Spring parents (the real ones) and the Johnson parents (the other ones) argued with Janie about her decision to attend college in Manhattan. "It's too much for you," they said. "You can't deal with the pressure. You'll drop out. You need to be with people who know your whole history."

No, thought Janie Johnson. I need to be with people who do not know one single thing.

The New York City dormitory to which she had been assigned held six hundred kids. She would be nobody. It was a lovely thought. She did worry that she might introduce herself ("Hi. My name is Janie Johnson") and they would say, "Oh, you're the one who went and found your birth family and then refused to live with them. You're the one the court had to order to go home again. You're the one who abandoned your birth family a second time and went back and lived with your kidnap parents after all."

Outsiders made it sound easy. As if she could have said to the only mother and father she had ever known, "Hey—it's been fun. Whatever. I'm out of here," and then trotted away. As if she could have become a person named Jennie Spring over a weekend.

One reason the kidnap story was so often in the news was

that Janie was photogenic. She had masses of bright auburn curls, and a smile that made people love her when she hadn't said a word.

For college, she wanted to look different.

Her sister, Jodie (the one Janie hadn't met until they were both teenagers), had identical hair, but Jodie trimmed hers into tight low curls. Janie had enough problems with this sister; imitating her hairstyle did not seem wise. So for college, Janie yanked her hair back, catching it in a thick round bun because it was too curly to fall into a ponytail.

Back when she'd first arrived at her birth family's house, Janie had shared a bedroom with the new sister, Jodie, and a bathroom with all the rest of the Springs. There were so many of them—a new mother, a new father, an older brother Stephen, an older sister Jodie, and younger twin brothers Brian and Brendan. If there was a way to say or do the wrong things with any of these people, Janie found it.

Now, when she looked back—which wasn't far; it had happened only three years ago—she saw a long string of goofs and stubbornness. If only I had been nicer! she sometimes said to herself.

But being nice in a kidnap situation is tough.

Janie's college essay spilled more truth than she had ever given anybody but her former boyfriend, Reeve. Still, it omitted two other reasons for going to college.

She wanted to make lifelong girlfriends. Sarah-Charlotte would always be her best friend, but at some disturbing level, Janie wanted to be free of Sarah-Charlotte; free to go her own way, whatever that was, and at her own speed, whatever that was.

And she wanted to meet the man who would become her husband.

Janie still loved Reeve, of course. But the boy next door had hurt her more than anyone. Whenever he was home from college (he was three years ahead of her), Reeve would plead, "I was stupid, Janie. But I'm older and wiser."

He was older, anyway. And still the cutest guy on earth. But wiser?

Janie didn't think so.

Reeve was a boyfriend now only by habit. She and Reeve texted all the time, and she followed his Facebook page. She herself didn't have a photograph or a single line of information on her own wall; she was on Facebook solely to see what other people were doing. She never posted.

Janie's other mother, Miranda Johnson, was excited and worried for Janie. Miranda's life had collapsed, and this year, she was living through Janie. Miranda was so eager to see Janie launched at the university. It was Miranda who drove Janie into the city on the day her college dorm opened.

Later, Janie learned that each of her Spring parents had arranged to take that day off from work so that they could bring her to college. But Janie said no to them, which she had pretty much said ever since they first spoke on the phone. ("Is it the only syllable you know?" her brother Stephen once demanded.)

On the first day of college, Janie and her mother took the

dorm elevator to the fifth floor and found her room. The single window had a sliver view of the Hudson River. Janie could hardly wait for her mother to leave so she could begin her new life. She refused Miranda's help unpacking and nudged her mother back into the hall, where Miranda burst into tears. "Oh, Janie, Janie! I'll miss you so, Janie!"

Janie tried to stand firm against her mother's grief. If she herself broke down, she might give up and go home.

The hall was packed with everybody else moving in, each freshman glaring silent warnings to their own parents: *Don't even think about crying like that woman.*

"Good-bye, Janie!" cried her mother, inching backward. "I love you, Janie!"

At last the elevator doors closed and Janie was without a parent. She sagged against the wall. Had she done the right thing? Should she run after Miranda and somehow make this easier?

A friendly hand tapped her shoulder. "Hi. I'm Rachel. And you are definitely Janie!"

Everyone in the hall was smiling gently. In minutes, she knew Constance and Mikayla and Robin and Samantha. Nobody bothered with last names. I can skip my last names! thought Janie.

"I'm actually Jane," she said. "Only my mother calls me Janie." She had never been called Jane. She felt new and different and safe, hiding under the new syllable along with the new hair. "Jane" sounded sturdier than "Janie." More adult.

Her actual roommate appeared so late that Janie had been thinking she might not even have a roommate. "Eve," said the girl, who flung open the door around eleven o'clock that night. "Eve Eggs. I've heard every joke there is. Do not use my last name. You and I will be on a first-name basis only."

"I'm with you," said Janie.

Her new friends—girls who seemed so poised, and whose grades and SAT scores were so much higher than Janie's—were nervous in the Big Apple. They thought Janie was the sophisticated one. Everybody she knew back home would think that was a riot.

Rachel loved ballet and wanted Janie to help her find Lincoln Center.

Constance wanted Janie to teach her how to use the subway.

Mikayla had planned to study fashion, but her parents said fashion was shallow and stupid, so Mikayla ended up here, and wanted Janie to take her to fabulous New York stores and fashion districts that dictated what women would wear.

Eve had a list of famous New York places, and wanted to see them with Janie.

She did it all. She even managed to alternate weekend visits with the Springs in New Jersey and the Johnsons in Connecticut. Every Sunday morning, she'd catch an early train and go for brunch with one family or the other.

When she met her academic advisor, the man did not seem to know her background. In fact, he kept glancing at his watch, resentful that thirty minutes of his precious time was being spent on her. She loved it. Maybe the sick celebrity of being a kidnap victim was over.

When her sister, Jodie, came into the city for a weekend

visit, Janie primed her. "They know nothing. They don't even know my last name! I'm just a girl named Jane. It's so great. Like having my own invisibility cloak."

Jodie was always prickly. "You enrolled here as a Johnson," she snapped. "Which happens to be your kidnap name. If you really don't want to be a kidnap victim, you would use your real name. You'd be Jennie Spring."

It's true, thought Janie. *I'm* the one extending the situation. I shouldn't have changed my name from Janie to Jane. I should have changed my name to Jennie Spring.

And if she said that out loud, Jodie would point out that being Jennie Spring was not a name change. It was her name.

When their weekend came to a close, Jodie said, "I have to admit that I thought being away from your Connecticut home would destroy you. But you're doing fine. You're Miss Personality here."

"I had plenty of personality before," said Janie.

"Yes, but it was annoying."

They giggled crazily, and suddenly Janie could hug Jodie the way she'd never been able to. "I *was* annoying," she admitted. "I was worthless and rude."

"Totally," said Jodie. "But now you're fun and rational. Who could have predicted that?"

Janie laughed. "I'm coming home for the summer," she told her sister.

"Home?" Jodie was incredulous. "You mean, my house? That home?"

"If you want me."

"Oh, Janie, we've always wanted you. *You* never wanted *us*!"

· · ·

The wonderful weeks of freshman year flew by.

Eve began talking about Thanksgiving. Eve's family had several hundred traditions, including who mashed the potatoes and who chopped the celery for the turkey stuffing. "I have the most wonderful new family here," Eve said, "especially you, Jane, but I can hardly wait to get home to my real family."

Even Eve, with whom Janie shared every inch of space and many hours a day and night, did not know that Janie Johnson had both a real family and another family. Like everybody else in the dorm, Eve vaguely assumed there had been a divorce and remarriage.

In contrast, Mikayla and Rachel acted as if they barely remembered home, family, and Thanksgiving. Janie could now see why parents might dread the departure for college: their beloved child could put away the last eighteen years like a sock in a drawer.

For Janie, the last eighteen years was more like clothing she had never been able to take off, never mind forget.

Janie telephoned her real mother. "Mom?" she said to Donna. It had taken her three years to use that word with Donna and just as much time to think of the Springs' house as home. "May I come home for Thanksgiving?"

"Yes!" cried her real mother. "Everybody's going to be here. Stephen's coming from Colorado and Jodie's coming from Boston! Brian promised not to study on Thanksgiving Day and Brendan promised not to have a ball game."

The twins were still in high school. Brian was still academic and Brendan was still athletic. Brian was always part of the Sunday brunch when Janie came out to New Jersey, but Brendan never was. If he didn't have a game, he went to somebody else's.

Next, Janie planned the difficult call to her other mother.

A few years ago, her other father had had a serious stroke. Miranda was not strong enough to move and lift Frank. Over the summer, while Janie was preparing to move herself to a college dorm, she had also moved her parents into an assisted living institution, where Frank was much better off. For poor Miranda, it was prison. Miranda should have found herself her own apartment close to all her girlfriends and volunteer work and ladies' lunches and golf. But she could not bear to live alone or to abandon Frank to loneliness.

Miranda would be counting on Janie's presence for Thanksgiving.

Miranda did not know how to text and rarely emailed. She loved to hear Janie's voice, so in this call, as in others, Janie started with gossip about Eve, Rachel, and Mikayla. Finally she came to the hard part. "For Thanksgiving, Mom?" Her throat tightened and her chest hurt. She hadn't even said it yet and she was swamped by guilt. "I'm going to take the train to New Jersey on Wednesday and spend Thanksgiving Day and Friday with them."

"New Jersey" was code for Janie's birth family; "them" meant the Springs.

"Saturday morning I'll get myself to Connecticut and stay until Sunday afternoon with you," she added brightly. "Then you'll drive me to the train station Sunday night so I can get back to the city."

Miranda's voice trembled. "What a good idea, darling. If you came here, we'd have to eat in the dining room with a hundred other families and the cranberry sauce would come out of a can."

Normally, Janie caved when her mother's voice trembled. But Jodie's visit had been profound. The name change, and the soul change, could not be from Janie to Jane. It had to be from Janie to Jennie. All the vestiges of the kidnap, even the ones she cherished, needed to end. She wasn't ready yet. But in her mental calendar of life, becoming Jennie Spring was not too many months away.

"I know it won't be the perfect Thanksgiving for you, Mom," Janie said, which was a ridiculous remark. It would be awful for Miranda. "But I'll see you on Saturday, and that will be great. I love you."

"Oh, honey. I love you too."

Vacation by vacation, Janie slid out of the Johnson family and into the Spring family. The Springs rejoiced; the Johnsons suffered.

When freshman year ended, Janie divided her summer. She lived Monday through Friday with her birth family. She got a job at a fish fry restaurant. She came home with her hair smelling of onions and grease. Fridays, she worked through lunch, went home, shampooed the stink out of her hair, and caught the train from New Jersey into New York. From there, she took a subway to Grand Central, and another train out to Connecticut, where her mother picked her up at the station. Her father always knew her. Frank could smile with the half of his mouth that still turned up, and sometimes make a contribution to the conversation. But mostly, he just sat in his wheelchair.

A few years ago, when Frank suffered the first stroke, Miranda stayed at the hospital while Janie handled the household. Janie was struggling with bills when she stumbled onto a file in Frank's office. To her horror, she found that Frank had always known where his daughter Hannah was and had sent her money every month. Of course, for twelve of those years, neither he nor anybody else dreamed that Hannah had kidnapped Janie. But when the face on the milk carton was produced and the truth came out, when the FBI and the police and the media and the court got involved, Frank Johnson knew exactly where the criminal was, and he never breathed a word. He had been writing a check to Janie's kidnapper on the very day the FBI interrogated him.

It had been such a shock to learn that she was a kidnap victim. But Janie almost buckled when she understood that her father was aiding and abetting the kidnapper. Only to Reeve did Janie spill the secret. One of the comforts of Reeve was that he knew everything. It was always a relief to be with the one person who knew it all.

And then came another surprise: at college, she found out that it was more peaceful to be among people who knew nothing.

During freshman year, Janie saw Reeve only at Thanksgiving and Christmas. The summer after freshman year,

Janie saw him only once, at the fabulous college graduation party his parents gave him. It was so much fun. Reeve had more friends than anybody, and they all came, and it was a high school reunion for his class. He and Janie were hardly alone for a minute. During that minute, he curled one of her red locks around a finger, begging her to come back to him.

She didn't trust herself to speak. She shook her head and kissed his cheek.

He didn't know why she couldn't forgive him. She didn't know either.

The following day, Reeve left for good. He had landed a dream job in the South and had to say good-bye to her in front of people. His departure was stilted and formal. She said things like "Good luck" and he said things like "Take care of yourself." And then it was over: the boy next door had become a man with a career.

Her heart broke. But she wanted a man she could trust, and she only half trusted Reeve. It was so painful to imagine him lost to her, living a thousand miles away and leading a life about which she knew nothing. She kept herself as busy as she could. One good thing about her parents' move to the Harbor was that they no longer lived next door to Reeve's family: she no longer used the driveway on which she and Reeve learned to back up; no longer saw the yard on which they raked leaves; no longer ran into Reeve's mother and got the updates she both yearned for and was hurt by, because she wasn't part of them.

By July that summer, Janie was not visiting her Connecticut parents until Saturday mornings. By August, she was borrowing her real mother's car, driving up for lunch on Saturdays, and driving home to New Jersey the same night. As her visits dwindled, so did her Connecticut mother. Miranda became frail and gray.

Is it my fault? thought Janie. Or is it just life? Am I responsible for keeping my other mother happy? Or is Miranda responsible for starting up new friendships and figuring out how to be happy again? I'm eighteen. Do I get to have my own life on my own terms? Or do I compromise because my mother is struggling?

The only person with whom she could share this confusion was Reeve. But she had decided not to share with him again.

THE SECOND PIECE OF THE KIDNAPPER'S PUZZLE

The food court had its own exit to the parking lot.

The woman formerly known as Hannah took the little girl's hand again. "Let's go for a ride." If anybody stopped them, she'd say she was trying to find the parents.

"What about Mommy?" said the little girl again.

The silly question annoyed Hannah. "She's meeting us," said Hannah. They had to cross a wide stretch of parking lot. The little girl's red hair blew in the wind like a flag: here we are!

But nobody stopped them.

It was so exciting.

Way better than stealing a car.

The little girl looked around. Still not afraid—just looking for Mommy.

"You know what?" said Hannah. "You can sit in front!"

The front seat was a privilege forbidden to small children. The little girl was thrilled. She climbed right in, so small she was hardly visible. It did not occur to Hannah to fasten the toddler's seat belt. The little girl even asked her to, but Hannah didn't have time for that kind of thing.

The mall was wrapped in parking lots. Hannah circled. She did not immediately see an exit to the main road. Racing toward her was a Jeep with a twirling light on its roof and a slap-on magnetic sign that read MALL SECURITY.

Hannah felt a wonderful thrill of fear, deep and cold and exciting. But the driver of the Jeep did not look at Hannah and could not see the small passenger in her front seat.

Hannah giggled. Guess what. Your mall is not secure.

"But what about Mommy?" said the child.

It was a stupid sentence. Hannah was sick of it. "She's taking a nap," snapped Hannah. "When we get there, Mommy will be awake." In moments, she was back at the interstate, choosing her direction by the usual method: whichever entrance came first. It happened to be northbound. Hannah changed the subject. "What's your name?"

Her name was Janie and she loved her shoes and she loved her doggy back home and basically she loved everything. Hannah quickly tired of this kid's happiness. "Put your head down," she said. "Take a nap."

Obediently, the little girl tipped over and curled up on the seat, and shortly the rhythm and purr of the car really did put her to sleep.

In less than an hour, they had reached New York City.

Hannah disliked paying attention to traffic, but now she had no choice. She really disliked paying a toll, but she had no choice about that either. Hannah hated things where she had no choice. It was typical of society that they were always shoving themselves down your throat.

Hannah's goal in life was to be free.

She emerged from the tangle of roads and traffic, merging lanes and shoving trucks; that was New York. The turnpike widened and she could breathe. Her eye was caught by a pile of red hair on the seat next to her. She had forgotten about the stupid little girl. She could not remember what her plans had been. What was she supposed to do with this burden?

Hannah hated responsibility. A kid! Next she'd have a utility bill and a factory job. She had to offload this kid.

A large sign loomed by the side of the road. NEW ENGLAND AND POINTS NORTH, it said.

Connecticut was the first Point North.

Hannah would dump the kid on her parents. She hadn't seen them in years, not since they tried to wrench her out of her group, which they viciously called a cult. It was her parents' assault on the leader that eventually led to his arrest and the end of the group. Hannah had never dreamed that she could avenge this.

I know! she thought, giggling. I'll pretend this is *my* kid!

"Wake up!" she said roughly. She had to jab the kid to wake her. The kid was confused and puffy-faced and tearful and Hannah had to sweet-talk her into a fun game. "A let's-pretend game!" she cried. "Let's pretend I'm the mommy and you're the little girl! And guess what! We're going to meet a whole new grandma and grandpa. It'll be so much fun!"

And it was.

The mother and father Hannah hadn't seen or communicated with in years kissed and hugged her. For a fraction of a second, Hannah remembered what love was. But then they centered their attention on the kid.

"This beautiful little redhead is our granddaughter?" they cried.

Now they really kissed and hugged. They rushed the little girl to the bathroom and cleaned up the sticky mess of the ice cream and fixed her a butter and jam sandwich with the crusts cut off, and found a cute little plastic glass with mermaids on it and poured an inch of milk in it and cooed proudly when she drank without spilling.

These people had not seen Hannah in years, and already, she came in second.

Hannah hated them.

They sang songs with the kid, and danced in circles, and rocked her to sleep.

Every now and then the little girl was puzzled and asked for her mommy and wanted to know when they were going home.

Hannah had mastered the art of lying. She explained to her parents that since they had lived in a communal situation, baby Janie had more than one mommy, and lots of brothers and sisters.

The new grandma and grandpa asked awkward questions. About, for example, the daddy. Hannah spun a long story about how a mate had been chosen for her by the group, and how the man's identity meant nothing, because no one had ownership over a child.

This was a pleasant thought. If nobody had ownership over a child, then New Jersey was not a problem. Besides, the actions of the day had fallen so easily into place. In the group, the leaders had often explained that some things were just "meant" to happen. There was a power out there. It ordained things and you had to go with the flow.

Hannah had simply gone with the flow.

The police would have another opinion. Police were like some kind of organized disease. They infected society. You could not lead your own life with them around.

She reached into her mind for more lies and came up with a one-night solution. She told her parents that baby Janie was not allowed to watch television. It wasn't good for children, said Hannah firmly, and she wasn't bringing up her daughter to find solace in silly television shows.

And so nobody turned on the TV and nobody saw the horrifying news of a kidnapping at a mall in New Jersey. And when the little girl Janie asked about her mommy, the Connecticut people thought she meant Hannah, and came up with excuses and explanations, and whisked Janie into another activity, and the weeks passed, and became months, and Janie didn't remember that mommy anymore.

CHAPTER TWO

Sophomore year was perfect. Janie's complicated past—except when she was with Miranda and Frank—was history. Autumn moved into winter. They had an early dusting of snow and then week after week of it—heavy, beautiful, and exhausting. It was April before the snow disappeared, leaving cold hard ground and cold hard weather.

The small, elegant city campus was a world of cell phones and texting. In class and out, at cafeterias and snack bars, on the quad and in the dorms, kids lived on their cell phones. Janie could be sitting outdoors on a bench, nibbling a bagel, surrounded by a dozen other students, and nobody would talk to anybody there because they were all on their phones.

It was slightly warmer than it had been in weeks.

Janie was perched on a long, low stone wall, playing a word game on her iPhone with Sarah-Charlotte. Sarah-Charlotte was in Boston, but they were in touch with each other so frequently that Janie hardly felt the distance.

When a man sat down on the same wall, Janie was barely aware of him. She concentrated on whipping Sarah-Charlotte with a very well-placed letter Q.

"I saw you the other day," said the man. "Walking by the river. I was on my bike."

She looked up, startled. He was a complete stranger. And very good-looking. He had shaved a few days ago, and the dark stubble was attractive. He had curly dark hair and a nice smile. He was a bit older than Janie. Perhaps a grad student. "It must be fun to have a bike in the city," she said. He did not have a bike with him now. Janie's Spring family were all bicycle enthusiasts. She herself was still afraid of being hit by cars.

"As long as it doesn't snow or rain, it's fun," said the man. "A bike can be faster than a taxi or a bus. Of course, that's going downtown. Coming back is uphill. But that's good too. Nice workout."

"That was one of the surprises of New York for me," said Janie. "How much walking there is, and how much of it is uphill."

"Want to walk over to Riverside Park with me?" he asked.

Riverside Park was a thin green strip that ran down the Hudson River for miles, dotted with softball fields and tennis courts, a marina and children's playgrounds, dog parks and hundreds of benches. It was patrolled constantly. Today the park would be packed with nannies pushing strollers, people of all ages and types sipping coffee, and high school ball teams practicing on dusty fields.

The man was smiling at her, a tender smile. A charming

smile. "I'd enjoy the company," he said in a careful sort of voice; a voice that said, *No risk. It's public. Plenty of people around.* "We have an hour of daylight left," he added.

This campus, thought Janie, has thousands of young women, and he saw me across the quad and wants my company. She felt the tiny weight of her cell phone in her hand. She wanted to text Sarah-Charlotte: Maybe I've met him!

Him. The elusive future boyfriend she and Sarah-Charlotte both dreamed of—perfect, of course, and madly in love.

No. She would not tell Sarah-Charlotte anything until she was sure. "That sounds nice," she said, although it sounded way better than nice—it sounded romantic and exciting and wonderful.

They did not exchange names. He adjusted his stride to hers. He was a talker, which was perfect. She could listen and gather her thoughts.

"I want to write," he told her. "I'm studying creative writing. It's harder than I thought it would be. But I have wonderful professors."

The only thing Janie had ever written easily was her college entrance essay. She was still amazed that she had written it at all, never mind sent it in. She was even more amazed that whoever was on that acceptance committee had given her exactly what she asked for: anonymity. Nobody had a clue that she was the face on the milk carton.

When they reached the park, they chose the paved path closest to the river and walked slowly. Janie usually watched the river traffic, and the passersby, the children and dogs and skyline. This time, she saw none of it. She took up her share of the conversation. She talked about college and classes and the dorm.

The sun was sliding out of sight. They had walked many blocks. They cut across the park to Riverside Drive and caught a number 5 bus going north. It was full. They jostled against each other. He caught her arm to steady her. "My name is Michael," he told her. "Michael Hastings."

"Michael," she repeated. She had always loved the name Michael.

But now it was her turn. He was waiting to hear her name.

What *was* her name?

If this was her future husband (she hoped the poor man did not know that she was way past their first date and planning their wedding), he ought to be told her real name. But the wonderful thing about him (aside from good looks, great body, and good conversation) was that he knew nothing. Michael did not want to bask on the edges of some ancient crime. He wanted the company of a girl he had seen across the campus.

"I'm Jane," she said at last, as if he had asked for information that would stump a *Jeopardy!* champion.

He chuckled. "It's good to know you, Jane."

He was tall and looked down at her, while she was medium and had to look up at him. She couldn't keep her gaze on him. He was giving her the shivers. Shivers she hadn't felt in a long time.

She thought of Reeve.

Her entire life since seeing her face on that milk carton had been about loyalty.

Did she need to be loyal to Reeve?

Reeve, her rock and her friend, had been the most disloyal of all. He had sold intimate details of her story on the radio to get himself a slot on a talk show. She had hated him for a while and needed him again for a while, and could not quite completely get past what he had done. I love him, she thought. But I don't have to be loyal. He's a former boyfriend.

A stab of pain shot through her heart at the thought of Reeve retreating forever to the past. When she caught her breath, it was like catching a glimpse of Reeve, with his moppy hair and his huge grin.

"Let me send you a text, Jane," said Michael, "and then you'll have my number."

Janie Johnson did not give out anything. Not real names, not real history, and not phone numbers. Why? she asked herself now. Do I think the kidnapper will come again? What am I afraid of? I want Michael to call me. I want to text him. Michael might matter. He might be the very first person after Reeve who will matter.

After Reeve felt like the edge of a cliff.

Michael was laughing. "It's okay, Jane. You don't have any way of knowing who I am. You don't know a thing about me. So instead of text messages, how about this? I'll be at that stone wall every day at that exact same time."

"You gotta love a guy willing to sit on an icy stone wall every day," said Constance, back at the dorm.

"Give him your number next time," said Rachel. "If you don't, *I* need a boyfriend. *I'll* meet him at the stone wall."

Mikayla said, "I'm going to wander by at that scheduled time and photograph him on my cell and we'll all study him."

"Don't do that!" snapped Janie, alarmed by her own anger.

Mikayla held up both hands, as if stopping traffic. "Just teasing."

Janie's heart was pounding. She knew better than anybody the power of one photograph. One tiny black-and-white photograph on a half-pint milk carton had changed the world for the Johnsons.

She wasn't ready for photographs.

Eve said, "Where is he taking these writing courses? Here?"

"I don't think he said."

"Check his student ID. He could be a creep."

Janie and Michael met at the stone wall the next day, and most days after that.

Michael usually arrived first, and he liked to bring a gift. A miniature sugar-dusted doughnut. A cup of hot chocolate. A single flower from a sidewalk vendor.

Janie ate the doughnut. She washed out the cup and kept it on her bookshelf. She saved the flower.

"There's something calculating about all these presents," said Eve. "He's buying you."

"He is not," said Janie, laughing. "It's so cute, all these little gestures."

Everybody in the dorm was eager for every detail of every meeting, and Janie loved telling her girlfriends all about Michael, but she did not tell anybody else. Not even Sarah-Charlotte, who knew almost as much of Janie's history as Reeve. She didn't tell one of her four parents or her sister, Jodie, who would have loved to know, and certainly not her brothers, whose interest would have been zero.

Even Reeve would not have understood how she was feeling. Like the trees and shrubs of New York, Janie was beginning to thaw; she was ready to bloom. In Michael's company, she had a fresh new existence, without the stain of the kidnapping. For the second time in her life, she was teetering on the brink of true love.

Michael was definitely in love with her. He wanted to know everything about her. He quickly learned that she would not discuss her family or childhood. "I know, I know," he would apologize. "You're very private. But I love every detail about you. Last Sunday you were busy in New Jersey with your parents. But the Sunday before that you were busy in Connecticut with your parents. My folks are divorced too, Jane. It's not so bad that we can't talk about it."

Both sets of Janie's parents had strong marriages. She wanted to say, "Nobody divorced. All my parents still love each other." But she was never ready to begin the real story. If she told, the sweet romance would sag with every dark question. Michael would become what so many people were: a voyeur of her nightmare.

"Tell me how your book chapter is going," she would say instead.

"Slowly. All I think about is you."

They would kiss.

He would say, "Jane, let me into your world."

She would say, "It's complicated."

Eve did not like Michael. "There's something off about that guy."

Janie would not fight with Eve. She just waited the conversation out.

"You don't know anything about him!" Eve would say. "It's creepy. You've never visited his apartment, he doesn't seem to have any friends of his own, he just adopts your friends, and you don't know for sure that he really is a grad student."

"He doesn't know anything about me either," Janie would say. "We're a perfect fit."

"You're one in a million with your privacy hang-ups, Jane. I do not believe there are *two* in a million who are so protective of their lives. And if there *are* two in a million, they didn't meet by chance on a park bench!"

"Stone wall," Janie would correct her. "And it isn't creepy. It's romantic."

Spring that year was beautiful. The leaves of park and sidewalk trees uncurled. Bulbs burst with color in the tubs by the entrances to stores. Tough, demanding New York City was soft and tender. Eve was not. She began inviting herself along when Janie and Michael went out.

One night, the three of them were at a restaurant. Over appetizers, Michael said to Janie, "So why don't you ever post anything on Facebook?"

Eve and Rachel had asked the same thing, of course. Janie couldn't remember what lame excuse she had given. There were dozens of Jane Johnsons on Facebook. Janie had chosen a photograph in which you could no more identify her than a tree in the woods. Basically, she just had an account so she could be a lurker.

"Jane's very private," said Eve, coming to her roommate's rescue. "I think it's adorable. She's not a conformist. She doesn't tell anybody anything and that's that."

"It isn't adorable anymore," said Michael. "It's frustrating." He hitched his chair away from Janie.

The inch was a chasm. Normal people shared. People in love shared. It was Janie's turn to share. But just remembering her first glimpse of her face on that milk carton made Janie's world spiral out of control. She could not quote herself, at age fifteen, whispering, "It's me." She could not describe the freefall into that hideous vortex: *Are my parents my kidnappers?*

I don't want to trust anybody with anything, she thought, chilled by that vision of her soul. Would life even be worth living if you did not have friends and family you utterly trusted?

Reeve's face wavered in her thoughts. Did she trust him again after all—or was he always to be a warning of what happened when you wrongly trusted?

Eve said to Michael, "You've made some interesting Facebook choices yourself. How come you didn't friend me when I asked?"

"I'm so sorry!" said Michael. "I didn't mean to do that. Of course I want you as a friend. You are a friend, Eve! But it's Jane whose friendship I crave."

Janie didn't like that word, "crave." It sounded—well—creepy.

They walked home. The streets of New York at night sparkled, full of people and action and noise. It was like a moving, drifting party. But tonight was awkward. Michael clearly just wanted the evening to end. Janie could not think of a way to smooth things over, and the image of Reeve made it impossible to do anything except offer her cheek for a kiss.

Michael didn't give one. He left Janie and Eve at the dormitory entrance and walked on.

Inside, the girls headed for the stairs, which Eve said were crucial to maintaining their figures, especially after so much dessert. Eve paused at the mailboxes, which she loved to check, although they hardly ever got mail. "Guess what?" said Eve. "You have real mail. I don't think I've had a paper letter since I got here. My parents phone, my sister emails, my friends text, we all use Facebook." She handed Janie the letter.

Together they ran up the first flight, paused at the turn, ran up the second flight, and trudged up the next three. "But we'll be skinny!" panted Eve.

They rested at the top. Janie studied her mail. "I never heard of the person on this return address. Calvin Vinesett. What a name. He's probably selling something, like all our other mail is. The expensive envelope is a sales trick."

They reached their room. Janie and Eve were neat. Eve kept her dirty clothes in a canvas sack, and now she dragged it out, stripped her bed, tucked the sheets under her arm, and headed for the laundry room. Janie threw the letter into the wastepaper basket.

But what if it really was mail and contained information she needed?

She retrieved the letter and opened it.

Dear Miss Johnson:

My name is Calvin Vinesett. I am a true crime writer. Like most of the country, I am riveted by your story. If you go to my website, you will see the kind of book in which I specialize. I have chosen you as the subject of my next book.

You are the victim of an act by a woman almost unknown to us; a woman who abandoned her family in her late teens to take up an unusual and rather hidden life with a group her family considered a sick and twisted cult. This woman briefly emerged here and there. During one episode, she drove you away from your rightful family. But you triumphed and are now a happy daughter and sister in two families, and going to a fine college.

Not only will your story be fascinating to millions of readers, but my book may be the route to finding that kidnapper at last. By helping me with this book, you will bring about justice.

A book! Bad enough there had been a TV movie! Bad enough there had been an *America's Most Wanted* episode. Bad enough the media came back on every anniversary or any slim excuse to invade Janie's life——eager to attack poor Frank and Miranda——quick to surround Donna and Jonathan Spring.

Janie threw the letter back into the wastebasket. It wasn't enough. She tore it in half and threw the halves back in. That wasn't enough. She carried the wastebasket down the hall and emptied it into the trash chute.

If she couldn't even tell Michael about her past, she could never, ever tell this Calvin Vinesett.

A book required many sources. All her friends would get a letter like this. Janie imagined them galloping over to Calvin Vinesett, begging to be interviewed, happy to contribute a morsel.

Janie did not worry that Reeve would tell. I haven't been loyal to him, she thought, but he will be loyal to me. He really did learn from his mistakes.

For a moment she wanted Reeve so fiercely she could have hiked to North Carolina.

On her iPad, she went to Calvin Vinesett's website. He seemed to write nothing but bestsellers, which sold all over the world in many languages. The books featured ghastly, brutal, bloody crimes. Long, riveting chapters (said the reviewers) revealed the psyches of the criminals and the suffering of the victims.

The media had mopped the floor with Frank and Miranda. How depraved they must have been to raise a daughter who became a kidnapper, said the media. *Really* depraved to have kept the kidnapped toddler. Who believed their pathetic story that they hadn't known Janie was kidnapped? And then, after the milk carton, those kidnap parents enticed Janie back into their clutches, so the innocent little child finished high school living with her kidnappers instead of with her actual mother and father.

Janie felt ill. Now, when Frank was no longer a rock to lean on and Miranda was at her frailest, she might have to face the media and their lies all over again.

Janie's cell phone rang with the piano glissando of her New Jersey mother's ringtone. "Hi, Mom."

"Did you get a letter from this Calvin Vinesett, sweetie?"

"Yes."

"So did everybody," said Donna.

Everybody, thought Janie, means Dad and Stephen and Jodie and Brendan and Brian. Who have been ruled by this kidnapping twelve years more than I was. Because I never even knew. They hate that kidnapping. Sometimes they hate me, too, since we don't have Hannah around to hate.

"A book like that might lead to Hannah Javensen's capture," said Donna Spring carefully.

She *wants* the book? thought Janie.

"But it is bound to focus on us as well," said Donna, "and especially on your poor mother."

Janie marveled that her real parent Donna Spring could refer to Miranda Johnson as "your poor mother." Sometimes she was so proud of being Donna's daughter. But she did not say so now. She did not say that in the last year and a half,

Donna Spring had become her real mother at last, and the Spring house, her real home. Not expressing the truth was second nature to Janie, because at the same time Donna would love hearing it, Miranda would be crushed by it.

"Are you going to help the writer, Mom?" asked Janie. It felt as if that ancient kidnapping had spilled acid on her beautiful spring and her sweet romance.

Get a grip, she ordered herself. It's not a big deal. It's the past. I don't live there. Let the writer do his worst. It won't touch me.

But she felt the cold fingers of the media stretching toward her. It was her face they wanted. They wanted to see her crumple and cry.

"The decision is yours, honey," said her New Jersey mother. "You do what you think is right."

Doing the right thing was harder than anybody admitted.

By no evil act of their own, two good people—Frank and Miranda—had been hurled into evil by Hannah.

Poor ruined Frank tried to do the right thing for his real daughter. He also tried to do the right thing for his other daughter, Janie. He wasn't going to know how it turned out. He didn't even know what he had for lunch anymore.

Poor ruined Miranda had tried all her life to be good, kind, and fair. She had been a wonderful mother to the little Janie who had suddenly appeared on her doorstep. Miranda had given Janie everything, from Christmas morning to cake decorating, from driving lessons to bedtime stories, and every minute of it had been just right. And so what? The media attacked her anyway.

Yes, Hannah should be caught. Yes, Hannah should be tried and found guilty and sent to prison. But Hannah's parents would be tried as well. Frank and Miranda would be found guilty on television and radio. Found guilty on the Internet and in newspapers. Found guilty by new neighbors and former friends.

"I can't always see what's right," Janie said to her real mother. "I hide out instead."

"There's no rush," said Donna. "We can all think about it and decide together sometime during the summer."

Summer.

That long lovely world of slow days and late nights, warm air and friendly sun.

But Calvin Vinesett would spend the summer writing of crime and filth, hounding Janie and her brothers and sister, tracking down Janie's high school friends, visiting her two sets of parents.

When her call from Donna ended, Janie held her phone for a long time, wanting to call Reeve and hear his voice and be comforted. Only Reeve would understand.

I believe Michael would understand, if I let him, thought Janie. Do I dare?

THE THIRD PIECE OF THE KIDNAPPER'S PUZZLE

In the group, no one used the name their parents had given them.

The group would be a family, strong and loyal and true. They would protect one another and be more pure and valuable than the men and women who accidentally gave them life.

All initiates the year Hannah Javensen joined were given musical names. She became Harmony and the other girls were Vivace and Glissando. She loved that name, Harmony. It meant she fit in everywhere, gently and perfectly.

One year, the group needed a post office box.

It was her job to get it.

She hated jobs.

She wanted them to do the jobs!

But they insisted. She was to pay a year's rent on the box using a false name.

But the false name had to be a real name, because to open a post office box, it was necessary to have proof of identity. (It was typical of American society that they were always trying to match you up with numbers and photos.)

Hannah had to find and use somebody else's identity.

The leader told her that as long as she obeyed him, she would always be safe. But Hannah was scared. What if she got caught?

Every night the leader would ask Hannah if she had done her job yet, and every night she had not, and every night she was dismissed from the group and had to sit alone.

Sitting alone! It was the worst punishment.

The leader screamed at her, "Harmony! Just steal a wallet! You're not pretty enough to be remembered and you're not different enough to be noticed and you're not plain enough to be interesting. You're just there! Nobody will notice you. Nobody ever has!"

The group laughed at her.

It isn't true! thought Hannah. They notice me! I'm their friend. They love me.

The next day, Hannah forced herself to wander through a nearby college campus. She followed various girls with long blond hair like her own. One girl was wearing pants so tight that she could have nothing in a pocket. She must be carrying everything in her skinny little backpack. The girl went into a ladies' room. Hannah saw the tips of the girl's fingers as she hung the backpack on the hook inside the stall. Hannah waited for the girl to sit down, and then she simply reached in over the door and took the backpack. The girl on the toilet screamed.

Hannah walked out. In the hall, she removed the wallet. She passed through a student center, where she left the backpack on a chair. In two strides, she was outdoors. She wandered across the grass, removed the driver's license and the cash, set the wallet on a trash can lid, and kept walking.

The leader of the group had been right. Nobody had noticed her.

But it was a good thing, not a bad thing.

In the post office, she gave the clerk Tiffany Spratt's driver's license and Tiffany Spratt's cash and in exchange they gave her a key. She could hardly wait to tell everybody how well she had done. She tucked the key into her jeans pocket and approached the leader. "About that post office box," she said timidly.

"I told you to do that last week! We've got a box now. Don't bother me." He never even knew that she had obeyed. He never asked for the key. He just walked away from her.

It was her parents' fault.

They had spoiled her, and done things for her, and helped her out, and now, when she had to be independent and contribute to the welfare of her group, she goofed.

Years later, standing in her parents' living room listening to her mother singing to that little girl, Hannah thought of that key. She had kept it. She had kept up the box payments too. The leader of the group used to say that things were meant to be. She had been meant to use that post office box.

It was time to get out of Connecticut, but Hannah did not want to leave broke. She took her father aside. "You bring

Janie up. It's too much for me. But I need money. I have a post office box in Boulder, Colorado. Send me a check every month."

Hannah could not miss the joy in her father's eyes. It was not his own daughter he wanted. It was that kid. He was perfectly happy to purchase a grandchild.

Hannah found herself giggling. They'll get caught, she thought. Probably in a day or two. They'll go to prison. Well, they deserve it, ruining my life.

Her father gave her lots of cash and Hannah drove away. She got rid of the car as soon as possible and took a bus. She took tranquilizers, too. She didn't like to be up and she didn't like to be down. She liked to be smooth.

Within hours, she barely remembered the little girl.

CHAPTER THREE

Calvin Vinesett would not give up.

Not only did he bother Janie with a second letter, he found her email address. Janie was not a big email user. It was not the end of the world to have some stranger connect by email. But her email appeared on her iPhone as well. She could ignore and even forget about emails on her computers. But on her iPhone, she could not help opening her messages and reading them.

Every communication included Calvin Vinesett's cell phone number.

Her beloved cell phone felt infected.

He had communicated with her brothers and sister. Stephen, Brendan, Brian, and Jodie seemed to be waiting for Janie to make the first move. As for Sarah-Charlotte and the rest of Janie's high school friends, Calvin Vinesett must not have known about them, because if they had gotten letters, they would have told her.

Michael chiseled away at her, wanting to know her better. "I still don't see why you won't use Facebook."

"Give it a rest, Michael! Just because you like to present a nicely edited version of yourself doesn't mean everybody wants to."

He backed off immediately. "You're right. I agonize over what to have on my profile. I'm showing off the guy I want to be, not the guy I am."

She loved him for that confession.

Six weeks, she told herself. I've known him only six weeks, and because it's me, it's been a careful six weeks. But that's okay. There's no reason to rush into my history.

Michael did not share this belief. His smile was forced. He's getting sick of this, Janie thought. I have to do more of what he wants and less of what I want.

Sophomore year was nearly over.

They were well into the month of May and final exams were beginning. Michael was irritated because Janie insisted on studying hard—and alone. "I promised in my application essay to be a good student," she told him. "I've pulled it off for three semesters, and I'm determined to get good grades again this semester."

"Oh, come on!" said Michael. "Your professors didn't read that essay! They don't know what you promised. I want to study with you."

"You're too much of a distraction."

He did not take this as a compliment. He left the city for a job interview and Janie tried to remember why she had wanted to study alone.

Her second-to-last exam was early on Friday morning. With her last exam scheduled for the following Tuesday, a much-needed three-day weekend lay in front of her.

The exam was easier than Janie had expected. She wafted out of the classroom. No need to return to her dorm to pack an overnight bag, because she kept stuff at her mother's. She took a crosstown bus through Central Park and then the subway down to Grand Central, where she bought a Metro-North ticket to Connecticut. "Hi, Mom," she said on her cell. "I'll be at the station at eleven-fifty."

"Oh, darling, I'm so excited. I can't wait to see you. And I think Frank knows you're coming! He's been smiling all morning."

"Give him a kiss," said Janie.

Grand Central was one of her favorite places in New York. She crossed the great room slowly, enjoying it like a tourist, and then walked down the long concrete platform to her train. She liked to ride facing forward, and she liked a window seat. This train was relatively empty; most people would not head out of the city until after lunch. She found a good seat in a clean car where nobody was yelling on a cell phone or eating something smelly. She sat down, tucking her bag between herself and the window, and took out her e-reader. She was on chapter six of some historical fiction novel Eve had loved. So far, Janie didn't love it. It was yet another wives-of-Henry-VIII thing, and there were probably ten chapters until the beheading, which would most likely be detailed and gross.

The train left the station.

She got her ticket out even though the conductor wouldn't collect it for quite a while. They slowed for 125th Street, where they would pick up passengers and then continue express to Greenwich.

Janie stared out the window.

Leaving the city always gave her a sort of heart stoppage, as if she were leaving a safety zone. As if anything could happen out here.

And anything did happen. Michael sat down next to her. She was too startled to be polite. "Michael! What are you doing here? Where did you come from?"

He kissed her cheek, put his arm around her, and settled in. Very close.

She felt smothered. The kiss did not feel like love. "He's buying you," Eve had said. Janie shook off Eve's negative aura. "How did you find me, Michael?"

"Eve said you were headed out to Connecticut. I thought I'd catch up."

But Eve had finished her exams two days ago and left the city. Eve didn't know Janie's plans for today. Even if Michael had texted Eve, she couldn't have told him where Janie was.

She stared at Michael.

"Okay, that's a fib," he admitted. "I didn't see Eve. I stalked you. Don't be mad. I love you, Jane. I haven't seen you in three days and you didn't even answer my last text!"

This was what her past had done to her: she suspected people of things. Janie relaxed and leaned against him after all. It felt good.

"So where are we going?" said Michael. "Are you visiting your parents or do I have a rival I don't know about?"

His only possible rival was Reeve, but Reeve was far away and occupied another world. Michael was this world.

Janie Johnson took a deep breath. It was time. "I'm going to have lunch with my parents. My dad had a serious stroke and a heart attack a few years ago. He's in a wheelchair, and if it's a good day he knows me and if it's a bad day he doesn't."

"That's awful," said Michael. "I'm so sorry, Jane. He must have been very young."

"No. My parents are pretty old." Janie still wasn't ready to approach the central theme of her life. She talked alongside it. "We used to have a lovely big house, but my dad couldn't go up and down the stairs anymore, and even after they re-built the downstairs bathroom, my mother couldn't manage, so the summer before freshman year—"

"Before we met," said Michael, as if referring to some other century.

"Exactly. Sad times." Janie rearranged his arm to snuggle herself even more safely inside his affection. Safe, she thought. How often I use that word. I remember feeling safe senior year in high school. Here I am with my boyfriend's arm around me and I don't feel romantic; I feel safe. "Anyway, my parents had run out of money. I got the house re-painted inside and out, held tag sales, sold stuff online, and then sold the house for enough to move them into an as-sisted living facility, which Daddy needs but my poor mother doesn't. She's got an easier life because the staff takes care of him but a harder life because she isn't with her old friends and can't do all the things she used to do. She's very brave."

"She must really rely on you," said Michael. "I'm looking forward to meeting them."

"I'm not sure that's a good idea," said Janie. "My parents aren't very good company these days."

"Maybe I could make it better. Sometimes a new face makes conversation easier."

Tears pricked her eyes. Michael could put anybody at ease. And her mother would rejoice that Janie had this sturdy fine man in her life. Since Mom never referred to the kidnapping or the New Jersey family, Janie wouldn't find herself dealing with an angry Michael, stunned and hurt that Janie had neglected to tell him all the important aspects of her life. "Taking you to meet my parents is heavy," she said to Michael. "Freighted with meaning."

"Wow. Big vocabulary. You sound like a college girl. And speaking of college, your university costs a ton of money. If your parents are so broke, how are you paying for it? Did you get scholarships?"

"No. My grandmother set up a trust for my education. If I could have given my parents every dime of that money to help them out, I would have, but the trust pays directly to the university."

"Your mother's mother?" asked Michael.

"Yes."

Her grandmother Barnette had been one of the very few who knew that Hannah Javensen had shown up one day, handed her little daughter Janie over to her parents to bring up, and vanished. Grammy approved the plan to change the name Javensen to Johnson. Grammy believed that Janie was her real true great-granddaughter, and she died before they ever knew about the kidnapping, one of the few blessings in the nightmare.

Janie sometimes wondered if her grandmother would have left all that money to a little girl who wasn't related to her after all.

It was the kind of thing that could still make Janie's heart hurt.

They ate in the private ell of the big dining room at the Harbor.

Michael had beautiful manners. He helped Janie's father with the wheelchair and with his glass of water. He complimented Janie's mother on her pretty scarf and glittery earrings. Miranda blossomed under his attention, and Frank gave Janie a smile that seemed real, that seemed to know things and to love her.

Michael took pictures of everybody. "We'll want to remember this," he told Janie.

Her heart double-timed in her chest.

For the rest of our lives, she thought.

She had no photograph of Michael, although of course a cell phone took photographs effortlessly and well. For everything else in her life, she took pictures and immediately sent them on to Sarah-Charlotte or whomever. She hadn't even told Sarah-Charlotte about Michael, although Michael knew all about Sarah-Charlotte, and loved reading her tart little texts. Janie could not believe she had never taken a picture of Michael. What had she been thinking?

While Michael was laughing, telling her mother a story, Janie snapped his profile, so sharp and strong, and sent it to Sarah-Charlotte: The man I love, she wrote in the text. Can't wait to tell you about him. Which was quite a fib, since Janie had waited six weeks already to mention Michael to Sarah-Charlotte.

Before dessert, Janie and her mother went to the ladies' room while Michael took her father to the men's room. It happened easily, and without anybody having to say anything.

"He seems like a wonderful man," said her mother excitedly. "Though part of me will always miss Reeve."

"Part of me will always miss Reeve too." In fact, the image of Reeve was all but in the mirror with her. Do I still love him? Janie asked herself. Yes. But do I love him enough?

When they returned to the table, Michael and her father were already seated and apparently having a conversation. Janie and her mother exchanged hopeful looks. Daddy could surface now and then, though rarely with a complete sentence.

"Barnette," her father was saying.

"Goodness," said Janie's mother. "How did you two get on the topic of my mother?"

"I was just asking about family," said Michael, beaming.

Janie's mother beamed back.

"College money," said her father thickly, but with a grasp of the topic.

Janie was so pleased! She circled Michael to reach her chair.

His cell phone was in his hand. On the tiny screen was a photograph he had taken of Janie's father in the men's room. Frank's clothing and hair were in disarray and the half-fallen side of his face looked warped and deranged.

Janie opened her mouth to say, *Delete that! Take a better one right now, while he knows us and he's part of the conversation!*

But Michael was clicking through his contacts, preparing to send the ugly photo.

Janie had always been able to memorize phone numbers. The number to which Michael was sending Frank's picture was Calvin Vinesett's. This demeaning picture of Frank was for a book.

A few hours ago on the train, Michael had told the truth.

He had stalked her.

He had stalked her from the beginning.

From the first powdered doughnut, Eve had known. *He's buying you.*

And Calvin Vinesett was paying.

In Boston, at Sarah-Charlotte's campus, the winter had been bleak, icy, and long.

Not until last week had there been one beautiful day. And on that day, Boston enjoyed a slice of summer. Sarah-Charlotte, a group of kids from class, and some grad student friend of somebody's had gathered around a tiny café table on the sidewalk. Sarah-Charlotte had been feeling the peace of warm weather. How wonderful to be wearing no coat, no scarf, no hat, no mittens, and no snow boots. She slumped in her chair, as comfortable as a cat curled up in the sun.

One of the boys gestured toward the grad student and said to Sarah-Charlotte, "I was telling Mick how you're the best friend of Janie Johnson, that kidnap girl."

"Ancient history," said Sarah-Charlotte. Her caramel latte slid sweetly down her throat.

"Not really," said the man named Mick. "It's only a few years ago that she recognized herself on the milk carton. That must have been weird. Were you there?"

Everybody wanted to cozy up to that old crime. Sarah-Charlotte would have to present a few tidbits or they'd chew at her ankles like annoying toy terriers. "We were all there," she said. "The same crowd of kids had lunch every day at the same table in the same high school cafeteria. Janie waved a half-pint milk carton at us and said, 'See this picture of a missing child on the side of the milk carton? It's me.' We laughed. Finished lunch. Went back to class. A few months later we found out that Janie hadn't been kidding. It *was* her."

She had told this much of the story a hundred times and it still spooked her. Sarah-Charlotte sat up straighter, as if to fend something off.

"I keep thinking about those kidnap parents," said Mick. "Here we have a mother and father, a Mr. and Mrs. Javensen. They're estranged from their daughter, Hannah, now about age thirty."

Sarah-Charlotte put on her sunglasses to separate herself from the summary of a story this person Mick could not possibly understand.

"Daughter Hannah is living with a bunch of weirdos, basically a religious cult. The fringe kind that might attack society with poison gas or just become drug dealers and prostitutes. Hannah has chosen to have no contact with Mom and Dad and claims to despise them. But one fine day, after years of absence, she shows up at their house with a little girl, tells Mom and Dad that this three-year-old is *hers* and therefore their grandchild."

Sarah-Charlotte had always loved Mr. and Mrs. Johnson; loved spending time at their house with Janie. After the milk carton, Mrs. Johnson got thinner and grayer and shakier, while Mr. Johnson moved slowly toward the stroke that would leave him half alive.

There were so many victims of Hannah Javensen.

Sarah-Charlotte had even thought of herself as a victim, because Janie had not shared her horrifying guess (*the people I love and call mother and father are my kidnappers*). She had often wondered if she and Janie really were best friends. They were sophomores in college now, and being left out of Janie's search for the truth didn't hurt any longer, but it was there. As if her friendship with Janie were a pie chart and a dark wedge had been cut away.

The others were glued to Mick's story. He obviously loved an audience—he spoke loudly enough that people at the next two tables leaned forward so they could hear too.

"And guess what?" said Mick. "The Javensen mom and dad *believe* Hannah! Next day, daughter Hannah drives away, never to be seen again. And what do Mom and Dad decide? They'll vanish too! So they change their names from Javensen to Johnson, a name so common that, even online, they'll share an identity with a million others. Then they bring up this unknown little girl as their own. Hah! If you ask me, those Javensen people are coconspirators in the kidnapping. They wanted another child, so they assigned their grown-up daughter to pick one at a shopping mall. They got off, you know. Those Javensens never even spent a night in jail. Miscarriage of justice, if you ask me."

Sarah-Charlotte's fury was so intense she wanted to kick Mick to the ground and then kick him some more. How dare he be entertained by Janie's nightmare? How dare he, without a speck of actual knowledge, pass judgment on anybody?

"There was no trial," she snapped. "And nobody 'got off.' It was clear all along that Mr. and Mrs. Javensen never knew what their daughter, Hannah, had done. If the Javensens had known that this toddler had been snatched from a shopping mall and that there was a real family out there, crazed with worry, they would have called the police in a minute. All they knew was that Hannah would make an unfit mother. The only good thing Hannah ever did was to bring her baby girl to the household where Janie could grow up properly loved and cared for. The Javensens didn't change their names to hide from the law or from a kidnapping they didn't even know about. They changed their names to hide from *Hannah*. Hannah was a rotten person who lived with rotten people and did rotten things. Rotten like a fish lying dead on a riverbank, crawling with maggots. Because that's what kidnappers are. Maggots!"

She was screaming.

People were staring at her.

The word "maggot" reverberated in the little group.

Nobody met her eyes.

Sarah-Charlotte stood up. On an icy day, she'd have a thick coat to wrap around herself, and keep her safe from invading worms like Mick.

She strode away.

Mick followed. "Sarah-Charlotte?"

She said nothing.

"I'm sorry. I didn't mean to be a jerk. I want to be friends. Can I at least walk along and make up for saying stupid stuff? I didn't know it was stupid, but maybe you can explain it to me."

He was taller than she was. Bending down, shoving his face near hers. She could smell his coffee breath. She had a fleeting sense of fear.

Ridiculous. She was on a busy street in a busy city with a man her classmates knew. "I'm in a hurry." She ran to catch a bus without caring where it went, and when he did not get on with her, she was weak with relief, and also embarrassed.

A sidewalk meltdown would be another episode in the long list Sarah-Charlotte did not share with Janie. Like that letter from the true crime writer. The author had found everybody. At least three of Janie's other high school girl-friends had gotten letters from Calvin Vinesett.

But here in Boston, the group Sarah-Charlotte had left on the sidewalk were acquaintances, not friends. She never saw them except in a lecture hall, and after the final exam, she might not see them again. Boston was too big. Her freshman year, Reeve Shields had been a senior on a different campus and Sarah-Charlotte never once crossed his path.

She still could not believe that Janie was ignoring Reeve.

Reeve was 110 percent the boy every girl wanted. If Janie really did walk away from Reeve, what a wonderful guy would be available. Sarah-Charlotte generally blocked daydreams in which that wonderful guy sought *her*. But the daydreams were there.

As she did on and off all day, Sarah-Charlotte went to Facebook. Reeve had more friends than anybody in the entire world, except maybe Adair, another high school girlfriend. Reeve stayed in touch with everybody from high school and everybody from college. Anybody who wanted to know anything just went to Reeve's Facebook page.

In honor of Janie's desire for a low profile, and in spite of the fact that she was the most important friend in his life, Reeve had no photograph of Janie on his wall.

Get over it, Janie, thought Sarah-Charlotte. What could happen now, after all these years? Reeve loves you! Stay in his picture, for heaven's sake!

Sarah-Charlotte got off a bus she hadn't needed to take, barely able to remember why she had leapt onto it. The man Mick vanished from her mind.

At the Harbor, Janie quietly took Michael's cell phone out of his hand before he could click Send. She walked over to her own chair, sat down, and deleted the photograph of her father. She checked for other photographs of herself and her family and deleted them. She dropped the phone into her own purse. She did not glance at Michael. She would cry.

She had loved him.

And he was a tool for Calvin Vinesett.

Had this happened as they were dating? Or had he introduced himself to her at that icy stone wall because Calvin Vinesett wanted him to?

Or maybe he *was* Calvin Vinesett!

No. The writer had published half a dozen bestsellers. Michael wasn't old enough to have done that.

Her mother did not observe these cell phone moments. Miranda Johnson was more comfortable with a landline and found the constant cell phone use by Janie's generation annoying and rude.

Her own phone signaled a text from Sarah-Charlotte, to whom she had just sent Michael's photograph. The caption no longer fit. Michael was definitely not the man she loved.

She was going to need Sarah-Charlotte to get over this. How wonderful to have a best friend in reserve. She felt a flicker of shame. You didn't keep a best friend in reserve for bad times.

She read Sarah-Charlotte's text: Janie—something's wrong with this picture. I've met this guy. He called himself Mick. He's very nosy. Be careful.

Dessert arrived. She couldn't touch hers. She couldn't even touch her fork. She couldn't breathe, for that matter.

"I love this," Michael was saying. "Chocolate cream pie? I could live here."

Miranda was laughing. "You could *not* live here, Michael. You'd die of boredom. I'm practically dead of boredom. Chocolate pudding, even with real whipped cream, does not compensate."

Somehow lunch ended.

An aide took her father back to his room. Janie and Michael and her mother went to the car. "You take the front," Janie told Michael, and he got in front with Miranda. The two of them chatted happily during the long drive back to the train station.

Janie stared at the back of Michael's head.

How could Sarah-Charlotte have met him?

Was Michael stalking more than one girl?

This was the man who had meant life after Reeve. Before Michael, "After Reeve" had seemed like the edge of a cliff.

And it was. Michael would have shoved her over. She had caught herself in time.

Janie's mother dropped them off at Stamford station. Their side of the tracks was almost empty because on a Friday afternoon, people were coming out of New York, not heading in.

"May I have my phone?" asked Michael politely.

She handed it over.

"Jane, what are you mad about? I had a great time. I love your parents."

"You are doing research for Calvin Vinesett. You took that hideous photograph of my father for that book."

He took a step away from her. Wisely, it wasn't a step closer to the tracks. She wanted to kick him down and watch the next train flatten him like a penny.

"What are you talking about?" he said. His voice was belligerent.

"You think I don't know Calvin Vinesett's cell phone

number when he's included it in every single message to me? You took that horrible photograph solely for Calvin Vinesett's book."

Michael looked around, as if there might be a cue card somewhere, and a script. "Listen," he said.

"I deleted myself from your contact list. Don't add me back. You've always known that I'm Janie Johnson, the face on the milk carton. Calvin Vinesett told you to find me."

His poise was gone. He didn't know what to say. Even when she had taken his phone, he had not realized that she knew about Calvin Vinesett. He just thought she didn't like the photo. He couldn't meet her eyes. "Okay, that's partly true. But what's really true is that I'm in love with you. Anyway, maybe I didn't tell you the truth, but you didn't tell me anything! I was closemouthed, but you were sealed shut. I brought you little presents and we went on walks and—"

"You were paid to do it, weren't you?"

He glared at her. "You know I want to be a writer. It hasn't been going well. I answered an ad. The guy's doing a book about the kidnapping and not everybody in the family is cooperating. He needs a little help. It's good money."

I gave up Reeve? she thought. Who has apologized and asked for forgiveness a hundred times? In order to have a guy who dated me for money? For future fame? For a paragraph? A guy who's not even going to admit that was wrong? "Add it up," she said. "I'll pay you back. There's your train. Get on it."

"But Jane—"

"Get on that train, Mick."

He flinched.

"And don't stalk Sarah-Charlotte again either!"

"Listen, Jane."

Janie did not listen. She stepped onto the escalator to the upper level of the station. She did not look back. I loved you, she thought. How will I ever survive in this world, now that I know I am a lousy judge of character? I couldn't judge character when I was three years old, and I can't judge now that I'm twenty.

She checked the schedule board for the next train.

She didn't want to get on a train. She wanted to throw herself on the floor and sob. She wanted to beat Michael/Mick up. Even more, she wanted him to explain how he really did love her, and he had not stalked her, and he had not been paid to get information from her.

Her cell phone rang. One of the lovely things about cell phone technology was that you always knew who it was.

It was Reeve's ringtone.

She almost wished it could have been Michael, pleading. But if he wanted to plead, he would have taken the escalator after her.

Back at the Harbor, only an hour ago, she had asked herself if she still loved Reeve. Her answer had been yes—but not enough. She stared at his face on the screen. *Reeve* loves *me* enough, though. This man to whom I have been rude and unforgiving—he loves me enough.

A wave of knowledge passed through Janie. Reeve's voice on the radio was nothing. Reeve in her life was everything.

It was a true gift. Not a powdered doughnut. A gift in her

soul. She trusted Reeve again. It was like taking off a winter coat. She was light again. "Reeve?"

"Sarah-Charlotte called me," shouted Reeve. "What's going on? Who is this guy? Are you all right? Do I have to kill somebody?"

Oh, Reeve, she thought. I've leaned on you for so long. And here you are again.

"Keep talking," she said. "I need your voice." The sobs she had been holding inside defeated her. She held the phone at an angle so Reeve couldn't hear her cry. She curved her elbow over her face so strangers couldn't see her break down.

"Some creep dated you in order to pass information to that true crime writer?" yelled Reeve. "He's using two names? Michael for you, Mick for Sarah-Charlotte?"

"You knew about the book?" she whispered.

"We all know. We all got letters. We knew you wouldn't want it. Nobody's talked."

A sentence of Michael's came back to Janie: *Not everybody in the family is cooperating.* Which meant that somebody was.

"Where are you right now?" asked Reeve.

"Train station. I don't know what to do next, Reeve. First you betrayed me and then I fell in love again and now he betrayed me."

"Ah, Janie. I grew up. That was the worst mistake I ever made, and I thought you had sort of taken me back. Listen. Get on a plane. Come down here for the weekend."

"I can't do that."

"Yes, you can. I'm on my computer right now getting you a plane ticket. You're about two blocks from the airport limo pickup. Take a taxi to that hotel or walk over. I'll make your limousine reservation too. Okay, there's a seven-forty flight from JFK to Charlotte. And an aisle seat. Bingo. Got it."

"I don't even have a toothbrush with me."

"It's Charlotte, North Carolina, not Antarctica. There are stores. The only thing you need to get on the plane is an ID. Are you headed for the airport limo, Janie? Pick up the pace."

"Why do you want me there?"

"Because I love you. I've always loved you. I always will."

Janie Johnson walked over to the taxi stand. "Don't hang up."

"I won't."

"I'm not taking the limo, Reeve."

"Janie! Please! I don't want you crying up there without me."

"I'm coming for the weekend, Reeve. But the limo is too slow with all those stops. It's too annoying. I'm taking a taxi all the way to the airport. I have lots of money. Even if I did inherit it from a grandmother who thought I was somebody else. With you I don't have to be somebody else."

Why hadn't she noticed that when she was with Michael, she was in a constant struggle to be somebody else? Somebody without a history? Somebody whose soul was unmarked by tragedy?

She slid into the backseat of a cab. "JFK, please," she told the driver, holding up a sheaf of bills to prove she could pay.

"Janie, I can't wait to see you," said Reeve.

"You don't have to wait." She loosened the red hair from its tight tension in that silly fat bun. She took off the drugstore glasses. She had hidden the real Janie Johnson for two years. She shook her head hard. For a moment the hair stayed tight, and then it relaxed, taking up its portion of the backseat. Janie focused her cell phone camera on herself, took her picture, and wrote,

xoxoxoxo, Janie

THE FOURTH PIECE OF THE KIDNAPPER'S PUZZLE

After the mall event, and the Connecticut event, the woman formerly known as Hannah drifted around the country, trying to find the old members of her group. But they had all moved on. Briefly, she traveled by train. She wouldn't mind spending her life looking out a window and showing up in the dining car a few times a day while somebody else drove.

The train trip ended, and Hannah found herself on the West Coast, that day in New Jersey as remote as elementary school.

In California, the weather was perfect but the loneliness deeper.

How did everybody find all those friends with whom they laughed and ate?

It didn't matter.

Her father would send money to Tiffany Spratt's post office box. Hannah wouldn't be the only one back in Boulder who skied and hiked, took a class or two, and then picked up their checks. Well, except she didn't plan to ski or hike or take a class. What would she do? With all that money, she would have choices.

And so Hannah made her way to Colorado and the post office box.

The post office box anchored her to the world. Stuff filled the box. It was so packed she had to pry everything out. Ads and flyers. Requests for donations. Giveaway newspapers. Even free credit cards, although they never worked when she tried them. She unfolded every piece of junk mail carefully, because her check was in there somewhere.

Yes!

The envelope was crushed, but the check was safe.

She headed for a bank, her Tiffany Spratt ID in her hand.

But they would not cash it.

In the end, she had to open a bank account with that check and wait day after day for the bank to decide it was real. Only then could she have the money. But not all of it! They insisted that she had to leave some in the bank, and furthermore, they charged a fee.

The establishment was so greedy!

But the real shock was, Frank's check wasn't enough money to live well.

It wasn't even enough money to live poorly!

Frank was probably lavishing money on that little girl. But would he pay Hannah's bills? No! She would have to get a job. And that had never worked for her. She was too fragile.

Back there in Connecticut, she had forced herself to give

the little Janie creature a hug and a kiss when she was leaving, as if she really were its mother. As Hannah had gotten into her stolen car, Miranda's voice had floated after her: "We have to go to the store, Frank. We need sippy cups and pajamas and a car seat. We need . . ."

Frank and Miranda were out there buying things for somebody else's child while refusing to give enough to *Hannah*! Their *real* daughter!

Hannah hated them.

She wondered if the police had found her parents yet, and if they were headed to prison. It occurred to her that if her parents were imprisoned, they could not support her.

On the other hand, if they were in prison, their money was hers.

Hannah did not read newspapers, and when she was in the location of a television, she certainly didn't waste it on the news. She did not know if her parents were doing time for kidnapping.

She didn't feel like talking to them, but the telephone was her only choice.

Dormitories always had public phones, and sure enough, she wandered into a student lounge and found three wall phones, each in its little cubicle, waiting for her coins.

If the police hadn't found Frank and Miranda, she'd threaten her father: *Give me money or I'm coming for my little girl.*

If the police *had* found them, the police might even answer the phone. But they couldn't find Hannah even if they traced the number. This was a dorm; hundreds of people used this phone.

She dropped her coins into the slots and poked the little buttons, oddly pleased that she remembered the number after all these years.

But the phone number of Frank and Miranda Javensen had been disconnected.

CHAPTER FOUR

Brendan Spring had been the most successful person in his family, and the least liked. Brendan thought of sports first, and everything and everyone else second. To be precise, he thought first of himself excelling in sports.

In his dreams, Brendan was courted by Big Ten schools, flown in to tour campuses, treated as a prize. In high school, he rarely concerned himself with books and academics, because he was going to be a star on the basketball court. His grades were low, but so what?

His favorite dream was the television interview where he was introduced as a legend. He would duck his head in a humble fashion, although he would be such an icon that sneakers were named for him.

His kidnap sister's boyfriend, Reeve, had graduated from college and gotten a job with ESPN. Brendan liked to imagine the day Reeve would beg for an interview. "It will help my career," Reeve would plead.

When Janie had been found—or rather, when she had

found them—her appearance at their house, her failure to thrive, and her return to the kidnap family had hardly made a dent in Brendan's life. The missing Jennie Spring was just an annoying girl who increased the wait time for the one bathroom. She wouldn't even use her name, but insisted she was a person named Janie. She left before Brendan had really noticed that she'd arrived. In his mind, he referred to her as J/J.

His older brother, Stephen, his other sister, Jodie, and his twin, Brian, pursued Janie, following her up to Connecticut and even becoming friends with the other parents, Frank and Miranda, and hanging out with the boyfriend, Reeve. Brendan couldn't work up any interest.

It had no longer been necessary for the Springs to keep the shabby little house with the street address they hoped a lost child might somehow remember. The lost child *had* remembered, had come home, and didn't like it there.

So the Springs moved to a big house, with a bedroom and bath for each kid.

A separate bedroom changed everything. Brendan no longer had his twin to hold him back. Brendan wanted success more than he wanted kindness. His family suspected this but pretended it wasn't so. The Spring children were supposed to have all the virtues and think of each other first. But the minute the twins were no longer confined to a single bedroom, Brendan forgot he even had a twin.

Anyway, his twin was embarrassing. If Brian had been a computer nerd, that would have been acceptable. But Brian just sat around reading stuff nobody cared about, like medieval history. While Brendan dreamed of being a sports legend, Brian dreamed of getting an e-reader to load with history books.

Senior year in high school arrived and Brendan waited to be courted by the finest basketball coaches in the country.

But they did not come.

He waited for the athletic scholarships at the top schools.

But he was not offered any.

Brendan was not even accepted at a Division I school.

He endured the end of senior year pretending to be proud that he was going to some loser college nobody had ever heard of.

When his mother said, "Well, you never did study; you're lucky you got in anywhere," he wanted to leave his family forever.

When his dad said, "Make the best of it," Brendan wanted to shove him.

When Jodie snapped, "Oh, stop whimpering," and Stephen said, "So life isn't fair; so you just noticed?" Brendan thought, Who needs these people, anyway?

His twin got into the school of his choice.

I'm going to Nowheresville and he goes to Harvard, thought Brendan. Brian probably did it on purpose to show me up.

More than anything, Brendan hated his twin's sympathy.

He seriously considered joining the army, which would have been better than showing up at that stupid college. But that summer, he was lethargic. This had never happened to him before. He was usually exploding with energy. His parents didn't notice. They were dreaming of how it would be when, the first time in decades, they would have no kids at home. They were either packing suitcases for Brendan and Brian or rejoicing that old J/J showed up once in a while. Then didn't his crazy sister Jodie decide to go off on some mission year to Haiti? Jodie got treated like a goddess because she was giving a year to the poor. Who cared about the poor?

In August, Brendan Spring found himself on the stupid campus, surrounded by stupid people and a stupid coach. Coach had the nerve to tell Brendan he wasn't trying. Preseason began with Brendan sitting on the bench.

"I'm better than any of them!" he shouted at the coach.

"You *could* be better," the coach said. "But you're not."

Brendan struggled to make friends. The rest of the team was lukewarm. His roommate hardly noticed him.

When he looked into his future, the only thing Brendan could see for himself was teaching elementary school gym.

Every hope and plan had rotted. The taste of failure would not leave his mouth. He was losing weight.

He did not bother to communicate with his family. They had gone to every game he played in high school, telling him how wonderful he was. Making scrapbooks. Filming him. It was their fault he had big dreams. It was their fault he was struggling in some loser dump of a college.

Brendan hardly ever even opened his parents' emails, and half the time he didn't bother with Facebook. He never had anything to post, and the shock of that was so great he couldn't stand the whole concept.

By February of his freshman year, Brendan's basketball team had lost too many games to make the playoffs. They were losers among losers.

Sometimes the only thing Brendan did after he woke up was go back to sleep. He was vaguely aware that the second semester was drawing to an end and that other guys were making summer plans. He did not want to go home to New Jersey. But what else could he do? Where else could he go?

When a researcher approached Brendan about a book on the kidnapping, Brendan chose not to consider that he didn't know much. He'd been even younger than toddler Jennie when it happened. He had no memory of her before the kidnapping and no memory of the events after it.

Brendan Spring said to the researcher, "Sure. Whatever."

In Boulder, Colorado, Stephen Spring was sitting at his computer, staring at a list of unopened emails. Stephen didn't check email often, but professors communicated via email, and so did his parents. And now, Calvin Vinesett had Stephen's email address.

"Dear Mr. Spring," the first message began. It described the author's plans for his book on Janie Johnson. It featured links to websites and bookstores.

Calvin Vinesett did not refer to the central person in his story by her real name, Jennie Spring. He planned to write a "true crime" book about a person who never even existed! Janie Johnson. It made Stephen crazy.

Stephen deleted the messages, but he could not delete them unread. It was like needing to know your enemy.

Today's email was from another person. Not Calvin Vinesett himself, but a hired researcher.

Dear Mr. Spring,

I know that you and your family have mixed feelings
about a book on the kidnapping of your younger
sister. I applaud how protective you are of her and
of each other. But I remain hopeful that you and I
can meet and talk.

The more I research, the more shocking aspects I
uncover.

I have learned that the father of Hannah Javensen
sent her support checks for many years, and that
he mailed those to a post office box right here in
Boulder.

Stephen was rattled. How had this guy found out about
the support checks? Janie herself hadn't known until a
few years ago, when Frank was hospitalized with a stroke.
Janie had gone into his files so she could handle some of the
household finances and stumbled upon years of canceled
checks.

Stephen hadn't even known what a canceled check was. It
seemed that at one time, banks mailed your used checks back
to you, because you didn't have an Internet site to keep track
of them. Stephen had a checking account, but only so he could
have a debit card. He wrote maybe one paper check a year, but
Mr. Johnson had written paper checks for everything.

Mr. Johnson hadn't used the name Johnson or Javensen on those checks, so when Hannah got her check, she could cash it but she couldn't locate the sender.

How creepy it was. The daughter hiding from the parents and the parents hiding from the daughter.

From that old file, it was clear that Frank began sending money to Hannah soon after she dropped toddler Janie off. Hannah had probably asked him for money and her father had probably still loved her. Stephen was okay with that. But a dozen years later, when Frank and Miranda were faced with the fact that this little girl had been kidnapped by that same Hannah, Frank should have told the FBI. Should have said, "You can stake out the post office branch in Boulder, Colorado, and catch her."

But he hadn't. He'd never missed a check.

When Janie had figured that out, she'd been furious. Janie had given up her real true birth family to return to the mother and father who had brought her up. She had done it out of love and loyalty.

And now she had proof that her other father's heart belonged to the kidnapper.

But Janie did not call the FBI either! She believed that Miranda had never known about the support checks. She believed all that was Frank's doing. Now that Frank was borderline dead in a hospital room and Miranda had all she could handle, Janie was not about to hurt her even more. Instead, Janie had decided to hurt Stephen.

She'd faked interest in him and pretended that she too might attend college in Colorado. She'd even brought her boyfriend, Reeve, and Stephen's little brother Brian into her scheme. What she really wanted to do was confront Hannah herself. But in the end, she chickened out.

Eventually Stephen and his parents learned the whole story.

"I hate her," Stephen had said. "How can she be loyal to her kidnapper's disgusting father?"

"She's your sister," said his mother. "We are not going to hate her. And everybody is doing the best they can."

"Janie never does the best *she* can!" yelled Stephen. "And Frank Johnson sure wasn't doing the best *he* could!"

"Janie wrote a final check and a final message," said Stephen's mother. "Janie ended it."

"Janie could have arranged for Hannah to be caught!"

"I'm sure Janie would love it if somebody *else* caught the kidnapper," said Stephen's father. "But Janie still calls the Johnsons Mom and Dad. Put yourself in her place, Stephen."

Janie definitely stood where Stephen never wanted to be.

Stephen had staked out the post office for a while after Janie's visit. He never saw anybody who looked like Hannah. But Hannah wouldn't necessarily pick up her own check. She could ask somebody else to do it for her. Next Stephen sent a letter to her box, pretending he had money for Tiffany Spratt, and giving his own cell phone number, a risk he took only because he was changing providers and would be getting a new number.

But his letter was returned unopened. A rubber stamp listed possible reasons a letter might be returned to the sender. Two were checked: Box closed. No forwarding address.

When Calvin Vinesett contacted the family, they all knew Janie wouldn't want them to talk about her and her lives.

Stephen understood that the only thing he could give his difficult sister was silence.

Now, in his apartment, his girlfriend, Kathleen, was reading his mail over his shoulder, a habit Stephen detested.

Kathleen gasped. "What! Mr. Johnson was sending money to Hannah? Here in Boulder? Even after he knew she was Janie's kidnapper?"

Stephen nodded.

"And you didn't tell me?" she shrieked.

Stephen froze.

"I'm sorry," she said instantly, "of course you didn't tell me, it's none of my business."

"Correct."

Kathleen backed away, literally and figuratively.

How had the researcher found out? Stephen wondered. The pool of informants was small. It wouldn't have been Janie herself. It certainly wouldn't have been Mrs. Johnson, whether she knew about it or not, and Mr. Johnson was all but a turnip.

That left Stephen's family. Mom? Dad? But Stephen thought that their desire to win Janie back into the family would trump any desire to share with a true crime writer.

Jodie was in Haiti, and although she could still text and email, Stephen couldn't imagine that she'd bother, and he wasn't sure she had ever known about the checks anyway.

The twins? Brian had known. Brian and Reeve had flown out with Janie to Boulder on that trip to find Hannah. Brian was the one who had spilled the facts to Stephen. But Brian was Janie's big supporter. It was hard to picture him telling all to the writer. On the other hand, Brian was all about books. Maybe he couldn't resist meeting a famous author. Maybe he wanted to be a writer himself and was eager to work on the project. As for Brendan, he never paid attention to family matters. Stephen doubted that Brendan knew about the checks.

It wasn't that Stephen minded the author finding out. It proved that the author was not a dummy. Knew how to research. Did thorough interviews.

It was just unsettling.

Maybe it isn't family, he thought. Maybe it's friends. We all have friends who know a little or a lot. Janie's best friend is that Sarah-Charlotte. I don't know her well enough to know if she'd keep secrets for Janie's sake. Janie's former boyfriend is Reeve. I do know Reeve. And we all know Reeve will sell secrets in order to hear his own voice. Janie broke up with him. Mom says she's dating somebody else. Maybe Reeve is mad and getting revenge.

The trouble was, Stephen liked Reeve. He did not want Reeve to be the bad guy. And Reeve had spent the last few years desperately trying to convince Janie that he would never behave that way again.

Reeve had gone into broadcasting. But in sports. ESPN was never going to refer to a face on a milk carton.

Now, in his apartment, with Kathleen hovering nearby, Stephen wondered if his girlfriend, who was fascinated by every detail of the Spring family history, might be talking to the researcher. Kathleen, whose father was an FBI agent.

But it was hard to imagine. She had not known about the

checks, and Stephen was pretty sure she wanted him more than she wanted interviews with strangers.

Kathleen did not dare give advice. If she said, "It would be good for you to talk about it, Stephen. And a bestseller could flush out the kidnapper," this romance would be over.

Kathleen breathed quietly so Stephen would not remember she was there. Stephen liked a girl who was somewhat in his life, not a girl who dominated it.

Stephen wouldn't let Kathleen live with him or even spend the night. He felt that if she moved in, she'd feel all permanent and expect stuff. He'd run out of oxygen and have to throw himself off a cliff.

Kathleen's mother didn't think Stephen even loved her.

"He loves me sometimes," Kathleen would say.

Stephen and Kathleen were both twenty-four. Stephen was getting a graduate degree in engineering while Kathleen was still inching toward her undergrad degree. She loved college. Why rush it? Who cared how long it took? Well, her parents cared, since they were paying, but Kathleen tried not to worry about that.

She had a sad fleeting thought that she should break up with Stephen. College was prime husband-hunting territory. This very semester, she would finally finish college and have to find work in an office somewhere, and she'd have no hope.

Marriage and children are not what I want, she reminded herself sternly. I'm going to have a great career, if I can just think of one. I'll worry about marriage and children some other decade.

She was lying. She wanted Stephen.

Like all his family, he had red hair. He had a buzz cut right now and looked completely different from the boy she had fallen in love with a few years ago. She liked to run her hand over the bristles.

He was muscular, because Boulder was an outdoor kind of place, and the two of them were constantly outside: skiing in winter; bicycling, playing tennis, and hiking in summer. And right now, tough strong Stephen Spring was afraid of an email.

When they first met, Kathleen had pushed hard for details about the Spring family saga. She demanded facts and photographs of the kidnapping. Stephen found out that Kathleen's father was an FBI agent, and dumped her. It took Kathleen the whole next year of college to inch back into Stephen's favor.

Janie, the kidnapette, as Kathleen called her, with her mass of auburn curls, must have been adorable in her role. Kathleen could perfectly imagine Hannah, too, because of the well-publicized high school photograph—a slender, sober girl with long blond hair. Kathleen imagined pretty, wispy Hannah on a stool at the ice cream counter with this cute little toddler. Whisking her away for a fun little drive. And then Hannah thinking, Uh-oh. This is called kidnapping. I think I want to get out of this.

Kathleen imagined Hannah driving all the way to Mommy and Daddy's house and trilling a little song of need. "Oh, I know I've been away for years without calling or writing, and I know you've suffered, but after all, life isn't fair, and meanwhile, here's my darling baby girl. You bring her up! Won't it be fun! Well—I'm off! Enjoy!"

She could imagine Hannah giggling as she drove on.

What vehicle had Hannah used? They never knew.

It was a big country. Lots of stolen cars. Hannah had probably dumped hers somewhere, and after seventeen years, that getaway car had long ago come to the end of its road.

Stephen pushed his rolling desk chair away from the screen. An expensive swivel chair with adjustable padded back, arms, and seat, it had been abandoned on a sidewalk on trash day because it was missing one caster. Stephen had lugged it home and bought another caster, and the chair worked fine. He loved adjusting it. So did Kathleen. She couldn't help herself. When she sat at his desk, she had to change his chair, even though she knew it annoyed him.

"You know what I think is the most startling part of the whole kidnap?" said Stephen suddenly.

Stephen never discussed the kidnap. Kathleen listened eagerly.

"Janie never had nightmares," said Stephen. "She was the victim, but she never had nightmares. The rest of us—nightmares swarmed us for years after she disappeared. The terrible things that could happen to small children and the terrible things that probably had happened to our baby sister. The worst memory I have is the first day, a few hours after Jennie disappeared. The police were there. Half the shoppers in the mall were there. Security found this suspicious car on the side of the parking lot. It was an old four-door sedan. I was too little then to identify cars. But it was heavier and longer than the cars I knew. It was filthy. Its upholstery was torn, like something had chewed it. One of the policemen took a metal stick from his car and pried open the trunk. When my mother screamed, I realized that the policeman thought my baby sister might be in there. I remember looking around, quick, counting the rest of us. Yes, Jodie was there. Yes, Brian was there. Yes, Brendan was there. I remember Daddy's car shooting into the parking lot. I remember how he leapt out of the car and forgot to close the door and ran over and it was like his face had fallen off and I didn't know who he was. And I remember my mother tottering toward the abandoned car, making these little noises, like an animal, but there was nothing in the trunk after all, and we were supposed to feel better. I looked out at that huge parking lot, all those hundreds of cars, and all those trunks. For years, I kept counting my brothers and sister, to make sure the rest of us were all still here."

Kathleen sank down on the hard surface of Stephen's IKEA sofa. She had pictured a giggly Hannah and an adorable Jennie/Janie. But it had been hell, and pieces of hell still lay around, waiting in ambush.

She took Stephen's hand. It lay hot and feverish in hers.

Over the years Jennie was missing, there might have been days when Donna Spring did not worry about her baby.

But she didn't think so.

The FBI believed that her missing daughter had been dead from the first day. Kidnappers rarely had long-term plans.

From the beginning, Donna had been swamped in her

guilt. *I'm the mother. It's my fault Jennie wandered away. My fault I didn't notice until it was too late.*

Nobody had had cell phones the year Jennie was kidnapped.

The minute they became widely available, Mrs. Spring bought one for each child, although at the time there was no such thing as a small child with a cell phone. Teachers and other parents disapproved. Donna and Jonathan Spring didn't care. It was the duty of Stephen, Jodie, Brendan, and Brian not just to text or call several times a day, but also to send photographs to establish that they were alive and well in a known location. On their contact lists were the numbers for their family's own personal FBI agent, local policeman, and state trooper.

Cell phones siphoned off some of Donna Spring's ongoing fear for her four remaining children.

After a decade or so, guilt receded an inch and fury moved in.

It was not *my* fault! It was the fault of the kidnapper. That hideous evil cruel woman who snatched my baby.

Fury came in rounds, as if Donna Spring were being executed by the firing squad of her own rage.

They had descriptions of that woman from the ice cream servers, and a fuzzy video of the back of a woman leaving the mall, holding Jennie's hand.

But they never had anything more.

Twelve years had gone by when Donna and Jonathan Spring decided to put Jennie's face on a milk carton.

And then came the wonderful, awful year when Jennie

was back so briefly and left so quickly. The year Donna sank into despair. She had no place to put her love for this child. And this child had no love for her.

Almost as bad as losing Jennie a second time was the attack of the media. The media never failed to point out that Donna "let" one of her children wander off in a mall. They loved to dwell on their vision of Donna twelve years later, driving her child back to live with the "kidnap parents" again.

The media loved that phrase, although Frank and Miranda had kidnapped nobody. But the media rarely mentioned Hannah. The success of the face on a milk carton and the endless unrolling of Janie's saga were more interesting than some criminal who was never found and whose life was guesswork.

Over time, Donna and Jonathan's lost daughter seemed less and less a girl named Jennie Spring and more and more a girl named Janie Johnson.

And then, unnoticed by the media, a day here and a weekend there, Janie began to come home again. It was the most wonderful, unexpected gift in seventeen years: Donna Spring was getting her daughter back.

Janie became close to Brian, the sweetest of the five Spring children. She even began getting along with Jodie, the prickliest. Stephen, the oldest, rarely came home from Colorado, and was hardly aware that Janie was reentering the family, while Brendan was always at some stadium or locker room and didn't care.

Brendan.

In the end, Donna thought perhaps Brendan was her lost

child. She had cheered him along through life, hoping that his daydreams were rational, but knowing in her heart that he would never become a professional athlete.

She knew his freshman year at college was agony. She prayed he would grow stronger through adversity, but that didn't always happen. They had a hideous example in Hannah Javensen. A child who never quite found friendship, scholarship, or even fun, and who, blaming the world, had left the world. Hannah had found comfort in a group of manipulative adults who hid her away, warped her mind, and eventually sent her out to earn money on the street.

Donna knew that Brendan had given his second interview. He had texted her, his brief note a jab, as if he were saying, "Hah! So there!" She knew why he was giving interviews: they let him be important for an hour.

Donna Spring gave a lot of thought to the concept of a true crime book.

Most true crime books were about murders and, specifically, the murderer. Most featured in-depth analyses of the families and childhoods of the murderers and their victims. The problem Calvin Vinesett faced in writing this book was that the primary victim, Janie, would never consent to an interview. Janie wanted it over with, not reconstituted and served up in bookstores and online.

But for Donna, a book was the last remaining tool to draw out Hannah Javensen. And Donna wanted this criminal behind bars.

By now, Hannah Javensen was well into her forties. Was she fat, haggard, and a smoker? Or thin, wasted, and a druggie?

Had she reformed and become a successful real estate agent, resembling any other suburban housewife?

Donna imagined Calvin Vinesett's book stacked in piles on bestseller tables, flying into e-readers, rushing into libraries.

What if Hannah Javensen read it? Because Miranda and Frank's daughter was still literate, whatever else she had lost.

A shadow of fear landed on Donna Spring. It was physical, as if the kidnapper had tapped her on the shoulder. She whirled around to see who was there.

Nobody, of course.

And yet she felt the kidnapper's presence, like a poison gas.

She checked the front and back doors, to be sure they were locked and nobody was out there.

The worst thing in life is to be nobody.

If Hannah Javensen is still nobody, what might she do in order to become somebody? wondered Donna Spring. You don't wake sleeping predators. You don't poke a lion or throw stones at a rabid dog. You don't knock on the door of a murderer.

My daughter's kidnapper is sleeping.

Suppose the research for this book wakes her up.

Suppose she remembers what fun it was, and wants to do it again.

Suppose the book not only tells us things about her. . . .

Suppose it tells *her* something about *us*?

THE FIFTH PIECE OF THE KIDNAPPER'S PUZZLE

Hannah could not understand how her parents' phone number could be disconnected. Had they moved away from her childhood home? From the house where the three of them had planted tulip bulbs together and had her birthday parties and decorated Christmas trees and painted her bedroom?

At pay phones, for weeks, she asked Directory Assistance to locate the new phone number of Frank Javensen. She named towns close to where she had grown up. But the mean phone company would never search more than a few towns at a time and she never located the Javensens.

Yet the checks continued to come to the box, so wherever Frank and Miranda had gone, it wasn't prison.

The checks angered her. They expected their daughter to live on this measly amount of money? The one in prison, as far as Hannah could see, was herself. She had to work long nasty hours at long nasty jobs. She could not get jobs at fast-food places because she had no social security number. Tiffany Spratt's driver's license was not enough. Hannah had to slave at low-class motels or load dishwashers at greasy little diners. When she was so fragile!

She held jobs that only undocumented and illegal immigrants took.

But then, she too was undocumented, and probably more illegal than anybody sliding over a border in the dark.

Sometimes, when she was scrubbing a toilet in a motel or pots and pans in a stinking kitchen, she remembered her childhood dreams. To be a ballet dancer or a high-fashion model. A poet or an ice skater. An archaeologist or a movie reviewer or a yacht captain. She remembered that she had meant to write the Great American Novel and get a 10 in an Olympics competition.

The years passed.

The world changed.

The Internet exploded.

Suddenly, a person could research with amazing ease. Hannah spent a lot of time at the library, where computers were free. But you could sit for only thirty minutes and then you had to give your seat to the next person. There was so much regulation in this world! She despised the librarians, who had those fake smiles and always, eventually, made her give the computer to somebody else.

But no matter where and how she searched, and no matter how good at searching she became, she did not find Frank and Miranda Javensen. Javensen was such a rare name it should have popped up instantly.

But it never popped up.

She did find old newspaper articles on the kidnapping at

that mall in New Jersey. She did not use the word "kidnap" herself. It sounded so criminal. She just thought of it as "that day."

"That day" had gotten a lot of coverage. Hannah devoured every word. She added to the list of people she hated. Those ice cream clerks, for example. What did the kidnapper look like? they were asked. "Long hair," said the ice cream people. "Dishwater blond. But it was the little girl we looked at. She was totally adorable. We hardly noticed the woman."

Dishwater? Her beautiful yellow hair? How dare they?

It turned out that the little kid's name had been Jennie.

Oh, thought Hannah, giggling. I thought she said her name was Janie. Oh, well.

She scoured the online archives for follow-up articles. But it was a story without an ending, and interest in the disappearance of little Jennie Spring tapered away. The police never connected Hannah with it and therefore never connected Frank and Miranda.

She wondered if Frank and Miranda had made the connection. Or had they been too busy shopping for the sippy cup, the pajamas, and the car seat?

If she could figure out where Frank and Miranda had moved, she would just go there. She was in the perfect blackmail position. "Give me money," she'd say, "or lose the kid." One year she tried Houston, to see if life was easier there, but it wasn't. Another year she drifted east and tried New York City. A bad experience. She'd been arrested.

Well, it wasn't her fault, she'd thought, sitting there in the cell.

Jail was a scary stinking noisy place with scary people. She sat, trying not to be noticed, thinking of the group she had joined when she was young. What had she been looking for?

Not independence. She did not want to be free to choose. She wanted somebody else to do the choosing.

Not fashion. She did not want to worry about clothing and hair and nail polish. She wanted a uniform in which she would be invisible.

Not fine restaurants or good cars or sparkling jewelry. She did not want stuff. She wanted a lack of stuff.

She didn't want to search for friends and work to keep them. She wanted people assigned to sit next to her who would automatically be her friends.

The other women in that cell in New York got out quick, because somebody was posting bail for them. Hannah didn't know anybody who would do it for her. Her very own parents didn't know she was here and obviously didn't care, or they would have kept in touch.

She served her time. When the jail term was finally over, she'd gone back west, where the sun was warmer and the questions were fewer. A little pile of checks was waiting in Tiffany Spratt's post office box.

Life dragged on.

She found a grim little place to live and bought a used television at a thrift shop. She had once despised people who watched television. They had no lives. Their friends were the emcees of quiz shows and the interviewers on talk shows. Their social life was the situation comedy, the drama, or the police series.

But over the years, her own life dwindled to the screen in front of her.

Sports saved her.

It was the only bright and happy thing she had.

Somebody always won.

It was so mysterious, the way somebody always won.

She had never won anything.

Couldn't there be a day, sometime, somewhere, when she would win?

Hannah couldn't remember what year she had been in that mall in New Jersey. At least a decade ago. Probably more than that, she thought.

Her new hobby had been going into big-box stores that sold all kinds of electronic stuff and had whole walls of televisions. She loved to pretend she could afford a big-screen TV and pay the monthly fee for hundreds of channels.

One day she was drifting past the television displays, wishing they weren't all tuned to the same boring news station. Each screen showed the same news anchors sitting behind the same desk. Their huge gleaming smiles had beamed at Hannah. She herself could not afford a dentist. She had terrible teeth.

"After twelve years, Jason," the beautiful newswoman was saying, "the kidnap victim recognized her own face on a missing child picture on a milk carton!" The camera focused on a tiny white milk carton that sported a tiny black-and-white photograph.

It was that New Jersey mall kid! Hannah had put her hands over her mouth to keep the giggles from splattering out. At last, Frank and Miranda were going to pay big-time for liking a strange toddler more than they liked their own daughter.

"It is amazing, Abby!" gasped the handsome male anchor. "The little girl has not yet been reunited with her birth family. Heartbreakingly, the kidnap victim, now almost fifteen years old, snatched from a shopping mall at age three, wishes to stay with her kidnap family."

I did not snatch her! thought Hannah indignantly. She took my hand.

"A judge is considering the situation, which is complex, and if I may say so, Abby, the claims here are difficult to believe."

They beamed at each other.

Hannah was so excited she dropped her hand from her mouth and beamed right back at Abby and Jason. In thirty seconds, she would be told where her parents were.

"The alleged kidnapper," said Abby, "is a woman named Hannah Javensen."

Her name leapt out of dozens of televisions. And there was her high school yearbook photograph! Oh, she had been so pretty! Look! Her yellow hair, shining like silk. Her sweet smile. Her elegant swanlike neck. The pearls nestled at her throat.

"Allegedly, after snatching the toddler, Hannah Javensen delivered the child to her own parents, Frank and Miranda Javensen. This couple—you can see them here, trying to shield their faces—allege that they did not know the little girl had been kidnapped. They allege that their daughter, Hannah, claimed the little girl was *her* daughter and therefore their granddaughter." Abby and Jason exchanged skeptical looks. "The couple further allege that this daughter, Hannah Javensen, asked them to bring the baby up for her, and drove away."

It worked, thought Hannah, a little dazed. Everything I did worked.

It was meant to be. I was guided.

She preened a little, enjoying her moment of fame, and found that she was not the only one looking at those screens. Customers and clerks were also staring. Did they know? Did they guess? Did they recognize her as the beautiful high school girl? Was some slimy little clerk this very minute calling 911 to turn Hannah in?

It took all her self-control to drift out of the store instead of run.

Of course, she had always had superb self-control.

Once she was out on the sidewalk, she glanced back to see if anybody was following her, but all she could see was a reflection in the window wall. Some fat woman in saggy clothes.

CHAPTER FIVE

The most wonderful weekend of Janie Johnson's life was coming to a close.

Janie prayed for something to delay the moment Reeve dropped her at the airport. Traffic jams! Snow! Although here in North Carolina, it was eighty-four degrees.

She wanted to cry, "Let's change the ticket, Reeve! I don't have to fly out Sunday afternoon! I can leave tomorrow morning!"

But she could feel Reeve turning toward work, thinking of Monday. All weekend, Reeve had talked about his job. In high school and college, Reeve had struggled. School didn't delight him and sometimes defeated him. But he had landed this dream job with ESPNU, and in real life—as he called work—Reeve excelled.

Janie was here because she did not excel at real life. Reeve had rescued her, but he always had. No surprise there.

She felt as if she had met him all over again. The good, solid Reeve, whose love had been steady. She had met herself, too—a person who could revel in what she knew about Reeve. Everything, really.

Janie sat squarely in the front passenger seat of Reeve's car, feet on the floor, shoulders restrained. On the other side of the cup holders and gears, Reeve's seat belt kept him upright and distant.

This was how they would part: neatly and safely.

When he pulled up to the terminal, she would release her belt and lean sideways to deposit a good-bye kiss on his cheek. Reeve would not release his seat belt, but just kiss her back, his fingers still on the wheel. He would wait until she was inside the terminal before he sped off. In half an hour, he would be at the job he loved and Janie Johnson would become a person he texted now and then.

I will not cry, Janie told herself. Reeve bought my plane ticket. He gave me every minute of a perfect weekend. I will give him my best smile so we can separate easily and he can get on with his life.

She distracted herself by thinking about his tiny apartment. She had felt so domestic there, wanting to furnish it and buy better towels and stock the kitchen.

Unlike New York City airports, which you only reached after driving forever in ghastly traffic, crossing bridges, and paying tolls, the Charlotte airport was right here. In only a moment, Reeve was turning into the Departures lane.

She stole a glance at him. He was frowning slightly. She had a sense that Reeve was on the cusp of something important, something he had chosen not to share with her.

Janie swallowed hard. She was simply going back to an

exam at college, but he was moving on. She wanted to fling her arms around him, tell him that she loved him madly, trusted him wholly, never wanted to leave.

No.

A simple smile was best.

At the door she would turn and blow him another kiss.

But what if she turned, fingers lifted, and he was already driving away?

No.

She would not turn back.

Reeve Shields did not think anybody on earth was as lucky as he was: production assistant in an ESPN office that concentrated on college sports. It didn't get any better. Even when it was hard, Reeve's job wasn't work. It was joy.

Of course, they didn't pay much for a job that everybody else in the world wanted too. Reeve didn't care. Renting a tiny apartment in Charlotte, North Carolina, was not expensive. His at-home entertainment was just to watch more sports on TV, or else go to a sports bar and then talk about those games with everybody else in the office the next day. Every day he learned something. Reeve had never been all that fond of learning something, or even anything. It was a treat to find himself galloping into work every morning, eager to learn more.

It was no forty-hour week, either. It was usually sixty. Sometimes eighty.

He'd had Janie since Friday afternoon. Almost forty-eight hours. Perfect hours, but it felt as if he hadn't been in the office in months.

They reached the airport in no time.

He wasn't ready.

He had thought he would be eager to put her on the plane. He would forget her the minute she was out of sight, drive straight to the office in Ballantyne, spend Sunday evening catching up. But he was swamped by an emotion he had not expected. His mouth was dry. His heart was racing.

No wonder that smooth New York City graduate student had pretended to be dating Janie instead of admitting he was researching her. Who wouldn't lie in order to stay in Janie's life? Janie turned down all interviews from all people, up to and including the FBI, so Calvin Vinesett had probably told this guy Michael to weasel his way into Janie's life.

Reeve was proud of himself. He hadn't even demanded the guy's last name or address so he could go kill him, which the guy deserved.

Reeve considered a bigger problem. Michael was history, but Janie had two more years of college, where she would be surrounded by guys more intelligent and more interesting than Reeve, and she'd pick one. How often were Janie and Reeve going to see each other? Not often enough.

"You can just drop me off," said Janie, her eyes on the signs, looking for her airline.

Reeve shot into short-term parking instead. It was such a small airport that Reeve could park only steps from the terminal. "We're early. We can spend another minute together." He found a space and turned off the engine. He reached for Janie's bag, which they had gotten at the mall when they were buying her clothing for the weekend. But she had already retrieved it, and was slinging the slim, dark red canvas tote over her shoulder.

I can't even carry something for her, he thought.

He circled the car and could not even take her hand, because she was patting her stuff, the way travelers did, reassuring herself that she had her purse, her ID, her sunglasses, and her cell phone.

Heat slammed down on them when they left the shade of the parking garage. Moments later came the icy shock of the air-conditioned terminal.

Departures were on the upper level. Reeve knew that Janie would take the stairs, not the escalator. For her, the hard part of flying was sitting still. She liked to stretch her legs before the prison of the airplane.

Her perfect legs, he thought.

Charlotte to New York was only an hour and a half. She wouldn't suffer much.

I'm the one who will suffer. I'll be alone.

He had not previously noticed that he lived alone. Now he was grateful he could return to the office instead of his silent, partially furnished little apartment.

Since she had checked in online, and had no luggage, Janie had nothing to do upstairs except go through security. Reeve wanted to talk, but Janie had gotten through this weekend without a tear. In fact, they had done nothing but laugh and love. She refused to break down now.

They stared at each other for one helpless emotional moment, and then kissed lightly, as if they had recently met and were mildly fond of each other.

Reeve stayed where he was.

Janie got in line.

There were dozens of people, the line curving back and forth in divisions marked by stretched ropes. When she looked at Reeve, her heart clutched. What am I panicking about? she asked herself. Michael's not going to bother me again. Yes, he's still in the city. Yes, I'm going back where he slimes around, like a slug in a garden, smearing my life. But Michael is history. He isn't worth panic.

She could not settle her lungs. They fluttered.

She could not still her heart. It banged.

The line moved. She was halfway to the TSA official who would check her ID.

I'm panicking because I'm not going to see Reeve again for ages. Because he's perfect, and perfect guys don't just sit quietly in front of their televisions watching ball games. They get snagged by perfect girls.

She set her jaw and blinked back the wetness in her eyes. She could not ruin this weekend by sobbing.

When she turned to wave, Reeve did not wave back. He just stood there. Oh, but he was the handsomest thing on earth. He was perfect.

Well, no, not perfect. Reeve had his flaws. Janie knew them well. He had worked past some of them, and others he had outgrown.

He seemed so much older. A good job and responsibility

had made him grow up, as if adding inches. He was taller and leaner and straighter.

"I love you," she said softly, and although he could not hear in the hubbub of the airport, he should have been able to read her lips.

But he barely nodded.

Reeve had spent a lot of time this weekend running his fingers through Janie's beautiful red-gold hair. Her hair had darkened, no longer vivid auburn but a deeper color, and she too was deeper; little Janie was gone. He would see the old Janie now only in photographs. This was a woman, and in some ways, he knew her better than anybody, but in other ways, Janie was still a mystery.

I love you, she said soundlessly.

Around her, families and businesspeople, conventioneers and tourists, children and wheelchairs moved slowly forward, everybody holding their hand luggage and their identification. Reeve shifted position so he could still see her. All that was left to him was a few minutes before she walked past the guards and vanished from his sight. "Janie?" he said.

His voice was drowned out by loud airport announcements, the talk and phone calls around her, a sobbing baby, and a wildly laughing trio of travelers.

"Janie!" he repeated loudly.

Janie had heard him the first time. She steadied herself so that she didn't leap over the carry-ons, shove the guards out of the way, and land on top of Reeve. When she could face him without excess emotion, she gave him a controlled smile.

"Janie?" he called, edging closer.

A guard frowned slightly.

Reeve was probably going to ask her to visit again one day soon and she was certainly going to say yes. She smiled for real, no holding back.

But Reeve Shields did not ask her to visit.

Across the bodies and the luggage of strangers, Reeve Shields yelled, "Janie! Will you marry me?"

The whole long line turned. Businessmen in suits turned. Businesswomen in pencil skirts, tired fathers and irritated mothers, a tour group of fat elderly women in sweat suits, Indians in saris, and salesmen with cases turned. Teenagers turned and ticket agents turned.

Travel tension vanished.

The crowd waited for Janie's answer, and their smiles waited too. Even the guards waited.

Marry! thought Janie. Marry this boy? But he's a man now. He's three years older than I am, and I am twenty.

Marriage.

More than a thousand times she had thought about marrying Reeve Shields.

But people her age didn't get married.

They lived together.

How incredible and wonderful that Reeve had asked her to marry him.

Reeve, who had stood beside her through so many episodes

of the long sad kidnap drama. Reeve, who had betrayed her as much as anybody.

She thought of every reason to get married and every reason not to.

A hundred travelers held their breath.

Reeve held out his arms.

Janie held out hers.

Yes! thought Reeve, giddy with joy. She's going to say yes!

"Yes," said Janie Johnson softly. And then she yelled, "Yes, yes, and yes!"

A guard released the rope that kept the passengers winding toward the security X-rays. Janie ran to Reeve and he wrapped his arms around the girl he wanted forever. The entire line clapped and cheered and one man gave that splendid arena-filling whistle of appreciation.

Reeve never wanted to stop kissing her but he did, and he said, "Let's get married now. Move here with me. Finish college here. I miss you already. I want to be together."

Get married *now*?

Impossible.

Janie had two more years of college.

And she wanted a real wedding; the kind that takes months to plan. People couldn't show up for a wedding now. If they got married *now*, her mother would kill her.

Which mother? thought Janie, her face buried against Reeve's shoulder. Which mother will be my mother for a wedding? Which father will be my father?

"Wedding" was such a beautiful word, full of silk and

white veils, flowers and long aisles, trumpets and church. Friends and family. But the wedding of Janie Johnson, aka Jennie Spring, might be a little too full.

If we marry now, thought Janie, I get to live far away from both sets of parents. I will not have to juggle both sets. I will not have to deal with my Johnson parents.

She loved the Johnsons. She understood. She forgave. But remembering what her Johnson father had done could still leave her trembling with anger and hurt. Was it right to get married just to solve family problems? Maybe it was an excellent reason. Maybe it was no reason.

If we marry now, I will be hundreds of miles from Calvin Vinesett and his hired stalkers, who can write nothing without me, because it's my story. Is running away from a problem a reason to get married?

She thought of Reeve's tiny rooms and his three pieces of furniture. The apartment would be hers, and she had always wanted to decorate her own place. Reeve would think anything she did was perfect. Was it right to get married just so she could paint a living room?

She was deafened by the clapping and calling and whistling of the crowd. Sort of a prewedding reception.

Reeve whispered, "I'll get us two puppies. You can call them Denim and Lace."

When she was in middle school, Janie had wanted to have twin daughters someday whom she would name Denim and Lace. Later on, of course, she knew that if she really did name her little girls that, they would sue her for bad parenting and call themselves Emily and Ashley instead.

Janie certainly wanted children. As many kids as her New Jersey family. But not now. She hadn't figured out how to take care of herself yet, never mind babies. And puppies were babies. Perhaps Reeve wanted to marry her so that there would be somebody home to walk the dogs.

It made her laugh.

Laughter was good. It broke tears. "When exactly is 'now'?" she asked.

"How about the Fourth of July? Because this deserves fireworks," said Reeve.

"That's six weeks. Do weddings come together in six weeks?"

"My sister's wedding and my brother's wedding each took a year of planning. Let's not have that kind of wedding. Let's just race down the aisle, say I do, and run off together."

Janie and Sarah-Charlotte had passed many an hour planning their weddings, leafing through brides' magazines and designing invitations. And now it was here, and Reeve just wanted to race down the aisle.

"That," said Janie, "is the best wedding gift I will ever have. My guy just wants to race down the aisle and shout yes."

They sealed it with a kiss.

"Ma'am?" said a guard courteously.

Janie had never been addressed as "ma'am." Had she aged a couple of decades just because somebody proposed marriage?

"I don't want to interrupt your whole future, ma'am," he said, "but when does your plane leave? The other passengers are holding your place in line."

Janie let go of Reeve. She backed into the line.

There were final cheers from the audience. Several people yelled, "Give me your cell phone number! I took pictures!"

"I took a video," yelled somebody else. "Tell me where to send it."

Janie never told anybody anything, but Reeve shouted out his cell phone number and everybody who had taken pictures on a cell phone got busy.

In a moment, Janie was holding out her driver's license to be matched to her plane ticket. The license read *Jane Johnson,* which was not in fact her name. Had never been her name. It was just the name she used.

Who, exactly, will race down the aisle and say yes? Janie wondered. Somebody named Janie Johnson, who doesn't exist? Or somebody named Jennie Spring, who was kidnapped, vanished, and has only partly emerged?

Now I never have to decide! I will be Mrs. Reeve Shields instead.

"Congratulations," said another agent. "Take your shoes off, please."

Janie was out of sight.

Reeve shook hands with total strangers and got hugs from women crying "That made my day!" and posed with tourists who wanted the picture for their scrapbooks.

He opened his iPhone. His witnesses vanished along with Janie, past the X-rays and into the airport, but their photos and videos were already his. Reeve opened the pictures of himself and Janie and watched the video.

It was good that he had these.

Without proof, Reeve would never believe that he had actually asked Janie Johnson to marry him, let alone that she had said yes.

He emailed the photographs and video to Janie. She was at the gate, she texted back, surrounded by well-wishers.

Reeve sat on a metal bench and emailed practically everybody whose number was stored on his phone. He didn't write any messages. He attached the pictures and let them speak for themselves.

Then he uploaded everything to Facebook.

Then he watched his video again.

Janie was still saying yes.

THE SIXTH PIECE OF THE KIDNAPPER'S PUZZLE

In the trailer where she was living at the time, Hannah followed the milk carton story, glued to the news and talk shows on her little television. She even bought newspapers, especially ones with tall fat headlines, and scoured each article. They all referred to the Jennie/Janie as a "victim." It was so annoying. The little girl had never protested! She had been perfectly happy to eat the ice cream Hannah had bought for her. Hannah was the victim! One afternoon taking a kid for a ride had led to a ruined life!

But the talk shows were stymied. Even though every professional and amateur psychologist out there had opinions, nobody in either family would give interviews. The New Jersey mother and father said things like "We're confident everything will work out." Hannah's own mother and father were cowards; they turned their faces from the cameras and wore sunglasses.

Hannah could not get over that Frank and Miranda had believed her so completely. They knew she was a liar. They knew she never bothered with the truth. And yet when it came to this huge thing—an actual living kid—they went and believed her. What was up with pretending to be the Jennie/Janie's mother and father instead of her grandmother and grandfather? Maybe they wanted another shot at raising a daughter. Maybe they just wanted to fit in at the PTA meetings.

But one thing was for sure: two families were fighting to the finish to keep the Jennie/Janie. Nobody but the police wanted Hannah. In fact, in all the coverage of this case and the custody of the Jennie/Janie, the most important person was hardly ever mentioned.

Just about the only people who mentioned Hannah were the Spring parents. "Stop focusing on us," they would tell the media. "Find Hannah Javensen."

It was not healthy to want revenge like that. It was better to understand and forgive than to nurse anger. The whole thing had happened years ago. Hannah had hardly thought about it when it did happen and hardly thought about it after it happened, and anyway, that Jennie/Janie girl was fine.

Hannah came close to calling up some of those reporters. She yearned to tell everything. She would put an end to that "victim" nonsense. She would laugh in her parents' faces and smirk at those Springs. But satisfying as that might be, it would end in jail. Hannah had done short stretches. She didn't want a long one.

At the library, she tortured herself by gathering more details. You had to be careful at libraries. Librarians were always leaning over your shoulder. Other patrons liked to gab about their projects, and the librarians followed everybody's passion and scurried over with some new angle or book. You had to be especially careful when printing something out. They were bound to hover. Hannah had a fat folder with every photograph she had cut from a library newspaper and all the printouts from online sites. She didn't want any snoopy librarian seeing it.

She liked to study those Spring people. There were so many of them, and they all had red hair. They looked like Easter rabbits dyed for the occasion. Some of them had curly red hair and some of them flat red hair and some of them redder red hair, but they were all healthy and freckled and proud of themselves.

Hannah had been too busy following the news to go to the post office. It had been fun, but now she had to get her money. She was not many blocks away from the branch when it occurred to her that her father would give her up. Now that the FBI knew that the Jennie/Janie wasn't Frank and Miranda's daughter and that their actual daughter had driven the Jennie/Janie up from New Jersey, Frank would tell! Frank would save himself, because he had always put himself first, and never Hannah.

Close to the post office, right this very minute, cops were probably hiding in parked cars, slumped behind steering wheels, sipping cold coffee, looking for a slim golden-haired young woman.

But she was smart and they were stupid. She swung away from the post office branch. She would have to go to Denver for a while. But wait! Denver was very close. The police would think of looking in Denver!

She had no choice. She left the state. She was forced to travel a long way. She was forced to steal. The one good thing about all the publicity was that Hannah did not need a library or a television. She could just read the headlines in tabloids.

Nothing happened to her parents. No arrests. No trials.

The weeks became months. She was desperate for money. Shortly before the annual rent on the box was due, Hannah made her way back to Boulder, walked quietly into the post office lobby, and put her key in the lock of the little box—and there lay her checks.

Her father had not turned her in. He was still sending money. It wasn't because he loved her. It was to buy her off.

She cashed her checks at her old bank and at last managed a nice long visit to a library. She had missed an important episode in the life of the Jennie/Janie. Through the courts, the Spring family had finally gotten their kid—but the Jennie/Janie left them and went back to Hannah's parents.

Frank and Miranda *still* wanted these other people's little girl more than they wanted their own little girl.

If only Hannah could make them suffer the way she had to suffer.

CHAPTER SIX

Brendan Spring's first interview had been fun. He knew that Janie—always the star in her own personal soap opera—would hate it that he was talking to the media about her. Brendan rather enjoyed sticking it to her.

The second interview was difficult, seeing as Brendan had already told everything he knew. He wanted another free dinner, though, so he pretended he had more to say and was holding back.

The night before the third interview, Brendan had trouble sleeping. The long year of anger was over. He was just confused. He could not think of anything to do all day. He wasn't interested in going to class. It hardly mattered now anyway. Classes were mainly over.

He wanted to pretend that he had never wanted success.

He wanted to pretend that success would come in the morning.

He wanted to have a better life handed to him.

A few hours before dawn, Brendan Spring realized that he was not the strong one in his family. He was the weak one.

When it was finally time to meet the interviewer at the restaurant, he remembered that Mom always said a good hot meal solved many problems.

Maybe she was right, but Brendan couldn't eat. He didn't know what he was doing here. He didn't even know what he was doing on Earth.

For a while the researcher did the talking. Perhaps he couldn't stand the silence. Perhaps he was hoping to jump-start Brendan. He told Brendan about the support checks Frank had been sending Hannah all these years.

Somebody in his family had done some serious talking. Brendan only knew about Frank's checks because he knew there was some secret about that trip to Colorado that Janie and Reeve and Brian had taken. Brendan had pounded his twin until Brian gave it up. "How come we're not telling the FBI?" Brendan had asked him.

"Because the one who'd be in trouble is Janie's father, and she loves her father, and in fact, I like him too," said Brian. "Frank is a good guy."

"Good guys send money every month to kidnappers?" Brendan demanded.

His twin had been uncomfortable. They were always uncomfortable with Janie's reality. But here in the restaurant, Brendan was really uncomfortable. This researcher knew more about the checks than Brendan did. Who had told him this stuff? Janie herself?

But Janie had practically hidden under the couch that day the FBI came and Dad kicked them out. Okay, sure, years had passed—she was older—but still. Brendan could not believe Janie had talked.

Stephen?

Stephen regarded the kidnapping and its effect on them as poison. Stephen wanted the kidnapper caught and imprisoned, but Stephen would not share intimate details with anybody about anything.

Jodie?

Brendan didn't understand this sister. He could see taking a year off to hitchhike in Europe, although he personally didn't care whether Europe even existed. But Jodie had gone to a third world island with no economy, fresh from earthquakes, waist-deep in rubble, where she was teaching English and tooth brushing. Yes, her cell phone worked and yes, she communicated all the time. You couldn't tell she was living in another world. She could have dealt with this guy by texting or whatever. But Brendan doubted it. Jodie had been hurt more than any of them by Janie's dislike of her real family. Jodie had made peace with their younger sister, but Brendan believed she was in Haiti partly to put serious distance between herself and the family. He did not think Jodie would tell a researcher anything.

Brian?

His twin was very bookish. Maybe he was in love with the idea of being part of a book. And for sure, Brian loved talking.

And yet, as the researcher moved into other topics and Brendan played with his food, he had a weird sense that the researcher was quoting a woman. It just didn't sound like a guy.

There was only one other female in the family.

Mom.

He tried to imagine her in a restaurant pouring out her heart to this man. What would be the point? Mom could talk forever about the kidnap and it wouldn't change the fact that her kidnapped daughter preferred her kidnap family.

And Brendan himself could talk forever—although he'd never talked once—about being a failure, and that wouldn't make him a success.

Brendan poured A1 sauce on his steak. Like everything else, it reminded him that he had not turned out to be A-one.

"How do you picture Hannah now?" asked the interviewer.

Brendan never thought of stuff like that, although the rest of his family was obsessed with the kidnapper. Hannah Javensen had been his age, and also in her second semester of freshman year, when she'd joined that cult.

Brendan felt a stab of sympathy for Hannah. She too had probably expected to be special. But no—she was just another invisible mediocrity. They probably offered her steak too, he thought. She probably dipped a bite in A1 sauce and knew she was actually C minus. And they probably said to her, "Come to us. We're your new friends. In our group, you'll be A-one. Which you deserve! Your parents were bad. They placed unfair demands on you. We will never do that."

"Lemme read some of the book," Brendan said roughly.

"I have a few chapters because Calvin Vinesett thinks it'll

help me do the interviews. But they're first drafts. He hasn't polished them yet."

"Listen," said Brendan Spring, "I read a book about every third year. Tops. I'm not gonna know if it's polished. Give it over. I wanna read some."

Jodie Spring had brought her sewing machine to Haiti, along with a suitcase of bright cotton cloth and dozens of yards of trim. The children who flocked to the church for food had old, torn clothes. Jodie could whip up an adorable smock-type dress and edge it with lace or a row of hearts. She set her sewing machine on a table next to the bottled water, the only safe water around, and sometimes the only water at all. The next little girl in line would choose her cloth from Jodie's stack. Jodie would cut it into two rectangles and string these on a collar made from the same fabric. She'd stitch up the sides and run the hem. The little girls were so happy in their new dresses.

Jodie ran out of cloth. Her church back home shipped more, but somebody stole the sewing machine. Jodie wept and the little girls who were not going to get dresses comforted her. She managed to hand-sew one dress, but each seam took a long time.

She used the rest of the trim for hair bows and bracelets. Her church shipped another sewing machine, but it never arrived. Somebody probably opened the crate and decided to keep it. She just hoped they were using it, instead of letting it rust.

She was utterly exhausted by Haiti.

Earthquakes had damaged so many buildings that her eye never rested on anything whole or painted or safe. Pieces of ruined structures stuck up in the air or lay in piles over yet more rubble. It seemed impossible that anybody could even walk down a street—that they could even locate the street! And yet people laughed and danced and wore bright clothing and thanked Jodie for coming.

The first few months had been so exciting. The next few months had been so busy. By the end of spring, she was drained. The nuns said Jodie had done great things.

But Jodie could not think of any.

Sometimes she played kickball with the kids. They did not have a ball. It was kick the can, which she had heard of but hadn't known people did literally. The church sent whatever Jodie requested, and sometimes it arrived, but people were so hungry for stuff that it never stayed at the mission. Soccer balls vanished in a knot of little boys joyful to have a real one, and books left the school shelves never to return.

"It's useless," Jodie said sadly.

"You were not useless," said the nuns. "You gave a year of your life to God and to the people of Haiti. You were a blessing, and you are blessed."

But she did not feel that way. On her life list, she could not write: *Save the world. Check.* She could only write: *Struggled in Haiti. Check.*

Thank God (literally; she thanked Him daily) for her cell phone. Every time she charged it (not always possible, in a place with occasional electricity), she went first to the calendar and stared at the date on which she would fly out.

I'm so proud of you, her girlfriend Nicole texted. Nicole was studying fashion design in New York City, which meant Nicole's life was the polar opposite of Jodie's. I ran into your mother, Nicole added. All excited because Janie stopped in.

That was EVER SO generous of Janie—to stop in, Jodie wrote back.

You're still mad at her, aren't you?

I'll ALWAYS be a little mad at her.

I haven't forgiven her for not loving us more than she loved the Johnsons, thought Jodie.

Jodie was standing within the convent walls. Well, not really, since most of the walls had fallen. She was standing within the rubble. But there was still a sense of enclosure. She could hear the noises of the town—different noises from at home: less traffic, more shouting; less machinery, more laughter—but she was wrapped inside the mission wall and had the faint sense of knowing what a real convent might be like for a real nun. You served God and the world, but you were enclosed in a wonderful way, with walls around and God above and sisters near.

Not that being enclosed with her real sister had been wonderful.

Maybe because it was a convent, Jodie could kneel easily. On her knees, she said silently to God, I want to forgive. Help me love Janie all the way through, all the time.

Nicole texted:

118

Would you still want to find the kidnapper, if you could?

In a heartbeat.

My cousin Vic is on the local police force now. They'd love to resurrect that cold case. They need some new thing to justify it.

And so, in Haiti, where wrong was so huge and pain so present, where Jodie could not solve a thing, where all she had to offer was a smile and a bowl of soup and a day of pointlessly shifting rubble, Jodie Spring decided there was one thing she could do: she could give the police a boost.

Frank Johnson always knew where Hannah was, and always sent her money.

Jodie texted: **Stephen knows which bank branch.**

Reeve Shields left the airport terminal and stood for a minute in the intense sunshine, letting it bake his body.

Janie phoned. "They delayed boarding. We can talk again."

Reeve entered the stuffy shade of the parking garage, sat in his car, and turned on the air-conditioning. They spent ten minutes getting mushy.

The Fourth of July turned out to be a weekday, so they settled on Saturday, July 8. "Today is May twenty-first," said Janie. "Seven weeks."

"Tons of time," said Reeve. "What do we do first?" He figured that whatever they did first would involve shopping. Reeve was not fond of shopping, but Janie loved it. Once they were married, she'd probably do all of it. Division of labor was good.

Of course, it's easier to shop when you have money.

Reeve knew to the dime how much he had in his checking and savings accounts. A week ago, he'd been rich, since his sixty-hour workweeks and required television left no time to spend money. No problem buying Janie a round-trip ticket for the weekend. But if he hoped to furnish a life, it looked tricky.

Janie moved on. "The big problem is," she said, "what is my name?"

"Don't let airport security hear you. They hate when people fly under false names."

"It isn't false. I do have two names."

Reeve put the phone on speaker, drove out of the parking garage, paid, and headed for the highway.

"I want to get married under my legal name," Janie was saying. "Because marriage has to be true all the way through. So here's the plan."

Reeve loved that Janie would make the plans. She'd make a list, he'd follow it, that would be that. None of the boring discussion that had absorbed his sister Lizzie month after month. Like flowers. How much could you actually worry about flowers? You called the florist and they delivered, right?

"When we get to that part of the ceremony where you say 'I, Reeve, take you, Janie, for my wedded wife,' " Janie told him, "you will say 'I, Reeve, take you, *Jennie*, for my wedded wife.' "

Reeve didn't drive off the road, but it was close.

Wife?

Wife?

He, Reeve, was going to have a wife?

That meant he would be a thing called a husband.

A hideous drumming infected the wheels. He had drifted off the road onto the warning cuts in the pavement. He found his way back into the lane. "I don't call you Jennie," he said. "You're Janie."

"It's not that big of a change. Two letters."

"Is this just for the wedding vows or is this for good?" Reeve asked. "Am I marrying some stranger named Jennie?"

"She is a stranger," agreed Janie. "We both have to get to know her."

"I know how I'll handle it," said Reeve. "My brother, Todd, will be best man. Along with the ring, he can hold up a cue card. JENNIE, it'll say, in capital letters. That will add a certain something to the wedding memories. Groom tries to think of bride's name."

They were both laughing.

Janie said, "You won't have to remember long. In a minute, I'll have turned into Mrs. Reeve Shields."

This was such a startling fact that for a while, neither of them could speak.

Janie boarded the plane.

She barely knew that there were other passengers, that the plane was full, that she had a middle seat. She watched the little video Reeve had forwarded and held it to her heart.

Reeve loves me. She had always known that. She just hadn't known how much he loved her.

"At this time, please turn off all electronic devices," said the flight attendant.

Janie never thought of her beloved phone as an electronic device. She touched the tiny switch at the top and then she was no longer connected to Reeve.

This is crazy! she thought. Why did I even get on the plane? Reeve wants me to live with him! He wants a wedding so soon there isn't even time to arrange one! And I'm flying away?

Janie groped for the seat belt release. She would get off. Everybody would understand.

But the plane was already taxiing toward the runway.

She had waited too long.

When the plane took off, she stared down at a city she didn't know. Somewhere down there, in the unknown city of Charlotte in the unknown state of North Carolina, she and Reeve Shields would start their married lives.

Without access to her beloved electronic device, she had to resort to the pencil she found at the bottom of her purse. The only blank paper she had was the leftover piece of her ticket printout.

Things to do, she wrote at the top.

#1 Tell parents.

A task with many subdivisions and pitfalls. Her flight would land at Kennedy. New Jersey and Connecticut were equidistant. If I'm getting married as Jennie Spring, she thought, I need to tell my Spring parents first.

Donna loved texting and tweeting, so Janie knew that her parents had gone to a movie this afternoon and were firing up the grill tonight. Her plane would land at 6:01. She would call as soon as they touched the ground. She would take an airport bus to Jersey, where Jonathan and Donna would pick her up. By eight o'clock tonight, they'd know about the wedding.

Janie did not have the faintest idea how they would react.

Next, she would tell her other parents.

Every time Janie dealt with one mother and father first, she dealt with the other mother and father second. The others always knew that they were second and it always hurt.

How many blows could Miranda sustain without collapsing?

Sarah-Charlotte and her roommate, Lauren, watched the video over and over.

Lauren said, "She is the prettiest thing on earth and he is the most in love. Look at him! He's such a puppy of a guy! You just want to cuddle him. The whole security line loves him too! I don't think anybody is ever going to love me that much."

Sarah-Charlotte called Janie but the phone went to voice mail. She had to leave a message. "Love the video," she said. "Love the future. Call me, Janie."

She was crushed. I'm the best friend and I find out along with the world? I didn't even know she was still seeing Reeve. I thought she was in love with that Michael/Mick. I don't even know what airport that video's in.

She texted Reeve. **Congratulations.** She wanted to add "How come Janie hasn't called me?" but stopped herself.

Reeve texted back immediately. **Thx. She's airborne. She'll call u asap.**

Lauren swooned. "Not only is he adorable, he's thoughtful! I want him too. How can we pry him away from Janie and have him for ourselves?"

Stephen Spring was still sitting in front of his computer, trying to process the researcher's request. Kathleen leaned over his shoulder and read the rest of the message out loud. " 'Would you consider having dinner with me while I am here in Boulder? I have found a clue to Hannah Javensen's location and you and I can discuss it.'

"A clue!" cried Kathleen. "That's so exciting."

And so unlikely. Stephen had done his share of hunting for the kidnapper. Some grad student hired online to do preliminary interviews for the actual author (which was insulting; was it beneath Calvin Vinesett to meet the people he planned to make money off?) had found something Stephen hadn't?

Kathleen bumped into the computer desk, and little florets from the dried bouquet she had insisted on putting there showered the keyboard. "Let's go, Stephen! Aren't you dying of curiosity?"

Stephen sometimes thought Kathleen dated him because she was still curious about Janie. He read on.

Based on the fact that Mr. Javensen (aka Johnson) used a Boulder post office, I have been searching Boulder public records for some time now.

Three women fit the profile of Hannah Javensen.

All three live alone in the greater Boulder area. All three appear to be the right age—late forties or early fifties. All have unclear backgrounds.

Three possible Hannahs. Here. In Boulder.

He had always assumed that Hannah didn't live here because it was so expensive. That she had traveled to the post office once a month. Certainly after Frank's checks stopped coming, living here would have been very difficult.

Now he pictured her, walking the same sidewalks he did, drinking coffee at the same coffee shop, sitting on the same bench in the same open-air mall, enjoying the same mountain views.

He could imagine Hannah living a marginal existence. Renting under a roommate's name. Living illegally in a warehouse, taking her baths in a sink. Getting paid cash. But such a person would not show up in public records.

"I have to know who those three possible Hannahs are," he said to Kathleen. "I think this is a scam to get me to an interview. But maybe not. If I lay eyes on Hannah, I'll know. I've studied her high school photograph all these years. Jodie and I even went to New York City with that photograph, believing we could find her. I know Frank and Miranda pretty well too. And we have the picture the FBI artists came up with, aging her. We know what Hannah would look like in middle age. We're going to get the names and addresses of the possible Hannahs and check them out."

We?

Kathleen was so excited. She'd get to meet these possible

Hannahs? The researcher was obviously brilliant, to have gotten information the FBI hadn't found. Of course, the FBI didn't have the little piece of news that Hannah had had a Boulder post office box all these years.

Stephen paced. Kathleen loved when he paced. He was so adorable.

What she really wanted to do with her life was teach skiing in the winter here in Colorado and guide kayak tours on the coast of Alaska in the summer. Once she'd suggested that to Stephen and he had just looked at her. "I'm an engineer. I don't like tourists, and people who can't ski will have to do it without me."

It was too bad. All his female clients would fall madly in love with him.

Like me, she thought. And what good will it do them? He won't notice.

"You call the researcher, Kathleen," he said. "I'm ready to meet the guy, but I'm not telling him anything. The goal is to learn everything he knows."

Kathleen called the number the researcher had given in his email. She made her own voice uncertain and girlish, although she despised women who were uncertain and girlish. "Hi, this is Kathleen Donnelly? And I'm Stephen Spring's girlfriend?"

The researcher's voice was warm and friendly. "I'm delighted to hear from you."

"Well!" said Kathleen. "I am very, very intuitive. And Stephen needs to talk. It is not good for him to tamp down his emotional needs. Stephen is very, very, very tamped down. Let's meet for dinner tonight. I happen to be broke, so you'll be the host. I'll tell a few teeny-weeny details that you can use to move Stephen into those painful spaces he's protecting. Stephen is very, very walled up."

The researcher was thrilled. "That's my skill," he told her. "Convincing people to trust me."

When Kathleen disconnected, Stephen was staring at her.

"He's taking us to the Boulderado," she said. "Tonight."

"Nice. Be sure to eat well. It sounds as if you can handle it without me."

"Oh, come on. Now he'll underestimate us. Think of something you can tell him that will make him pliable, while I get dressed. The Boulderado is luxurious." She was wearing hiking boots, camo pants, and an old sweatshirt. "I'm not sure I own a dress at all," she told him, "never mind one I'd wear to the Boulderado. I don't want to waste time going back to my own apartment, especially when I won't find a dress there. Oh, this is such fun!"

She ran down the hall of Stephen's grad student housing and banged on a door. "Mandy! I'm desperate! I have to borrow some clothes!"

"This isn't a game!" Stephen yelled after her.

When Reeve had called Janie Friday afternoon and insisted that she fly down for the weekend, he made it sound simple. But weekends were when games happened. He had been scheduled to work the entire weekend, day and evening.

He had begged, pleaded, and offered trades, but everyone said no. By the time Janie's plane was airborne, he hadn't managed to get a single hour off. He had had to ask the boss.

The office was informal. He didn't even know his boss's real first name. He went by the nickname Bick.

"Janie?" said Bick, looking excited. "Janie Johnson is coming for the weekend? This is great. I can't wait to meet the face on the milk carton."

Reeve was stunned. They knew the media story of his girlfriend? He knew he had never mentioned it. "She hates when that comes up. Please, whatever you do—"

"Right. Absolutely. I won't refer to it. But you know, I hired you because of the janies."

The janies.

Reeve's own boss—at his own job—in the town where he was bringing the real Janie—a thousand miles south of where he'd betrayed her—knew about the janies.

Reeve had been eighteen and a total jerk. All he had cared about was getting a slot on a late-night talk show at his college radio station. Almost immediately, he ran out of things to say on the air. He stumbled and flubbed. A failure in five minutes. And then he remembered that he possessed a story he could tell forever.

Janie's.

He had spun it out, ratcheted up the emotion, strung it along night after night. It gave him a weird celebrity. The radio station had little power. It reached a small urban audience. They were fascinated by the janie episodes. In no time, he had a following.

It came to a halt when the living Janie, her sister, Jodie, and her brother Brian drove up to Boston to surprise him with a visit. It had never occurred to Reeve that Janie herself might ever be in his audience. Janie, Jodie, and Brian didn't kill Reeve, but only because they had no weapons.

The worst of it was, he had used her real name. Everybody who listened to those episodes referred to them as "the janies."

In Bick's office, Reeve said thickly, "You hired me because of the janies?"

"Yep. I was in Boston doing college basketball games and that night I heard a janie live, and a friend taped the rest for me because I had to head back down here. You were really good, Reeve."

"I shouldn't have done them."

"No, but you did them so well. You built up an audience. That's what we're all about here. Audience. I was scrolling through the applicants for this job and recognized your name. I figured, a guy like that—worth interviewing."

Everybody always asked Reeve how he had landed this amazing job, since he did not have amazing credentials. Reeve had wondered too. Now he knew. He was surprised by how much it hurt.

What if Janie found out that Reeve's betrayal had won him this job? Did he have to tell her? *Guess what, Janie? That problem back in Boston we never refer to because it's so upsetting? That's why I was hired.* Out loud he said to Bick, "The janies are not a good part of my past. If you run into her, please don't mention them."

"Oh, yeah, sure, because she'd probably have to kill you. How come she didn't kill you back then?"

"She's nice," said Reeve.

Bick grinned. "Have a good weekend. See you Monday morning."

Reeve had raced out of the building, driven fast to the bypass, and taken the speedy back entrance to the airport, substituting the demands of traffic for the shock of the janie problem. When he parked and got out of the car, he imagined Bick playing the janie tapes for Reeve's colleagues.

But when he put his arms around the real Janie, when they were laughing again in a minute, like old friends, when she kept leaning over to give him a kiss, and when he hugged her fiercely at every red light, he forgot.

Now Reeve drove to Ballantyne, a massive planned area with handsome corporate buildings, sprawling golf courses, a resort, and attractively landscaped apartment complexes. Green grass surrounded tiny ponds and sidewalks curled around orderly trees, all planted the same day and, twenty years later, all the same height.

Too bad he hadn't planned that carefully.

I will have to tell Janie that my voice on the radio didn't go away, he thought. If I don't, somebody else will. We'll live right here. And this is a partying crowd. She'll see those guys all the time.

And when he told her, what if Janie decided not to marry him after all?

His phone rang. It was his mother.

Reeve loved his mother, but he liked to talk to her under controlled circumstances. This was not one. She always wanted his full attention, and at work, he could give outsiders only about 1 percent of his attention. He'd call her later.

He waited a minute, and then listened to her message as he opened the car door.

He had completely forgotten that he had attached the pictures and video and sent them to everybody. Including his mother.

"Reeve darling," said his mother, "of course I've always adored Janie. But you are far too young. Janie is much much much *much* too young! She needs to finish college and launch a career, and you're working sixty-hour weeks and have a splendid career in front of you, and you cannot blockade whatever wonderful things come out of this ESPN job by getting married too young. Furthermore, you have no money."

Good to know he was launching a new life with that many problems and that little support.

Reeve headed into his building. Along with catching up on the sports world, he had to arrange time off for the wedding. Most people went on honeymoons too. Where should he and Janie go? And how, precisely, would he pay for it?

Reeve walked in the door and found chaos.

Guys were shouting and laughing and stomping around. Sunday afternoons were busy because big games were scheduled then, but what was playing that would make everybody howl like this?

"Shields!" bellowed one of the guys, holding up his cell phone. "Man! You're only twenty-three! You don't wanna get married now!"

"But if you do get married now," said another guy, "this is the one. She's beautiful." This in a voice of amazement, as if they had assumed that only a loser would want Reeve.

Their boss raced up. "Lemme see this video!" shouted Bick.

Again everybody watched Janie, her red hair everywhere, her eyes wide in amazement, holding out her arms, the passenger line parting, the crowd going wild and the kiss lasting forever.

"Wow," said Bick. "Gonna be two faces on this milk carton!"

"No. Please," said Reeve. "That's history. I realize you all know about it, but Janie can't handle it if you bring it up all the time. Or even once. You have to leave it alone. She's just a girl named Janie, okay?" He corrected himself. "Jennie," he said. "She wants to be Jennie now."

The married guys gave him tender looks, whatever that meant. The single guys shrugged and returned to sports topics.

One of the job requirements here was "strong knowledge of college sports." Reeve had been glued to television sports channels since he was a toddler. The rest of his family also loved sports, but their TV watching branched out into other things. His sister Lizzie, who had become a lawyer, preferred legal/police/forensic series. His mother liked food and house stuff, as if anybody cared how strangers fixed dinner.

It occurred to Reeve that he and Janie had never sat in front of a television watching anything. Not football, not basketball, not extreme sports. Not even the weather. This whole weekend, they hadn't turned on the television. Reeve grinned, remembering this weekend.

But in fact, TV was a large portion of Reeve's life, and it was how he earned his salary. He had to see those games.

He had the oddest sensation that he did not really know Janie very well.

Maybe she didn't know him very well either.

Maybe all brides and grooms realized at the last second that in some ways they were strangers.

Maybe all other brides and grooms postponed the wedding till they knew each other better.

Reeve considered the forty-eight hours he had just spent with the girl he loved.

No.

He was not postponing the wedding.

He said to his boss, "We want to get married on July eighth. Any chance I could switch my vacation to that week?"

Bick's face changed. In a different voice, he said, "Better come into my office, Reeve, and we'll talk."

They're firing me, thought Reeve.

On the upside, I won't have to tell Janie that my boss has copies of the janie tapes.

Brendan hardly ever paid close attention to anything these days, but he was struck by the researcher's nervousness. What was wrong with letting Brendan read some of the book? The man pivoted his laptop so Brendan could see the screen, but he kept a grip on it. Did he think Brendan planned to snatch the laptop and throw it down a crevasse in a glacier?

Brendan used a thick stupid voice. "I don't read a lot. This'll take me a while."

The researcher seemed reassured.

Brendan pulled the laptop away from the man and began to read.

He had expected a sort of newspaper article. *At eleven a.m. that day,* etc. But instead he found a long, terrifying narrative about a mother and father who were sadists.

It didn't seem to have anything to do with Janie.

He was swept into the story. By the fourth page, he hated this mother and father.

The top of the fifth page began, *Frank and Miranda Javensen bear full responsibility for damaging their little Hannah so severely that . . .*

The sadists were Frank and Miranda?

But Janie loved them! And they loved her! And Jodie and his own twin, Brian, had spent tons of time in Connecticut visiting, and they loved Frank and Miranda! Even Stephen liked them, and Stephen had a pretty short list of people he liked. His own mom and dad thought highly of the way Frank and Miranda dealt with Janie.

Brendan read on. . . . *Hannah was forced to flee to the safety of a religious order.*

Religious order? Come on. She joined a sick, twisted cult whose leaders lived off the income their girls made being prostitutes. It wasn't a convent. It was the opposite of a convent!

Who could Calvin Vinesett be interviewing? Brendan didn't want to read any more. He closed the document.

Waiting behind it on the screen was the open application: a folder with the name *The Happy Kidnap.*

That was the book title?

The Happy Kidnap?

A book that proclaimed Janie had enjoyed her kidnapping? That Janie was happier with some other family?

It was a little bit true, a little bit of the time, thought Brendan, and it kills my parents. A book called *The Happy Kidnap* will destroy my mother and father.

For quite a while now, Brendan Spring had regarded his parents as losers: people who settled for suburbia and weight gain and pointless trips to a meaningless church. Jodie was a loser too—a cheerleader without a sport, running off to Haiti so she could cheer away poverty. Stephen was a loser— the silent engineer type, thrilled by geology textbooks and a girl not good enough at sports to play any, so instead she biked around Boulder wearing expensive pseudo-sports gear. Brian was definitely a loser, holding out his brains on a platter to the admiring professors.

Brendan saw his parents now as brave soldiers in a war they hadn't wanted, standing guard over the four children left to them after Hannah Javensen seized Jennie.

The book would be yet another enemy, piercing their armor.

Because it wasn't a book portraying an evil Hannah who must be captured. It was a book jeering at the families who had suffered. He couldn't begin to imagine how the book would portray Janie herself.

He had vaguely thought his mother could be behind it, in her zeal to have the kidnapper brought to justice. But his mother would never say things like that. She would certainly never cooperate with a book with that title.

Where was Calvin Vinesett getting his information?

Maybe it was not information. Maybe it was all made up. Calvin Vinesett might be writing stuff that would sell, instead of the actual sad truth.

Because the sad truth was, Frank and Miranda had done their best, but Hannah had not.

Like me, thought Brendan, shocked.

THE SEVENTH PIECE OF THE KIDNAPPER'S PUZZLE

A year after all that publicity when the Jennie/Janie recognized her face on the milk carton, a made-for-TV movie was advertised. Hannah was thrilled. She was supposed to work that night, but seeing a television movie about herself was way more important.

She had lunch at the soup kitchen that day and took three desserts, even though that was not allowed and they glared at her, but who cared about them, anyway? This was supposed to be a charity. They were supposed to be nice about things.

She wrapped the little squares of cake in paper napkins and took them home so she would have a special snack for the movie.

She had popcorn, too. She was so excited. How would they portray her? Who would play her role? Some famous beautiful willowy blonde?

The movie began in a high school cafeteria with a pretty little red-haired teenager about to recognize her picture on that milk carton. Okay, Hannah understood. She would appear in flashbacks. The teenage girl would remember that beautiful golden woman with whom she had had ice cream and a ride.

But in the movie, the teenage girl did not remember!

What the teenage girl remembered was her first family! That lineup of red-haired Spring people. The girl in the movie even remembered the dog! But she did not remember Hannah.

The movie was about the girl's agony when she found out that the parents she loved were not her parents.

And the movie was about Frank and Miranda! The movie felt sorry for Frank and Miranda. The movie dealt lovingly with the Spring family. The movie did not even name Hannah!

The next day, when Hannah showed up at her job, they said she had let them down. They had needed her last night and she had not even bothered to phone. She was always letting them down, they claimed, and they were letting her go. "Here's what we owe you," they said, handing her a skimpy little bit of money.

A few months after that, Hannah Javensen was featured on *America's Most Wanted*. The point of that TV show was for somebody out there to recognize the criminal. It still puzzled Hannah that anybody could think of her as a criminal. But they loved that word, and she had to prepare herself for their ugliness.

The good thing was, the show would be entirely about Hannah and could not feature the Jennie/Janie or Frank and Miranda.

Hannah didn't stock up on snacks this time. She wrapped herself in a blanket because her hands were icy. The first minute was very good. The reenactment had been filmed in the actual New Jersey mall. She recognized it.

But the woman playing Hannah was plain and whiny. In this version, the woman walked around the mall, eyes roving, looking for a victim. In this version, the woman snickered to herself when she spotted a cute little girl. The woman cooed and fussed over the little girl, which had not happened! They were making all this up!

They did get the ice cream right.

They had even located the actual clerks, who were fatter and dumber-looking after almost seventeen years. And the clerks said, "We mainly noticed the little girl. She was just adorable, with all those auburn ringlets."

Well, sure, when you had some dull stupid woman playing Hannah.

Frank and Miranda had not given interviews. The Jennie/ Janie had not given interviews. Even the red rabbit people had not given interviews! The TV people were obviously annoyed. So was Hannah. She would have liked to see them, and hear their lies and fabrications as they blamed everything on her.

At the end of the show, Hannah's last known photograph was "aged." "Have you seen this woman?" the announcer demanded sternly.

They had gotten it so wrong! She was not plain and thick and gray. Well, maybe a little gray. And missing a tooth, because how could she afford a dentist?

Hannah looked in the bathroom mirror, which she generally avoided. I'm not pretty anymore, she thought. I'm not anything anymore.

She tried to comfort herself with the childhood daydreams. When she could have been a ballet dancer or a high-fashion model, a poet or an ice skater. When she could have written a novel or captained a yacht.

But she wasn't even going to be a waitress in a good restaurant.

She was going to bus tables in a scummy little diner.

CHAPTER SEVEN

On the plane, Janie worked on her to-do list.

Had anybody ever packed so much into a three-day weekend? Tonight, Sunday, she'd be in New Jersey. Tomorrow, Monday, she'd go up to Connecticut, tell those parents, and hurry back to the city for her last final on Tuesday.

She had not studied over the weekend. When the plane landed in Charlotte, she clung to Reeve for a few minutes, and then, as always, the two of them started laughing. For years, that had been the pattern. Janie would tell him the latest (upsetting) news of her history and her families. He would listen. He would lighten her load with a smile. They would kiss. It would recede.

But now her past really would be history.

She would live in a city about which she knew absolutely nothing except that Reeve was there. All difficulty would stay in Connecticut or New Jersey. What a lovely thought.

#2, she wrote. *Tell Sarah-Charlotte.*

Even in elementary school, they had had such fun planning

their weddings, in which they would be each other's maid of honor. Janie could hardly wait to tell Sarah-Charlotte that it was coming true. She was going to go walk down an aisle and say "I do" to Reeve Shields. Was there time to order bridesmaids' dresses? Or did Sarah-Charlotte have to bring her own?

She knew what Sarah-Charlotte would think about getting married at twenty. Sarah-Charlotte was always pushing Janie to have ambition. "You could be a brilliant lawyer or a fine doctor or change the world in some significant way," Sarah-Charlotte would argue. "You shouldn't plan for some guy to have a life while you tag along."

"I'll have a life," Janie would defend herself. "But I don't want to be an attorney or a doctor. If I have a career, I want it second, not first. I want a family. One that isn't broken and kidnapped and hurting. Where nobody is angry or separated or feuding."

"There aren't families like that," Sarah-Charlotte would say.

"I'll make one. And that's how I'll change the world."

She knew that Sarah-Charlotte would be disappointed by Janie's choice to marry young. Sarah-Charlotte would feel that Janie was throwing away something important, while Janie felt she was taking on something important.

Janie visualized the inside of a church and the bridesmaids lined up. Eve! Her roommate and best friend at college. Eve had to be in the wedding!

She thought of more details and wrote

#3 bridesmaid gowns

#4 money

Somebody has to pay for this. Of course, I have my inheritance from my grandmother, but it was meant for college. I don't know what else I can use it for exactly.

She had never asked her real parents for money. She felt timid about asking now. Weddings cost a lot, even last-minute, thrown-together weddings.

A shivery panic rolled over her.

More important than money was how her parents would feel about Reeve. What if they said, "Reeve? The creep on the radio?"

She wanted her brothers and sister to be happy for her too. But she had made a lot of mistakes with her real family. She had not been a rewarding sister or daughter.

If I want my Spring family to love me, she thought, I have to put them first. It doesn't matter what Sarah-Charlotte and I planned all those years.

The maid of honor has to be my sister, Jodie.

"Siddown," said Reeve's boss.

Reeve sat.

Bick leaned back in his chair, which he never did. He was all forward motion, a living projectile, hurling himself into the next project.

Reeve waited.

"ESPN headquarters is in Bristol, Connecticut, Reeve. You're both from that area. With you getting married now, I was thinking. Would that be better for her? You know—given her situation? Stay near her family? You want me to look into a transfer for you?"

143

To work at ESPN headquarters. It was a staggering thought. He had not even dreamed of that, because working here was such fun he couldn't imagine anything better.

But the moment Bick spoke, Reeve knew Janie was partly marrying him because he wasn't in Connecticut. She could distance herself from both sets of parents and from all confrontations and sorrows of the last few years. Distance was what he had to offer.

"Sir, that's a great offer. But I love it here. And Janie— maybe a thousand miles is a good thing."

"It's a thousand miles?" said his boss.

"It's seven hundred. Janie calls it a thousand."

"I guess we won't hire her to handle stats. Congratulations, Reeve. I'm happy for you. I'll fix the vacation."

Reeve made it to his cubicle.

He looked at his watch.

Janie should have landed.

He tried to catch his breath. Maybe I shouldn't turn the Bristol offer down without talking to Janie first, he thought. If we're partners in life, we should be partners in decisions.

In his little cube, surrounded by all his stuff, amid a life led completely without Janie, he could not believe they had decided to get married.

With shaky fingers, he called her.

"Hi!" she said excitedly. "I'm off the plane. I'm looking for airport transportation. I'm so excited I don't think I need a bus. I'll just levitate home."

"Janie, did we really decide we're going to do it?"

"We really did. You panicking?"

"I'm something. I don't think it's panic. I think I'm reality-ing."

"Oh, totally. Reality is always a shock. All our parents will scream, 'You're too young!' "

He always felt better when Janie was talking. There was something buoyant and unstoppable about her voice. Some of his younger colleagues rested their elbows on the rim of his cube and grinned at him. He grinned back. "I'm in the office, Janie, so it's hard to talk. But vacation is arranged, so I hope the church is free on July eighth."

"What church did you have in mind?" she asked.

"That and most others are your decisions, Janie."

"Love when that happens. And I love you, too, Reeve. Practice saying Jennie."

"Jennie," he said.

They hung up.

He had not told her about the janies. Or the Bristol offer.

I'm like Frank, he thought. I'm planning to hide stuff from her.

Jodie never left her cell phone on because she didn't want to drain the battery, in case she had no way to charge it again. She went into the little chapel, open to the sky since the earthquake had destroyed the roof. In a terrible way, it was still beautiful. She stood in the shade of a remaining wall so there would be no glare on the screen. She wanted to study the phone's calendar again and confirm that she had only ten days to go.

She had messages waiting. There was even one from Janie.

Janie preferred to text, because it was somewhat removed, a perfect way for a somewhat sister to stay somewhat in touch.

Jodie read that first.

> Dear Jodie, Reeve asked me to marry him. Now. We will live in Charlotte. Wedding July 8. Jodie, will you be my maid of honor? Please? Will you be home in time to come shop for the gown? We'll be shopping in New Jersey. Love love love Janie

Reeve? Jodie had thought that was over.

Jodie had never forgiven Reeve for betraying Janie on the radio. Even though her faith emphasized forgiveness, Jodie found forgiveness an annoyance and hardly ever wanted to participate.

Wow, thought Jodie. Now I have to forgive Reeve. He's going to be my brother-in-law.

She found herself holding her hands up to the sun and dancing. A wedding! Her little sister in love! And Jodie would be the maid of honor.

Jodie was extra pleased because she knew that Sarah-Charlotte expected to be maid of honor. Jodie would rather hang out with a litter box than Sarah-Charlotte.

Shopping in New Jersey, Janie had written. It was code, the way everything involving Janie was code. It meant Janie was going with Mom—hers and Jodie's mother—the real mother—to buy that gown. How thrilled Mom would be! Not just because of the fun of wedding gowns, but because she was the mother Janie had chosen.

Janie was always going back and forth between her two families, apparently never realizing that every departure was a slap in her real mother's face.

Jodie admitted to herself, not for the first time, that she had fled the continental U.S. partly to distance herself from her ambivalence toward the kidnapette.

Kathleen's word. Jodie had not warmed to Stephen's girl-friend. But Kathleen had a way of seeing to the center of things. That little syllable "ette" included the spoiled-brat part of Janie Johnson.

Jodie took a break from the amazing text that Janie had sent and opened her other messages. Everybody wanted her to watch the attached video. The video was full of shadows and half faces as a cell phone swung its little eye over a crowd.

There was Reeve—looking as young as ever; definitely not old enough to get married—and there was Janie—as beautiful as ever.

Will you marry me?

Jodie saw Janie stumbling out of the crowd, people parting to let her through, a guard beaming, Janie burying her face against Reeve. It was what every girl on earth wanted—to be loved so much that the man could not bear to part.

It occurred to Jodie that Reeve was not the only one who had betrayed Janie. The minute Nicole told her cousin Vic about Frank sending money to Hannah, it wasn't a cold case anymore. It would be red hot.

Nice betrayal of your own, Jodie congratulated herself. The FBI will interrogate Janie while she's trying on wedding gowns. She might even be guilty of a crime for not telling them about the checks. It might be aiding and abetting a criminal. They might charge *Janie* with something!

How clearly Donna Spring remembered that day five years ago when she had answered the kitchen phone in the old house. It was a rectangular plastic box fastened to the wall and it had a long curly cord you could twirl as you paced the room.

The Springs didn't even have landlines anymore.

A girlish voice had said to Donna, "Hi. It's . . . your daughter. Me. Jennie."

She remembered how cold and white the telephone had been. She remembered steadying herself on the kitchen counter, whispering, *"Jennie?"*

In those days, they ate in the kitchen. She remembered how all the faces turned toward her. Her big broad bear of a husband gasped. Petite pixie Jodie's mouth opened in a silent cry of excitement. Stephen frowned and looked skeptical. Brendan and Brian weren't listening.

If it happened today, she would have her iPhone, and the missing child would send a photograph of herself, and they would all know instantly that she was one of them. Donna would do the same, and Jennie would have proof that she had called the right number.

Donna still remembered every digit of that old telephone number, the one they had kept year in and year out, hoping for such a call. Knowing in her heart that little Jennie had not had the phone number by memory when she was three, so it was pointless to hope that Jennie at age four or six or eight or fourteen would remember it.

Little Jennie never really came home. Instead they had the difficult, sometimes delightful, infrequent presence of Janie Johnson.

Janie had gotten closer to them during her freshman year in college, and Donna and Jonathan Spring had taken advantage of New Jersey's excellent access to Manhattan, going into the city to visit Janie a number of times.

The summer between her freshman and sophomore years at college, Janie spent most of each week with her real family. It had been friction-free. They attributed this in part to Janie and Jodie having bedrooms of their own. Neither girl shared well with anyone, but they really hated sharing with each other.

Donna and Jonathan had been busy getting the twins ready for college. Brian was accepted at his long-shot choice. Brendan's hopes were dashed. Last August, Brendan had been dark, silent, and stomping while Brian was light, laughing, and eager. They took Brian to Harvard first, and Brian hardly noticed when his parents drove away, his excitement was so great. They took Brendan to his school the following week, and Brendan couldn't wait for his parents to leave either, his humiliation was so great.

Stephen had not come home from Colorado at all last year, and Jodie had been busy planning for a mission year. The trip to Haiti had come through at the last minute, and there was a flurry of paperwork, purchases, and plans.

Janie had been the quiet member of the family.

"I'm sorry, sweetheart," Donna said one day. "It's crazy around here. I haven't spent the time with you I wanted to."

"This is the best visit I've ever had. I feel as if I really know everybody, and I'm happy or sad for them. Proud and hopeful. I helped pack. I was at every send-off. I was just one of the crowd, instead of that annoying interloper."

"You were never an annoying interloper," said Donna, although Janie had been that and worse.

And that year, all five of Donna and Jonathan's children were away from home. The Springs repainted rooms. They took carloads of stuff to Goodwill. They paid humongous tuition bills. Janie's sophomore year began with a lot of family time, but visits dwindled as her college schedule swept her up. In the spring she began dating somebody, but they knew very little about him.

Donna was afraid that Janie would marry somebody from some distant place. An Australian boy with a ranch in the outback, say. Janie would vanish just when Donna was starting to know her, and they would visit by Skype and say only pleasant things. Her father said to Janie, "Your mother and I want to meet this young man you're seeing."

"His name is Michael," said Janie.

"How about we come into the city and have lunch together? Nothing demanding."

"Dad, Michael doesn't know anything about me. It's so peaceful and serene, to be with a person who doesn't know anything. He thinks I'm just another pretty girl. I'm scared to have him meet you or Frank and Miranda, because he'll want explanations. And then it won't be the same. He'll be interested in the kidnapping instead of me."

"You have to tell him sometime," Jonathan pointed out.

"I know, Dad, but sometime isn't here yet."

"Can we meet under false pretenses?" asked Donna.

They had passed a silly pizza dinner planning how to meet Michael without Michael knowing.

Donna was thinking about all these things when her cell phone rang with its Janie code. They had had the children record their own voices and trill their names, instead of having ringtones, so Donna's phone sang, "It's Janie-Janie-Janie-Janie-Janie-Janie!"

"Hello, darling. Did you have a nice weekend in Connecticut?"

"Mom, I didn't spend the whole weekend there after all. I just stayed for lunch on Friday. You won't believe what happened. Michael followed me onto Metro-North. All of a sudden, he was just there—sitting down next to me. And you won't believe who Michael turned out to be."

"A Hungarian prince?"

"That would have been nice. No, he turned out to be a researcher for that true crime writer. Calvin Vinesett. Michael was hired to get information from me."

"Oh, sweetheart! How slimy!"

"But it turned out perfectly, Mom! I flew down to Charlotte instead. Reeve bought me a ticket. I spent the weekend with him. And guess what! We're getting married. He proposed! Look on Facebook. You can see the video. He proposed in the airport. The other people in the security line filmed me when I was saying yes."

Donna Spring was speechless.

"So I'm back from Charlotte. My plane just landed at Kennedy, and I'm taking the airport bus out to New Jersey. Can you pick me up? We can start sorting out wedding details. It's going to be July eighth with Father John, although I haven't talked to him yet and I don't even know if the church is free. And then tomorrow, Monday, I'll scoot up to Connecticut and tell them."

Donna was reeling. "July eighth?" she said weakly. "*This* July eighth? You mean a year from now, don't you?"

"No. Seven weeks. I think we can pull it off, Mom. And on the plane, I made a decision."

Donna pulled herself together. I'm the mother, she reminded herself. Janie has to finish college. Reeve is a sweet boy, but they're way too young. July 8! I can hardly do a load of laundry by July 8!

"My decision is," said her daughter, "that I will get married as Jennie Spring. Because that's who I am. I want to say in church, before God and in the presence of my family, that I, Jennie Spring, take thee, Reeve."

Donna Spring wept. *My daughter is home at last.* She spoke over the lump in her throat. "I think we can pull it off too, darling. Let's have the reception in our backyard, because it's too late to book a hall now."

"Mom, I can pay for it. I have money from Miranda's mother."

Donna's tears were unstoppable. *She* was the mother. The

Connecticut parent was "Miranda." "We'll pay for the first wedding in our family, Janie. You'll save that money for college, because you are not to drop out. You are just going to enroll in a different school in Charlotte. Right?"

"Sure," said Janie. "When does Jodie get back? It's in a couple of weeks, isn't it? Do you think she'll be back in time to go wedding gown shopping with us, Mom?"

Stephen had a minute of peace while Kathleen borrowed clothes. Tamped down? he thought. Walled up? Protecting painful spaces?

You bet.

He opened the door to his very small closet while he checked his messages. He took out a shapeless dark linen jacket he had probably never worn, because it didn't have a single wrinkle. He had a vague feeling this had been a birthday present from some relative. He draped it on his shoulder and thought he looked quite metrosexual with it hanging there, implying that any moment he would transform into a model.

From Haiti, Stephen received a text. **Go to Reeve Shields's Facebook page,** Jodie had written.

Reeve had the most impressive Facebook action of anybody Stephen knew. Not only did Reeve have more friends (actual and virtual) than Stephen by a hundred to one, but he was always putting some photo or sports information there, and his friends, riveted by his fabulous job (or at least, his fabulous employer), checked his page constantly.

Reeve was a nice guy, but Stephen did not care what Reeve might post on Facebook.

On the other hand, he didn't hear from Jodie much, and a person who texted from Haiti was serious.

He went to Facebook.

And there before him were photographs and a video in which Reeve Shields asked Stephen's little sister to marry him. Their embrace was something out of a movie.

Was Reeve insane? He was twenty-three, with a world-class career ahead of him.

And he wanted to fill up his life with a wife?

They didn't get more high-maintenance than Janie.

Reeve wouldn't just be getting a princess.

He'd be getting a kidnap princess, which was the worst kind.

Stephen sure didn't want Kathleen seeing this. She wasn't going to get movie-level romance out of Stephen. She wasn't going to get a proposal, either.

Stephen was watching the video for the third time when the ringtone on his cell announced his mother. She could only be calling about this video. He had a lot more thinking to do before he could talk about this development, but he could not let his mother down. He answered.

All these years, Donna Spring had waited, praying that her baby girl would come home. Even after Janie came home, Stephen's mother had to go on waiting and praying. And now Stephen heard her voice as it should always have been; the voice Hannah Javensen's crime had destroyed. "Stephen! Did you see the video? You did? You won't believe this! Janie's back from Reeve's, and she's staying overnight here! And not only is she going to marry Reeve, she wants to do it *here*. In our church! With Father John! And Dad will walk her down the aisle. And Jodie will be maid of honor. On July eighth! This very July! On the eighth!"

Stephen didn't care about any of that. But he choked with joy for his mother.

"You'll make it, won't you, Stephen?" she said anxiously. "You'll be here? I know it's short notice, but you'll come? You have to come!"

"I'll be there," he said, although the timing was terrible. But that had always been one of his sister's most notable qualities: the ability to destroy everybody's daily life.

"Only seven weeks to put a whole wedding together!" she cried happily. "And I have a hundred people to call!"

"I'll let you get started," said Stephen.

His mother had stepped out of the years of pain, which he was unfair to blame on Janie, because the blame rested solely and squarely with Hannah Javensen.

I will work with the researcher, he decided. Any chance to bring Hannah Javensen down is worth it. And if Kathleen or anybody else is giving material to the author, so what?

I want that book to exist. I want to capture Hannah Javensen. She's going to pay for how she hurt my mother.

"Janie, you're calling me before you called your parents?" shrieked Sarah-Charlotte.

"Well, I told my New Jersey parents. Frank and Miranda don't go online much. They don't use Facebook. They're not going to check Reeve's site. They don't live next door to Reeve's parents anymore either. So my New Jersey parents are meeting me here at the airport bus drop. I'll spend the night with them, and then Mom's loaning me her car to go to Connecticut so I can tell Frank and Miranda in person."

"And you've really and truly set a date only seven weeks away? What's the rush?"

"Reeve doesn't want to be apart."

"You could live together and have the wedding next year."

"I don't want to," said Janie. "I want to make those promises. For better or for worse. For richer or for poorer. In sickness and in health. I want to be just like my real parents, and Reeve's real parents, and my other parents."

This isn't pretend, thought Sarah-Charlotte. We're not seventh graders, lying on the floor cutting pictures out of brides' magazines.

"I want to say those vows in front of God and my family and I want to say them as the person I really am. No more pretending. I will really be Jennie Spring when I walk down the aisle and I will really be Jennie Shields when I walk back out."

"I don't know if I can call you Jennie," said Sarah-Charlotte. "Let me try it on for size. Jennie? Nope. Doesn't work for me. Jennie is somebody else."

"You are absolutely right," said Janie. "Jennie has always been somebody else. I never let Jennie come back. Today's the day."

Seven weeks, thought Sarah-Charlotte. How on earth are we going to choose, order, and receive my maid of honor gown that fast? With me in Boston and the action in New Jersey?

Janie's voice changed, as if she were turning into Jennie

Spring during this very conversation. "Sarah-Charlotte?" she said, in that asking voice; the one that comes before bad news. "You're my best friend. No one will ever be as good a friend. But a wedding is a profound thing."

I'm not in the wedding, thought Sarah-Charlotte.

It hurt so much she couldn't breathe.

"Now that I'm Jennie Spring," said Janie, "I have to have my sister, Jodie, as my maid of honor."

This is what it is to grow up. In one minute, it all changes and you can't use your childhood plans. "Of course," said Sarah-Charlotte.

"And you'll be one of my bridesmaids? Please? Will you accept being a bridesmaid?"

"Oh, Janie, you know there's nothing I want more!"

"And I just thought of it this second, but it's also Reeve's wedding! I totally forgot. He has two sisters and a sister-in-law. Maybe they have to be in the wedding."

The girls were giggling now.

Sarah-Charlotte said, "Have you ever even met the sister-in-law?"

"Yes. But I forgot her instantly. I'm sure she's a fine person."

"Do you think she's a fine person who's going to be free in seven weeks? Perhaps she's a fine person with a commitment. That's what happens when you jam a whole wedding into a minute."

"Sarah-Charlotte, the bus is taking the exit. I can see my dad. He's standing next to his car. He's jumping up and down! He's blowing me kisses! Oh, good! At least one person thinks my wedding is great."

"Then quick, we have to plan the bridal shower. I'm giving it. It'll be in Connecticut. I'm already thinking of the theme and the colors."

"Everybody's scattered all over the country," said Janie doubtfully.

"Planes? Come across one lately? Got a marriage proposal while waiting for one lately? Think your high school friends are bright enough to board one?"

"But who would come to a shower? They have to fly to the wedding, which matters more."

"Everybody will come. People will drive all night or hock their ten-speeds for plane tickets. I'll call Katrina and Adair and you'll bring Jodie and your New Jersey mother and you'll send me a list right now of your girlfriends at college. I only know about Eve and Rachel and Mikayla. What kind of stuff do you want for your shower? What does Reeve already have?"

"Reeve has some plastic forks from Chick-fil-A."

"That's wonderful," said Sarah-Charlotte. "That means you get to design his whole life while he just stands there. Don't ask him for an opinion because it would just be clutter. Are you thinking modern, classic, frilly, French, stainless steel, silver . . . ?"

"I haven't thought yet."

"Come on, girl. You and I spent middle school listing stuff like this. We even chose your kids and their names. Remember Denim and Lace?"

"Reeve wants to get me puppies and we'll call them Denim and Lace."

"Straighten him out. You'll be living in two rooms in a mountain of gift boxes and ribbons. You do not have room for puppies. Be firm. This is an important precedent."

Reeve's sister Lizzie got through to him next.

Reeve had no choice. He answered the phone.

Lizzie was a piece of work. She was a lawyer for a corporation that did nothing in particular Reeve could figure out, but they sure had a lot of litigation. Lizzie loved it. She strode around in her stern, sober suits as if she were being filmed or else facing the Supreme Court. Lizzie said, "Reeve, what is this nonsense about getting married? You are too young."

Reeve never argued with Lizzie. "I am young," he agreed. "So is Janie. But we've set the date. July eighth."

"That's too soon," said Lizzie. "That's ridiculous! At least wait until she's graduated from college. Give her two more years, Reeve."

"It is too soon," he agreed. "But can you come? We want you there, Lizzie."

There was silence. Lizzie was never silent. Then there was an odd snuffling sound.

"Lizzie? Are you crying?"

"Oh, Reeve," said his sister shakily. Lizzie was never shaky. "I want you to be happy, Reeve. But Janie Johnson? Reeve, Janie is high risk. Don't do it."

THE EIGHTH PIECE OF THE KIDNAPPER'S PUZZLE

Fourteen years after that day in New Jersey, Hannah was working in a coffee shop. The owners of the Mug were all chummy and gushy. Everybody pretended to be friends. They never pretended to be friends with Hannah.

She wasn't a waitress. She didn't pour coffee. She didn't get tips. The waitresses were supposed to share but they didn't.

The Mug had a promotion. After you had come ten times and gotten your Mug ticket stamped, the owner painted a coffee mug just for you. You chose your colors and spelled your name, and the owner had those plain fat mugs you could decorate at a paint-it-yourself pottery place, although Hannah never had, and the next time you came, your very own mug was hanging on a peg on the wall.

The customers simpered over their mugs. It was a pain to hang them back up on their stupid little pegs, because the pegs were just barely long enough. Once Hannah had dropped a mug and it broke and the customer actually cried.

The owners said if Hannah broke another one, she'd have to leave.

It was hard to find jobs where they didn't ask questions. Jobs where you didn't need a car. It was time to demand more money from Frank. Thanks to the publicity and the Internet, she knew Frank's address and phone number. Fear of the FBI had stopped her from calling. But so much time had passed! The FBI was too stupid to find her. And since Frank would be in plenty of trouble if Hannah got caught, because he could have turned her in, Frank would have no choice. He'd have to give her more money.

He still had a landline. She'd call until she got him. He was old and had to be retired by now, and he ought to be home in the evening.

Hannah did not recognize the voice that answered the phone. "This is Barnette Bank and Trust," said Hannah firmly, using the name she generally chose for scoping out tricky situations. "May I speak to Frank Johnson?"

"I'm sorry, he isn't home. May I give him a message?"

The female voice didn't sound like her mother. But it was years since Hannah had heard her mother's voice. "Is this Mrs. Johnson?" asked Hannah.

"No, I'm their daughter, Janie. How can I help?"

Even though Hannah had known that her parents loved the Jennie/Janie more than they loved her, she had not really understood that the Jennie/Janie thought it was *her* house, and that these people were *her* parents! She probably thought their money was *her* money.

Frank still had money, Hannah could tell. The girl's voice was all soft and serene, the way people's voices were when they had everything they needed and more.

Just because Frank hadn't turned her in didn't mean the girl wouldn't! And even though the girl was so grasping she even snatched *parents,* she wouldn't show any decency toward Hannah. She wouldn't be grateful that Hannah had given her these parents. She would want Hannah locked up.

"I'll email," said Hannah, proud of her superb self-control. "Can you give me his email address?"

"Sure. Who is this, please?"

Wait. The girl would tell Frank that the bank had called. Hannah often used her grandmother's name and had wrongly used it this time. There might be a Barnette Bank, or Frank or even the girl might be smart enough to make the connection. Hannah had no email address she could give the parent thief. Nor would it be safe to blackmail Frank by email.

Hannah had only one option now. She had to see Frank in person. Two thousand miles stood between them. When you did not have a car, could not afford a train, had no ID to get on a plane, and could not miss work or you would be replaced, how could you make such a journey?

It's her fault! thought Hannah. She kept the rage out of her voice. "I'll call again," said Hannah smoothly. "Good afternoon."

"Thank you for calling," said the sweet little voice of the vicious little parent thief.

CHAPTER EIGHT

Stephen did not think he had ever phoned Janie before.

"Stephen!" cried Janie. Her voice was exactly like his mother's. He had never noticed that. Perhaps Janie and his mother had never before been equally happy and excited.

He summoned all the affection he could. "Hey, little sister. Congratulations. I'm happy for you." And he was. He had always liked Reeve in spite of it all, and he thought Janie would be okay in Reeve's hands. Janie was not an independent sort, foraging for herself, striding out to conquer the world. Janie wanted her hand held.

Stephen loathed holding hands.

After Jennie had disappeared, Stephen's father had escorted Stephen and Jodie to school every morning. Not once had they been allowed to walk in or out of elementary school without their father tightly gripping their little hands. These days, Kathleen often reached for Stephen's hand and he often shoved it in his pocket and he never explained.

He said to his sister, "You've always wanted to be married."

"You're right. I want to be married just like all my parents. For better or for worse, for richer or for poorer, in sickness and in health."

"I have to admit," said Stephen, "that when the worst came, our real parents and your Connecticut parents stuck to each other. I'm not there. I love being with Kathleen, but part of me never wants to connect like that."

Janie considered this. "If Kathleen feels the same, you're okay."

"I wouldn't ask. I might end up having to make a commitment."

Janie said, "I'm making more commitments than just to Reeve. Outsiders wouldn't realize just how much of a commitment."

Stephen could never predict Janie. She could go in any direction. He hoped she did not intend to hurt their parents. However, with Janie, intent didn't matter. She hurt them all the time anyway, just by choosing to be with the other mother and father.

His sister said, "Our wedding will be in church, Stephen. With God as our witness. I'm not actually Janie Johnson, even though I graduated from high school as if I were, and I'm at college as if I were. But in church, for my wedding, I will be married as Jennie Spring. Father John will say 'Do you, Jennie, take this man, Reeve, to be your wedded husband?' And I, Jennie Spring, will say 'I do.' And a minute later, I will be Jennie Spring Shields. Janie Johnson will be finished. I'm retiring her."

Stephen said something he had never expected to say. He would have signed up for the Marines and made a commitment to them rather than use these words. But he used them. He said to his sister, "I love you."

Reeve was on the phone with his older brother, Todd.

"Wow, man," said Todd. "It took me years to work up to a marriage proposal, and then only because Lindsay gave me a deadline. I didn't even know you were still seeing Janie."

"Me either. She had a catastrophe. A true crime writer doing a book on the kidnapping hired a researcher and instead of being honest and just asking for an interview, the researcher pretended to be a grad student and he was dating Janie."

"So she's marrying you on the rebound, huh?"

"No, she's marrying me because she's loved me since middle school. And her name is going to be Jennie from now on. I don't know how that's going to work. I don't personally know anybody named Jennie. I'm thinking of writing her name on the back of my hand so I have ready reference."

"Speaking of hands, did you get Janie a ring?"

"No. It wasn't a ring situation in the airport."

"It's a ring situation now. Trust me. I know women."

"He doesn't really," said another voice. Todd had the phone on speaker, and his wife was talking. "*I* know women," explained Lindsay. "Congratulations, Reeve. Now go buy a ring."

"I don't have any money. Can't we just tattoo them on our fingers?"

"No," said Lindsay. "And if you don't have any money, get a loan. It doesn't matter how tiny the diamond is. She wants one anyway. Do you know her ring size?"

"I do, actually. Sarah-Charlotte dragged us to a craft show once and my job was to carry the junk they bought, and they spent like half an hour trying on rings at a goldsmith's booth even when they couldn't afford a single thing there. But Janie and I are going to be engaged for only seven weeks. She doesn't need a ring."

"You know nothing," said Lindsay. "Years can roll by and your bride will still be waiting for her engagement ring. Better you should buy it right now and when she flies back to Charlotte for her next visit, you'll do something incredibly romantic and give it to her."

"I already did something incredibly romantic," said Reeve. He was thinking—Janie's coming back down? Of course, I want her to, but I have to work. I just got assigned my first college baseball game. The College World Series is coming up. I can't be thinking about rings. I'll be putting in twelve-hour days. I'll be out of town half the time.

"And you have to come up here several days before the wedding," said Todd, "because you have to get a tuxedo."

"I have to wear a tuxedo?"

"Yes," said his brother. "You're in a church in the afternoon with your bride. You're going to see her at the far end of the aisle, all in white, the most beautiful princess in the world. She deserves to look down that aisle and see the handsome prince, not some slob in an old team jacket."

"That opinion doesn't sound like you," said Reeve.

"It isn't like him," said Lindsay. "It's like me. I dictated that sentence."

"Want to back out now?" teased his brother.

But Reeve found that he wanted a situation where the woman in his life would know how to handle stuff, the way Lindsay knew. Would give him instructions about what to wear and what to say. A woman who knew the puzzles of church aisles and tuxedos.

He and Janie would have an excellent division of labor. He would concentrate on sports stats; Janie would handle their lives.

Jennie, he reminded himself. I'm marrying somebody named Jennie.

Kathleen usually dressed in two minutes or less. It was one of the things Stephen appreciated about her. But she was not back yet. Obviously dresses, especially borrowed dresses, were not as fast. Mandy might even be suggesting makeup, and a special hairdo, and even stockings, which Stephen had never seen on Kathleen's legs.

Stephen's cell rang. It was Brendan. He hadn't heard Brendan's voice in months. Had Brendan broken a leg? Was his athletic career over? Did he need money? Surely Brendan didn't want to discuss weddings. "Hey, Bren. What's up? You okay?"

"I kind of wanted to talk about the book. You know. The true crime thing. I gave the guy a couple interviews. I read a few pages in a chapter."

"I decided to get involved too. We're meeting with the

researcher in half an hour," said Stephen. "Kathleen's coming with me."

"That's impossible. I just saw him."

"Either he hopped the next plane or the author has more than one researcher. Calvin Vinesett is really sinking money into this. Or the publisher is. So tell me. What's the problem?"

"There's just something off about the whole approach," said his brother.

Brendan was aware of approaches in book writing? Stephen began laughing.

"I feel like Calvin Vinesett doesn't care about the crime," said Brendan. "Like he's picked out some other crime. The crime of being a lousy parent. True crime books—well, I haven't read any, actually. I've hardly read any books ever. But they have to be about the crime, don't they?"

"I've never read a true crime book either," said Stephen. "I can't even watch police and attorney TV shows because we lived inside a crime for so many years. Crime rots you. A piece of me is rotten because of Hannah Javensen. I'm always fighting the rot. I'm always afraid it will spread."

Brendan would have said that his older brother had few emotions. He would have said Stephen was a sort of human tire iron; that Stephen could race right up to any kidnapper, shoot her dead, walk away, and party. "I bet Kathleen wants you to get all emotional and say stuff like that to *her*," Brendan told his brother. "I bet you don't, either."

"I've never said it to anybody. Even myself. Quote me and die," said Stephen.

They laughed. Brendan thought that maybe going home

this summer wouldn't be so awful after all. Of course, Stephen wouldn't go home. He'd moved his life west. People who wanted to see Stephen had to go to Colorado.

Stephen said, "You coming to the wedding?"

"Wedding?"

"You read your email, Bren?"

"Now and then."

"July eighth. Janie and Reeve. Our church. Our house. Go to Reeve's Facebook page and check it out."

"I'll look later. I gotta tell you something first. Why I called. The title of the book Calvin Vinesett is writing? It's *The Happy Kidnap.*"

Reeve watched as responses to the video popped up on his Facebook page.

—*Yeah, dude, like you'd compromise working at ESPN (whoever thought you'd be the one to get that job!) by getting married!*

—*Marriage? Like I believe you want to start taking out the garbage and unloading the dishwasher. Next you'll claim you're going to graduate school!*

—*Come on, man, Reeve hasn't proved to my satisfaction that he ever graduated college to start with!*

—*I'll believe it when I get the engraved invitation from Mr. and Mrs. Johnson.*

—*Reeve. A, You're too young. B, You're immature.*

—*But she IS the prettiest girl on earth. Congrats. Or is this April Fool's?*

—*Love what your high school friends are writing. And just as a sidebar, maybe this'll bring the kidnapper out! Maybe she'll want to come to the wedding and drink a toast to you. And you'll toast her back! After all, you wouldn't know Janie if it wasn't for the kidnapper.*

Jodie need not have worried about what to say on the phone to her sister. Janie talked enough for a dozen girls. ". . . and we'll get married in your church. My church. It's the only church I've ever been to. Mom's made an appointment for me with Father John. Mom says you can't put a formal wedding together in seven weeks. But at least the gown will be formal. And can you get here soon, Jodie? Mom says there's a really wonderful bridal mall. When exactly are you getting home? What color do you want for your dress? You choose."

"You're not asking Sarah-Charlotte?"

"Yes, but she's a bridesmaid, and probably also Reeve's sisters, Lizzie and Megan, and his sister-in-law, Lindsay, but maybe they'll have to buy their own dresses separately, just in whatever color you pick. We'll invite everybody we can think of to the reception, because Mom and Dad say that in a backyard we can be pretty basic. Chips and salads, and Dad will grill hamburgers and hot dogs. You should see Dad. He just can't stop grinning. He actually picked me up and whirled me around in the air. 'Father of the bride!' he kept shouting. And laughing."

Their father was a bear of a man—big, broad, wide, sometimes with a great bushy red beard and sometimes clean-shaven. His voice was the same size as his body—even his whispers were shouts. Jodie couldn't wait to get a bear hug from Dad. She knew just what it was like to be lifted up and swung in a circle.

"And you know what else?" said Janie. "Dad said that Frank can be father of the bride too. He thinks we can have Frank in his wheelchair, and we'll rent him a tuxedo, and Dad can have me on one arm, and push Frank in the wheelchair with his free hand, and both my fathers will walk me down the aisle."

Oh, her father was truly the best man, figuring out how to have the other father in their shared daughter's wedding.

"Because I have the best parents in the world," said Janie. "We do, I mean. You and me. Okay, so it took me a few years. But I'm proud to be Jennie Spring. Even if I'm worried about Miranda."

"You'll be in some beautiful white gown and everybody will be weeping and Miranda will be so happy for you, Janie. So you were at Reeve's for the whole weekend? What's Charlotte like?"

"Charlotte?" repeated Janie. "You mean the town? I think it had trees or something. Buildings. I'm sure I saw buildings. But who knows? I was looking at Reeve."

"What about college? You dropping out?"

"I'll register somewhere in Charlotte. Reeve says it has colleges."

They laughed hysterically.

Jodie said, "Remember how intent we were on getting into the exact right college? And we worried about our essays and our SAT scores and we visited campuses and wanted the exact right place for our personalities?"

"Exactly. And now, I'm like, whatever. They have courses? You get a degree? I'm there."

"I would have been horrified a year ago," said Jodie. "But Haiti brought me to my senses. Wherever you go will be fine."

"Probably, but I want to talk about dresses."

"Reeve must not think dresses are important or he wouldn't be scheduling your wedding in a minute and a half."

"He wants *me,* Jodie. He wants me in his life, and he wants me now. I can look forever and I won't find another guy who wants me to marry him right now, this minute, because he can't stand living without me."

Jodie had so much thinking to do after Haiti. What was sorrow in America compared to the suffering she had seen? And even living in Haiti, she only *saw* the suffering. She herself did not suffer. An American volunteer could always get on the next plane and go home.

Through Haiti, Jodie had caught a glimpse of eternity, and she did not want to lose her memory of it. When she got back to America, she would need to live alone for a while. Not at home. Not sharing a dorm room. Not sharing an apartment. Certainly not sharing a life. She would run from any guy who wanted her to marry this minute. If he couldn't hang on for a few years, who needed him?

But a sister's wedding, that was different. "I'm due to fly out in ten days," said Jodie Spring, "but I haven't saved the world here, and the new group of volunteers has arrived, and we're short of beds. I'll change my plane. Don't go to the bridal mall without me."

Kathleen had not worn high heels since forever. Mandy's stunning yellow leather heels, with a frosting of yellow leather roses, were so high Kathleen could hardly stand erect, let alone walk. But she conquered that in a minute and walked up to Stephen all slinky and sexy and grinned at him.

"Wow. Great shoes," said Stephen. "You have the best ankles in America, you know."

Kathleen was thrilled. Compliments from Stephen were rare. She might have to give up thick socks and Birkenstocks. "And the dress?"

"I like how it swirls."

Kathleen had to start wearing dresses now? If only she knew Stephen's sisters well enough to share this. Guess what! Every day I'm 1 percent closer to the girl Stephen really wants!

Stephen took her arm at the curb and held it. So romantic!

And then, to her amazement, a taxi stopped.

"I called one," he said. "Because of the shoes. Girly girls never arrive all sweaty with blisters." He opened the door for her, and she got in, taking care with the yards of fabric in the skirt.

"Don't forget that I'm strong and silent, and you're the talker, Kathleen. What are you going to tell him about yourself?"

"I'll start with my own family. I'll have to leave out what Dad does, since he's with the FBI. I'll have to leave out what Mom does, since she's with the IRS. I think Dad could be a bus driver instead. I can see him taking the exact same route for thirty years, can't you? And I think Mom might work a shift at McDonald's. Yes. She adores french fries. It's her calling. And she crochets a lot."

"Sending you to this university is a great sacrifice," said Stephen.

"Yes. They're suffering, but they love me and the other nine children."

Stephen stopped laughing. He said quietly, "Kath, this is the enemy. We can't give this researcher anything. Not one word. And we absolutely have to get what he has on the possible Hannahs." Stephen swallowed. "Because the title of the book this bestselling author has under contract is *The Happy Kidnap.*"

From the limousine depot, Janie's father drove back to the house, while her mom was on her phone telling everybody she knew about the wedding, and Janie was on *her* phone telling everybody *she* knew.

When they were both in high school, Janie had coaxed Reeve to skip school and take her to New Jersey. She wanted to find the house occupied by the unknown family who had put that face on that milk carton. Not so long ago, but another world. No GPS in that old car of Reeve's. No cell phones in their hands.

Janie could hardly believe they had existed without cell phones.

On that long-ago day, she and Reeve had stopped at a phone booth and used the phone book hanging inside it. Janie probably hadn't even *seen* a phone booth since that day.

As she talked with her parents, Janie bought a wedding app for her iPhone. It took little browsing to see that every other bride in America planned to spend a lot more time getting ready than Janie did.

For Janie, formal wedding invitations were out. No time

to get them designed, printed, addressed, or mailed. Spiffy receptions were out because reception halls were booked a year or two in advance. Caterers ditto. Special-order gowns were out. She had to get hers off a rack.

She texted Sarah-Charlotte. Looking for eloping app.

You're not eloping. You're racing. You're a track star bride.

Reeve's mother kept calling her son until she got through. It took hours and used up her patience. "Marrying Janie is a lovely idea, Reeve," she said brusquely. "And that video is so romantic. But she is young, young, young and so are you. You cannot get married in seven weeks. Seven years would be a better choice. You have just gotten started in your career, which requires a major time commitment and will involve travel as you are given responsibility for events at distant campuses. She herself has two more years of college. You must wait until she has her degree and has lived on her own and matured considerably prior to setting a date."

"Actually the date is Saturday, the eighth of July. Are you free, Mom? Did you check your calendar? We'll have the ceremony at the Springs' church, and then have a big party—a picnic, really—at their house."

"Better would be to wait, save money, have a lovely fashionable wedding, go on a wonderful honeymoon, and—"

"Mrs. Spring is reserving a block of rooms at a motel near the church," Reeve said.

"Donna and Jonathan Spring cannot be in favor of a marriage when Janie is so young and facing so many intense situations for which she is emotionally unprepared."

"Actually," said Reeve, "she's going to call herself Jennie from now on. She'll be Jennie Spring for the next month and a half and then she'll be Jennie Shields. It's a nice name, isn't it? If I can just remember it. Todd said, since he's best man, he'll hold up a cue card so I use the right name when I say 'I do.'"

"You've already talked to Todd?"

"I've already talked to everybody, Mom. Your line's always busy. So did you check your calendar?"

"Reeve, you do not have the money to do this."

"That's true. But we're doing it. And financial decisions will be made by Janie and me. I mean, Jennie. Listen, is Dad around? Can I talk to Dad?"

Kathleen shoved her place setting over and scooted her chair elbow to elbow with the researcher. "I'm so excited to meet you, even though you're not the author. Do you have any of the book with you? Tell me about yourself. How did you get this job? Did Calvin Vinesett do hundreds of interviews and you were the best?"

She was having difficulty thinking of this weedy grad-student-looking person as an enemy.

Anyway, Calvin Vinesett would have chosen the title. What did Calvin Vinesett care if it hurt anybody? He didn't even care enough about the Springs to do his own interviews. Probably he was accustomed to hurting the innocent people in his books and it was easier if he never met them.

"I'm taking writing classes," the man said, "and some of us applied to be researchers when we found an online request. I was the lucky one."

"I'm so thrilled for you! Think of the doors this will open! And you are brilliant to have turned up three possible Hannahs. I mean, how did you do that?"

He looked uncomfortable. "Well, public records in Boulder."

"Like ownership of houses? Do these Hannahs own a house?"

The researcher tried to take control. "Let's get to that later. Right now, let's start with you, Stephen. I guess what I find most surprising is that you and your brothers and sister became close to the kidnap parents. Frank and Miranda Javensen. I understand you visited them a number of times."

"Aren't you going to take notes?" said Kathleen. "You don't even have your laptop on the table. Stephen will want to be absolutely totally sure that he's quoted properly. I mean, that's not negotiable. Here, let's get your laptop open and powered up." Kathleen handed him his briefcase. "I can't quite see the screen," said Kathleen. She tilted his computer. "Oh, look! An interview with Miranda! I thought she *never* gave interviews. And you got one? I am so so impressed." Kathleen reached over the researcher's arm to open the file.

"Ms. Donnelly," said the researcher, "please remember that this is an interview with Mr. Spring."

"Oh, he's useless," said Kathleen. She yanked the laptop in front of herself and began to read the interview with Miranda.

The researcher looked around. They were in the middle

of a huge formal dining room. His chair almost touched the chair of a stranger at the next table. Unwilling to cause a scene, he said in a low voice, "Please give me back the laptop, Ms. Donnelly."

Kathleen's eyes flew down the page.

There were no quotes.

The writing did not seem to be the result of interviews. In fact, it sounded as if somebody had been following Mrs. Johnson. Had entered a store after her, and then a restaurant, and a bank.

Kathleen had a bad feeling about this. Not about snatching the guy's laptop—she felt great about that. But about the non-interview quality of the Miranda file. She closed the file and scanned the other document titles. She clicked on one called *Preface*.

What if there was a kidnapping, and the child was glad?

What if there was a kidnapping, and the child cooperated?

What if there was a kidnapping, and everybody was happier afterward?

That is the story of Jennie Spring, a child who joyfully became Janie Johnson and never looked back.

A child whose birth family later advertised on a milk carton, using a baby photo.

A child who reached her teens, saw that photo, and knew how to capitalize on it.

A good child—but a bad one.

This is the story of her kidnapping.

It begins with the parents of the kidnapper. What kind of people create a daughter like Hannah Javensen? What kind of upbringing did Hannah Javensen have? What kind of people pretend to adopt a stranger's child?

Let us examine the sad and twisted story of Frank and Miranda.

If he reads this, Stephen will kill Calvin Vinesett, thought Kathleen. She closed the document. Next to it was a little icon labeled *The Hannahs*.

"Give that back!" said the researcher.

Kathleen had an app on her phone, Evernote, whose purpose was to capture text. Once she'd opened the Hannah material, she didn't waste time reading it. She just photographed it.

The researcher yanked his laptop back. "Those names don't mean anything," he said. "You should not have those names!"

"You told us you discovered three Hannahs," said Stephen.

"I was exaggerating. I've been working my way through public records, trying to find women in their forties or fifties who match Hannah in some way. There's no reason to think any of them might really be Hannah. They just fit a little of the profile is all. I just mentioned them as bait so you'd give me an interview."

"Bait!" Stephen stood up fast.

Kathleen was afraid he would hit the researcher. She stood up too, ready to block her boyfriend. A fistfight wouldn't help.

But Stephen strode out of the restaurant. At the exit, he did remember to wait for Kathleen, but she had to slip off the yellow leather heels to keep up.

Outside, the air was wonderfully chilly. It tasted of mountains. The sky was bright and the stars hovered, as if they wanted to drop down and talk.

"I hate the media," whispered Stephen. "Bait! Imagine taking three names out of the phone book and using them for bait. And I'm the stupid fish who bit!"

They had gone two long blocks before he realized she was barefoot. "Sorry," he said. "Are your feet okay?"

"Yes. Just slow down, that's all."

They walked gingerly for another block. There was a bench. They sat.

Kathleen said, "I don't believe that the list is bait. He did not plan to show you that list, Stephen. He was not going to give you the possible Hannahs. So the names and addresses do matter. And we do have them."

"Why would he lie and pretend they don't have meaning?"

"Probably Calvin Vinesett wants to find Hannah himself. Think what a coup that would be. Every talk show in America would ask him to be a guest. Another million copies sold."

"We have to stop the book."

Kathleen was doubtful. "No court is going to prevent

publication of a book about a famous crime and a famous victim. Janie is public property. And even if courts got involved, so what? The writer just e-publishes and it goes viral."

Stephen groaned. "Kath, the timing couldn't be worse. There's a wedding coming up. I just found out. Actually, I got the news while you were borrowing clothes from Mandy. Then Brendan called and told me the book title and I forgot. Janie is marrying Reeve. In July! Janie has a shot at being happy, Kathleen. Happy all the way through for the rest of her life. We cannot have a book appear, using that word like that."

Kathleen thought of the vicious preface Calvin Vinesett had written.

What if there were a wedding, she thought, and the bride was destroyed?

THE NINTH PIECE OF THE KIDNAPPER'S PUZZLE

Fifteen years after that day in New Jersey, Hannah decided that she needed to be part of this thing called Facebook. She studied a tutorial before she opened her account. It said not to use her real date of birth because that might lead to identity theft.

It was the first laugh Hannah had had in a long time. Stealing credit cards was so much more fun when they called it identity theft. She had acquired a new ID from a careless college student named Jill Williams. Hannah loved that name. It sounded strong and aggressive. The real Jill Williams was already on Facebook, so Hannah acquired a new free email account and a new date of birth. She scanned good old Tiffany Spratt's driver's license photo and picked a university with a zillion students for her profile information.

The Jennie/Janie herself did not seem to be on Facebook. But the other Spring kids were. Stephen Spring turned out to be going to college right here in Colorado. That shook her up. Had he picked the University of Colorado so he could find her? But if Stephen Spring had known that Frank used a bank here, he'd have told the FBI.

The trouble was, you had to be a Facebook "friend" to get at the real information.

Hannah went to her extensive file. A local Connecticut paper covering the first week of the milk carton excitement had mentioned a boy next door. Reeve Shields. There he was. He had more friends than anybody, but only friends could get past the limited profile. She offered up Jill Williams. "Classmate of Brian," she notated.

But Reeve Shields did not accept Jill Williams as a friend.

The left-hand column of each profile—Stephen, Jodie, Brendan, Brian, and Reeve—showed the person's Facebook friends, and Hannah began making lists, looking for overlap. The first overlap was a Nicole who was friends with each of the Springs.

But Nicole did not accept Jill Williams as a friend either.

The next overlap was a Sarah-Charlotte Sherwood, who was friends with both Reeve and Brian Spring. Like Reeve, she had a huge number of friends.

But Sarah-Charlotte did not accept Jill Williams either.

She didn't even *exist* and they didn't want her!

Hannah's fists rained down on the computer. She didn't damage it; she hit the plastic casing, not the screen. And yet the librarian made her leave the building. The librarian told her not to come back. Two other computer patrons escorted Hannah out the door.

She walked a long way to another library branch. A brilliant decision. At that branch, on that computer, a girl named

Adair, who was a friend to Reeve and to Sarah-Charlotte, accepted Jill Williams as a friend.

Hannah was in.

Adair liked to post. She and Sarah-Charlotte were in the Jennie/Janie's high school class. Adair heard from everybody and uploaded everything that was interesting and everything that was not.

Now that she was a friend of Adair's, Hannah managed to be accepted by Sarah-Charlotte as well. On their walls, Hannah found plenty about Janie. The parent thief was popular.

I was supposed to have that life! thought Hannah. That girl grabbed it away from me.

After a few months, she had all their addresses and most of their home phone numbers. Jennie/Janie. Miranda and Frank. Reeve. Sarah-Charlotte. The red rabbits from New Jersey. She had a little map of the United States and used neon thumbtacks to mark the spot where each person was. She loved shoving the little nails into their hearts.

Stephen was right here. It wasn't that surprising that one of that bunch of red-haired children would end up in Colorado. She avoided his street, because he might recognize her. She hadn't changed much and she was strikingly beautiful.

Hannah had spent so many hours online at libraries, searching for more on the Springs and the Johnsons, that she knew way more than the stupid librarians. They led such cushy lives, darting around a comfortable heated or air-conditioned library; snacking in some nice cozy staff room; now and then showing somebody how to apply for a job via computer.

She hated those librarians. Even now they were asking her to go. Her time was up, they said.

She couldn't go yet. She was reading an amazing post from Adair, who reported that Janie, her brother Brian, and her boyfriend, Reeve, were all flying out to Boulder to visit Stephen and see whether Janie would like to attend college in Colorado.

That girl is flying here? To this very town? My parents must be paying for her ticket! With my money!

"Please," said the librarian. "We have another patron waiting."

Hannah gave up her computer and stomped out of the building. She could not make up her minds. Each of her minds had a different opinion. Should she stand in the shadows and watch the Jennie/Janie and the red rabbit brothers? Or lie low, because they couldn't help but recognize her?

Her minds collided and crashed. The next day it was difficult to work at the motel, and she got yelled at, and even threatened. If she didn't work harder, they'd let her go.

"Let" her go. As if she'd been trying and trying to go, and finally they would let her. Why didn't they just say out loud that they would fire her?

Fire. Like guns. Like flames.

In the end, she lay low. She even waited to visit her post office box until the scheduled trip to Colorado was over. It was fifteen and a half years since that day in New Jersey, but Hannah was still as intuitive today as she was back then. She got spooked just approaching the post office. She did not see anything irregular. But it was a trap.

If felt like a trap. Maybe they had lied on Facebook! Maybe they had not. They had not come here to see about colleges. They had come to catch her. Frank had told.

Her money was lying right there, right at the far end of that lobby, and she couldn't get at it.

She walked on by. It took effort. She was so proud of her amazing self-control.

The third week she was desperate for the money.

She went very early, which she never did because she usually had to be at the Mug; people who drank coffee often drank it before the sun even came up. But it was her day off, and she went to the post office before it actually opened; only the lobby with boxes was open.

It felt safe. She opened her box.

The usual envelope from Frank was not there.

Instead she found a big plain envelope with her real name on it. *Hannah Javensen.* Was it a letter bomb? Was the FBI about to pop out of the tiny doors and slots around her?

She rolled up the envelope in her hand to keep the name from showing. She left the building. She was almost throwing up. She took side streets and an alley and dealt with a scary dog and finally reached a bench by the river.

She opened the envelope. There was a check in it. But there was also a slip of paper with a hand-printed message.

This is the final payment.

CHAPTER NINE

Monday after lunch with her New Jersey parents, Janie drove up to Connecticut in Donna's car.

No matter which bridge she took over the Hudson River, it was the wrong one. No matter how she timed this trip to avoid commuter traffic, she hit traffic. No matter how often she told herself that once she hit Connecticut the traffic would thin out, it never did.

It was only four days since her last trip to Connecticut. Four days since Miranda met and enjoyed Michael Hastings. Miranda would want to talk about Michael. Which meant Janie would have to discuss Calvin Vinesett's book.

Michael was all lies, she thought, navigating the tricky connection from the GW Bridge onto the Henry Hudson Parkway. But that's true of many people in my life. My Connecticut parents—my sturdy suburban straight-arrow parents—are world-class liars. When I first recognized myself on the milk carton, they even told me about their decision to lead a life of lies.

Miranda had insisted that she and Frank never wrote to Hannah again. Never telephoned. Never sent their real daughter a birthday present or a Christmas card. "We let her vanish," said Miranda, who had wept.

Her father shed no tears. Janie had assumed he was too manly for weeping. But he was protecting yet another lie. A life built on lies must be shored up, day after day, fib after fib. Did the man inside Frank's ruined body know what he had done? Did he continue to believe that he had done the best and only thing?

As for Michael, Janie believed that he had not thought particularly about telling lies. He had a chance to sidle into publishing, and he took it. The fun of being a spy without the risk of going to war.

Michael had lost his gamble. Janie had given him very little. He could contribute nothing to Calvin Vinesett's book.

As for Frank and Miranda, she still loved them. But she loved them differently. She loved them sadly.

Last year she and her mother had had a terrible confrontation. Frank's illness had taken such a toll, and that day, Miranda cried, "You aren't helping me enough. You aren't visiting your father enough! You only loved him when he was healthy and handsome. I need you, Janie! We both need you!"

"I'm going to tell you the truth," said Janie cruelly. "Frank has always known where Hannah is. He's been supporting her all these years. I found the checkbook and the bank account he used. He sent a check every month to a post office box in Boulder, Colorado. For your sake and his, when I put a stop to that, I didn't tell the FBI, so they didn't catch Hannah. Every time I look at Frank, I know that he chose to take care of the woman who destroyed my real family. I love him, Mom, but not as much. It has nothing to do with his health. It has to do with his decision to protect Hannah."

Miranda did not ask for more information. She sat there and dwindled away, like a creature in a nightmare, getting smaller and smaller. She never said whether she already knew. She never said a word about Hannah. Did Miranda's heart and arms yearn to hold her real daughter again? Or was her heart frozen against the horror of what Hannah had become? Would Miranda have tried to find Hannah herself, if she had known where Hannah went every month? She never said, and Janie never asked.

Janie made it to the Merritt Parkway, a good road because it was so pretty and a bad road because it was so narrow. She ached to talk to Reeve, or at least text him, and know that he was emotionally at her side. But he was working. She could not bother him at work. He would tell her it wasn't a bother. But it would be.

She turned up the radio to distract herself.

At last, she arrived. The Harbor was a pretty place with a flowery front garden and tall trees. She signed in at the front desk. "Hi, Grace."

"Why, hey there, Janie. You were just here the other day. Your parents will be so happy to see you again so soon."

Janie went through the lovely sitting area and said hello

to people who had lost pieces of themselves; ancient decrepit people, struggling to breathe or remember. Her father needed to be here, but, oh, poor Miranda!

Janie took the stairs instead of the elevator, which was incredibly slow.

Few apartments at the Harbor were locked, because the aides had to go in and out so often. Michael had been fascinated by that. Would Michael tell Calvin Vinesett that there were no locks? But Calvin Vinesett had so little interest that he assigned somebody else to visit her parents. So what if the author of the book knew that not even a bolt stood between him and two helpless residents?

Janie knocked and went in. Her father sat in his wheelchair. Miranda was massaging her husband's feet, which had poor circulation and had turned a ghastly mottled purple.

This wreck was the wonderful dad of her childhood. Janie was glad that Frank himself did not know how bad it was. She flooded herself with the images of this once-fine man. Every picnic at the beach and ball game in the backyard. Every soccer game coached and piano practice timed. Every shared evening watching TV and fixing snacks and tucking under the afghan.

She looked at his big hands, which had held and thrown so many footballs, now trembling on his lap.

Abruptly and completely, she didn't care anymore that those hands had written the checks that paid the bills of her kidnapper.

It's okay, Daddy. You did the best you could. And now it's

over. And thank God I still love you. And I believe, wherever you are inside that body, that you love me.

Frank and Miranda looked up in astonishment. Janie was swept by love for them; by respect for their courage. She hugged them hard and found herself sobbing and her mother said, "Darling, tell me everything. What's wrong?" and her father mumbled, "N cry." *Don't cry.*

She kissed his cheek.

"I'm crying because I'm happy," she said, which was not true. Who could be happy, seeing Frank's destruction? "You will absolutely never guess what. I flew down to Charlotte Friday afternoon to spend the weekend with Reeve."

"Reeve?" said her mother. "What about Michael?"

"He turned out to be a dud. We never have to think about him again."

"I'm sorry, darling. Michael was charming. And so sweet to your father."

"He's history," said Janie firmly. "Here's the news. Reeve asked me to marry him."

Her mother's jaw dropped.

Janie handed over her cell. "Watch this video."

Miranda held the iPhone awkwardly and frowned at the first muddled moment of the airport scene and then gasped as it unfolded. "Oh, Janie! That is so romantic! That is *beyond* romantic!"

Janie took the phone back. "Look, Daddy. Can you see the screen? Do I have it at the right angle?"

He reached for the phone and managed to hold it himself.

They crowded together to see it again. Her father's eyes twinkled in the old way.

"Reeve can really kiss, can't he?" said Miranda, giggling. "You'll have a long engagement, won't you? You won't finish college for two years and I know you'll want to stay in New England. I'm sure Reeve is hoping to earn a transfer or promotion so he can get out of there anyway."

"He loves it there," said Janie. "And so do I. And here's the really big news. We're getting married July eighth."

"A month after your college graduation? That works. Two years is enough time for planning."

"July eighth right now," said Janie. "A month and a half from today."

"That's ridiculous," said her mother dismissively. "You can't get married now. You're barely twenty years old. What will your New Jersey parents say? I know Reeve's parents will disapprove. They have high hopes for Reeve and getting married too young is a poor decision. No. You must rethink this, Janie."

The door opened and in came two dietary aides. "Hey, Ms. Johnson," they said. "Hey, Mr. Johnson. Oh, look, your beautiful daughter is visiting for supper. We'll bring a tray up for you, too, Janie. It's such a good meal tonight. Lemon chicken, carrot-raisin salad, orzo, broccoli, a nice dinner roll, and chocolate pudding."

They set Frank's meal on a rolling hospital tray while Janie opened the card table for herself and her mother. A shocking contrast to the long slow meals in the formal dining room they had enjoyed for so many years.

When the aides had left, Janie said, "Mom. You know I love

you. I've managed to be two daughters at one time, but I can't have weddings in two places. The wedding will be at Our Lady of Grace, the Springs' parish. Father John will perform the wedding. The reception will be in the Springs' backyard. But you'll be there and you'll also be my parents. I will have two mothers of the bride and two fathers of the bride. Donna is reserving a wing at the motel for everybody to stay, and a handicapped room for you and Daddy."

Miranda swallowed hard. A few tears slid down her cheek.

Was Miranda wishing that she was the real and only mother of Janie? Wishing that her real daughter, Hannah, could have had a middle-class life and a wedding among friends?

Janie realized that she did not care. It was okay to love extra people and be torn. "Mom? Will you be okay? Tell me."

"A person always weeps over a wedding," said Miranda bravely. "Reeve is a lovely boy. He will be a delightful son-in-law."

But Reeve would not be Miranda's son-in-law. He would be Donna Spring's son-in-law.

They talked about Reeve and what fun it had been living next door to his family and whether Mrs. Shields was reacting well to the news of a wedding in seven weeks. Not likely. Mrs. Shields mainly reacted well to things she controlled.

When dinner was over, Frank took his wife's hand. Their hands were so old! Their joints had swollen and their veins had knotted. Her father patted Miranda's fingers, repeating something neither woman could understand.

"The ring," said Miranda finally. "He's tugging on my diamond."

"Reeve didn't give me a diamond ring, Daddy," Janie told him. "Maybe we'll do that some other year."

He mumbled a long sentence whose only clear word was "wedding."

"The wedding will be in New Jersey, Daddy. In church. You'll be there, because you're the father of the bride. We'll get a tux for you too. You'll look so handsome."

"Far de bide," he said.

"Father of the bride," she agreed.

"Come?" he said clearly.

Janie knelt beside him. "Oh, Daddy, yes. I need you there."

She met her mother's eyes. "But here's the thing, Daddy. I have another father. My New Jersey father. Jonathan Spring. And another mother. Donna Spring. And I want to get married as my real legal self." Janie clasped her father's hand and drew her mother's in and held their hands in hers. "I will say my vows as Jennie Spring," she told them. "The days of Janie Johnson are over. And then I will be Jennie Shields. So my name is Jennie now."

She had never asked these parents to call her Jennie. She had forced the real parents to say Janie.

I've been a terrible person, she thought. But I had terrible decisions to make. And I wasn't ready.

Maybe nobody is ever ready for a terrible decision.

"Even *I'm* not used to the name Jennie," she said, trying to smile. "Reeve is going to have cue cards so he can remember to say Jennie during the ceremony. But that's the wedding present I want from everybody. Even from you. My name. Jennie."

● ● ●

Reeve had lost himself in work. Mondays were especially busy. Right now they were preparing for the College World Series. It wasn't until everybody began knocking off that Reeve remembered he led a life outside of work. He had not checked his phone in some time.

Many people had texted and called. Especially Janie. He read her messages, following her through the long drive and difficult visit to Connecticut.

If I don't tell her that I was offered a position in Connecticut, thought Reeve, then I'm not letting her be part of the decision. Aren't wives and husbands supposed to share important decisions?

He wanted Janie to think about china and curtains and stuff. Where she would finish college and what she would do with that degree. He wanted her to have ordinary problems, like parking or shoes. He wanted to carry her away from the grip of the kidnap and the double parents.

They would live in his one-bedroom apartment, which was in a pleasant complex surrounded by trees and running trails. He even meant to go running one of these days. He had seriously been thinking of getting tableware, because the little plastic forks he got with takeaway food kept breaking. But then he'd have to find time to go shopping, and find out where you did that shopping, and somehow it never worked out.

Janie loved shopping. This was good. They would divide household tasks. She would shop. Of course, it's easier to shop if there's money.

Reeve had been in the weddings of one brother and one sister. Those weddings had been like architecture, undergoing design and revision for a year. At his wedding, all he had to do was show up with his shoes polished. He moved through Janie's texts, assuming that she had assignments for him. Her most recent text said, Want to visit again soon.

Can't afford another ticket soon, he wrote back.

I'll drive, she wrote. Only 14 hours.

Reeve did it in twelve. She obviously intended to drive the speed limit. He made a mental note that when the two of them went on trips, he would drive.

What do we need to talk about? he texted.

I wasn't thinking about talking. XOXOXOXO.

On the bench in Boulder, sitting in the dark, Kathleen watched the video yet again.

She had a wedding vision: herself in a white gown, and an aisle, flowers and guests and music. But she could not put Stephen into this vision. Stephen dreamed of being a geologist—going down shafts or up mountains; going to Mongolia or Tanzania or the isolated land of northernmost Canada. But basically, just going. On his own in a world of risk and tough odds. He did not dream of weddings.

"I mean, think about it," said Stephen. "Reeve's in a big city. Has a fabulous job. Famous athletes and coaches roam all over his office. He has no responsibilities except at work. And he wants to change all that and get married."

What would the wedding be like? Kathleen wondered.

Would it be formal? Would there be a bridal shower?

Would there be bridesmaids?

Would that snippy sister, Jodie, be a bridesmaid?

Would Janie remember that her older brother, Stephen, had a girlfriend?

Would Janie think of inviting the girlfriend?

Would Stephen think of putting Kathleen's name on the guest list?

Would Stephen even know there was such a thing as a guest list?

I want to be at Janie's wedding, thought Kathleen. I want to be at my own wedding.

She was glad it was dark and Stephen could not see her face or the tears shining in her eyes.

Stephen said, "So now we have the names of the three possible Hannahs. That's what we'll do tomorrow. Go look at them."

"We both have to work," said Kathleen faintly.

"I'm getting a substitute," said Stephen.

She was not going to be left out of Hannah hunts. "Me too," said Kathleen.

Jodie told her supervisor and the nuns that she wanted to leave now, because of an upcoming wedding. They hugged and kissed and told her how wonderful she was, and how of course she must go home for that great celebration! They gave her a party, and somebody somewhere managed to bake a cake, and all the children came, and she photographed them on her cell phone so she could keep them in her hand.

She loved Haiti. She loved Haitians. But now she was going home to party. The family's first wedding!

Jodie had expected to return from Haiti as the star of her family, the one who had handed her life to charity, done good work, and helped save the world. Everybody would want to see her photos and videos and hear every bit of her story. But no. The lost sister had center stage again.

From the nuns, Jodie had learned to pray for patience.

She smiled at God and said silently, So I need even more of it, God. Janie's a big patience taker.

At the airport, Jodie rejoiced because she was going home. Such a beautiful phrase.

Once again, she would have a life of comfort and safety. A life of electricity and friends. Cars and air-conditioning and washing machines. Libraries and malls. She could eat a salad without worrying about diarrhea. She did not have to think of the tropical diseases that came through the air, through the soles of bare feet, through water and dust and mud and rubble. She did not have to look at what passed for housing in the areas not yet cleaned up from the earthquake—housing so bad that if an American kept a dog like that, the American would be arrested.

They began boarding her flight.

She was just about to turn off her cell when a message arrived from that researcher who was helping with a book about the kidnap. It was so annoying that the man had her cell phone number. Who had given it to him, anyway? Probably Brendan, who had become such a pain. Mom said

Brendan was giving interviews. Jodie had asked her mother, "What do you think about the book?"

"I'm still thinking," Donna had said. A non-answer if there ever was one.

Jodie deleted the researcher.

Donna Spring floated on the joy of her daughter's wedding.

All those years of fury and fright; all those nights of despair; all that weeping and emptiness—and now her daughter wanted to be her daughter. She wanted to be Jennie again, and marry in the church where her real family went to Mass. She wanted her real father to be the real father and give her away in marriage. She wanted to become Jennie Spring Shields.

After all this time and all this pain, Donna's daughter finally knew who her family was.

What do good people do when there is no good thing to do? The question had haunted them from the day Janie recognized her face on the milk carton.

Frank and Miranda Johnson were good people. They had done a good job rearing the little girl they thought was their granddaughter. They had done good things in their community and they had done good things keeping the lines open when Janie could not be reconciled to her original life. Frank and Miranda had constantly invited Stephen, Jodie, and the twins to their house. They had driven Janie down to New Jersey for Christmas and Easter, keeping their distance, staying at the motel until it was time to leave.

The media savaged them. Parents of a kidnapper: it must be their fault. Janie had stood by them literally and figuratively.

Donna remembered her joy when Janie trusted her with information, and her outrage about that information. Frank had known all these years how to find the kidnapper and had been paying her bills.

"I don't think Miranda knows," Janie had said. "I don't want to tell her. I just closed the account. It's over."

But the FBI could have staked out that post office box! We'd have her by now! Donna wanted to shake her foolish child by the shoulders.

"My parents have been through enough, Mom. Capture and trial? No. I like to think that in the pieces of his mind he has left, Frank still has good things, like sunshine and football. I mean, who cares anymore?"

I care! thought Donna Spring. Hannah took a sledgehammer to our two families. I even care that poor Frank was crucified by that horrible woman, keeping his terrible secret, hiding money and accounts and staying anonymous until it gave him a heart attack and a stroke. I care for Miranda. I care for me! Every single night of my life, thinking if only I had held her hand in that shoe store in that mall.

I care that a woman of violence, like Hannah Javensen, could do anything to anybody. That even now she may be harming the innocent. And we could have locked her up!

But now, tonight, she thought, I care for you, my darling daughter. Imagine. You're getting married. To the very boy who betrayed you on the radio.

Donna had three boys of her own. In fact, she had married a boy. Boys didn't always think first. Or ever.

Donna gave Reeve credit for driving Janie to New Jersey five years ago to check out the Spring family. Janie and Reeve had parked across the street and stared at the front door of the house on Highview Avenue, watching four redheaded kids pile off school buses. Kids who looked like Janie. Donna imagined knowledge coating Janie like ice: she really was the face on the milk carton.

You're only twenty, thought Donna. But in some ways, you're as old as I am. You have suffered, you made difficult choices; every day you struggle to do the right thing, even when you can't figure out what it is.

But Hannah . . . not so much. Hannah wanted to do the wrong thing.

Oh, how Donna Spring wanted Hannah to pay!

In Boulder, Stephen and Kathleen found the street on which the first possible Hannah lived. It was a long road. The person did not live at the expensive end. She lived at the dumpy end. Stephen and Kathleen found themselves facing a small house divided into very small apartments. Probably rented to students, with 100 percent turnover every year or even every semester.

"What will you say to her?" Kathleen wanted to know.

"All I want to do is look at her." He walked right up and rang the bell. Nobody answered.

Stephen rang again and they waited again.

A woman walking a dog paused on the sidewalk. "I'm the

landlady. You wanna rent a room? I got an empty one. You gotta share a bathroom."

The woman was middle-aged. Somewhat heavy. Short puffy hair dyed blond, with gray roots showing. Bushy eyebrows. A big solid chin and very full lips.

"Thanks," said Stephen. He looked at the list and read the first name out loud. "So that's you, ma'am?"

"Yep."

Scratch her, thought Kathleen. The Hannah in the high school picture is thin. Thin lips, thin hair, thin eyebrows, thin shoulders, thin nose. Weight gain wouldn't change basic features. This was not Hannah.

Stephen said, "Did you ever rent to a woman named Tiffany Spratt?"

Who in the world was Tiffany Spratt? wondered Kathleen.

"Come on," said the woman, gesturing with her dog-poop bag. "You think I remember them by name all these years, coming and going and skipping out on their rent? Mainly I have boys, though. Girls, they're always wanting their own bathroom."

"Thanks," said Stephen. "Appreciate your time." He walked away.

Well, this was the shortest and least productive interview on record. Kathleen followed reluctantly. Down the block, Stephen opened his wallet and took out the photograph of Hannah.

Imagine carrying the picture of the criminal who destroyed your life right in your wallet! Imagine it sitting there, where you'd see it each time you used a credit card! Its little yellow hair and its little prim smile always staring up!

Sick, thought Kathleen. If we got married, I would put a stop to that. But we'll never get married. He's not the marrying kind. And my parents say you can't change anybody. Which is nonsense. I've changed myself a bunch to meet Stephen's expectations.

Anyway, who was she to judge him for toting old photographs around? She herself had two photos of Hannah from the FBI website, the same high school yearbook photo and the computer-aged portrait.

"Ever since Jodie and I went into New York City trying to find Hannah I've carried this," Stephen told her. "We were stupid kids, but it wasn't a stupid idea. Hannah was arrested in New York once, and she's out here somewhere. And a guy who writes huge bestsellers, who ought to know what he's doing—his research team thinks she's here in Boulder. So maybe the list exists as bait to get me, but I actually feel better about his research. He got some of it right. That can't be Hannah, but she is the right age, and gender, and I think the poverty fits too."

The reader of this future book wants way more than age, gender, and poverty, thought Kathleen. The reader wants description and conversation and analysis and photographs and background. Calvin Vinesett has a long way to go. Which is good. The book will take ages to write, and by then, Janie will be safely married and living far away under another name.

"Who's Tiffany Spratt?" she asked.

"That's the name Frank and Hannah chose for the post office box and the checks. I figure if we meet the real Hannah, she'll be a little shaken that we know the name."

It crossed Kathleen's mind that the real Hannah was a kidnapper. By definition, violent. Should they really be wandering around trying to shake up people who liked violence?

On Wednesday, Lizzie was on the phone to her little brother yet again. "Yesterday," she said sternly, "I visited the Harbor to see Mr. Johnson."

Reeve was startled by this news. But then, his family had lived next door to the Johnsons for years. He used to be very fond of Mr. Johnson. Now Mr. Johnson was a shell. It was hard to be fond of a shell. You had to be fond of the history of the shell.

"You will have legal in-laws," said Lizzie, the family attorney. "Donna and Jonathan Spring. And you will have emotional in-laws, Frank and Miranda Johnson. Instead of helping Janie with her burdens, you are whisking her away."

"Isn't that a form of helping?" asked Reeve.

"Does it help Frank and Miranda?" demanded Lizzie.

"Listen, Lizzie. Janie found that assisted living place, after searching everywhere for something her parents could afford. She cleaned up that big house and got it repainted and found the real estate agent and got it sold. She put on that huge tag sale. She arranged the move from nine big rooms to three tiny rooms. She got Frank into his teensy bedroom with his walker and his eleven medications and she got Miranda into her teensy bedroom with her three medications.

She got cable TV and telephone and Internet connections up and going. She arranged the furniture to fit and put the stuff Miranda wouldn't part with in a storage unit. Every two weeks, for two whole years of college, she visited. You didn't visit our parents every two weeks when you were in college. You didn't even come home for Thanksgiving!"

"And I salute Janie," said Lizzie. "But who will visit Frank and Miranda now that you're taking their only child to North Carolina?"

"You probably should do it, Lizzie," said Reeve. "Your house is closer. Yes, I think that's the solution. You visit."

Reeve rarely stopped Lizzie in her tracks. It was a pleasure.

But his sister had many topics to discuss. "Reeve," she said, "I understand the ceremony will be in the Catholic church. Are you becoming a Catholic?"

"I'm not sure. The priest is letting me meet with him by Skype. We have two talks scheduled, and one more in person in New Jersey before the wedding."

"It's a serious decision," said his sister.

"Getting married?" said Reeve. "I'm with you. How much more serious does it get?"

"I cannot support the pope's decrees in many situations," said Lizzie.

"And that applies to me how?" demanded Reeve. "Lizzie, I'm Christian. I can be a different variety of Christian. I know we're too young to do this. I know we don't have enough money and we haven't thought it through and we're crazy. But we'll have the blessing of God."

Totally fun. He had silenced her twice in one conversation.

Sarah-Charlotte's roommate said, "I read a lot of true crime, you know. It fascinates me."

Sarah-Charlotte did know. There was always some gruesome title lying open on Lauren's bed. Nothing would make Sarah-Charlotte read true crime. She knew how lucky toddler Jennie Spring had been that her kidnapper had not tortured or murdered her. She knew that a person like Hannah Javensen who would actually snatch somebody's baby would do anything. It was a chance in a million that when Hannah was ready to do worse than kidnap, she found herself near the one household where she could dump the kid and pretend the crime had never happened.

Lauren said, "Kidnappings are shocking because they involve innocent helpless children. But the Janie Johnson case is especially interesting. Janie was taken for no reason that anybody could discern. The kidnapper just felt like it. Imagine a woman so removed from normal human emotion that stealing a kid was no different from stealing a video game. The toddler survived, so it's not like that Smith case where the mother drove her car into the pond and purposely drowned her little boys so she could date somebody who didn't like kids. But I think Hannah Javensen is just as frightening. A kidnapper who presents a stolen child to her own mother and father like a birthday present. 'Here! A granddaughter for you! Auburn curls and a polka-dot dress! Well—I'm off! Bring her up for me!' The kidnapper wanted her own mother and father to get caught for her crime and suffer what should have been her punishment."

"Hannah pulled it off," said Sarah-Charlotte. "Frank and Miranda were hideously punished." Although Janie was punished the most.

"As for Michael/Mick," said Lauren, "it isn't safe for Janie to be stalked by some kidnap junkie. Let's investigate him. I'm so disappointed in Calvin Vinesett. I've read all his books, and I had no idea that he used researchers. I always imagined him going to the prison and visiting the killer and interviewing the sick and crazy parents—there's always a sick and crazy parent, you know."

"There is not," said Sarah-Charlotte sternly. "I love the Johnsons. The sick and crazy person is Hannah. She was probably born that way. Or her body chemistry shifted sideways and she became that way."

And then Lauren's parents arrived at the dorm to take her and her stuff home for the summer, and the girls hugged good-bye. Sarah-Charlotte hauled the last of her own stuff down to the lobby, turned in her room key, and waited for her parents.

Mick had followed her too, trotting down the sidewalk that day, hoping to become friends. He really is a stalker, she thought, and she was utterly confused. The guy had a New York City apartment. Why would he travel to Boston, figure out what classes Sarah-Charlotte was in, and edge into *her* life?

I can't tell him anything, she thought.

But what did he think I could tell him?

She had a thought so weird she couldn't breathe. No, she said to herself. Impossible.

She batted her hands at her head, to get rid of the crazy thought.

I need a second opinion. But whose?

Not Janie. Not Reeve. They don't need more kidnap in their lives. Not the Johnsons, for sure. Not the Springs, who are all kidnapped out. Reeve's lawyer sister, Lizzie? She helped Janie once.

But Sarah-Charlotte didn't like Lizzie, and the feeling was mutual.

A couple of times, Sarah-Charlotte had run into Brian, one of Janie's younger twin brothers, who was also in school in Boston. Well, not Boston, really; Harvard students always said Cambridge.

She called him, but Brian was not willing to discuss the true crime book. Either he had things to do or he was not a fan of Sarah-Charlotte's. Sarah-Charlotte learned only one thing: Brendan had given interviews. That didn't get her anywhere.

And then her parents arrived, and triple-parked, and they flung boxes and duffels and suitcases into the car, and Sarah-Charlotte forgot.

Jodie's plane was approaching Newark. She was pierced by the deep emotion of an American returning home after a long time. It wasn't joy, but joyful heartache. *Yes. I'm home. Oh, thank you! I'm home.*

The plane was coming down over New Jersey, her beloved state, and below her was an ocean of small roofs and wide roads, hurrying cars and fat green trees.

They landed.

She would have kissed the ground if she had been at ground level.

At the gate, she had a drink of cold water from a fountain, and thought how Haitians would love such a thing, and then went to the ladies' room and marveled at how clean and white and sweet-smelling it was.

She turned on her cell phone and called her parents.

"We're waiting at baggage claim!" shrieked her mother, as if she needed to project volume all the way to Haiti.

When Jodie got to baggage claim, hundreds of other arriving passengers were on their cell phones, describing exact locations, but Jodie could skip that step. Hers was the crowd of redheads. Mom's was getting gray and Dad's was vanishing to a curly rim around a bald head, but that massive mane of red hair could only be Janie.

The difficult sister cared enough to come.

And then they were all hugging and laughing and saying pointless things like "How was the flight?"

"I want to hear all about Haiti," said Janie.

Jodie thought, I could never explain Haiti. I didn't understand while I was there. "First, I get to hear all about the wedding," she said.

Haiti receded as if it had been a dentist appointment instead of another world and a year.

"Get in here, Reeve!" shouted his boss.

Reeve's gut tightened. He'd done everything, hadn't he? In the right order? In a timely fashion? Every detail correct?

He trotted into Bick's office.

"So, how far have you gotten with these wedding plans? Because we have a problem."

"We do?"

"I shouldn't have okayed July eighth so fast. We've got the Big East preview that weekend and I want you on it. I can give you the second week in September, or else next weekend. June third. I figured things were gonna be pretty loose, seeing the way you proposed and all. You didn't engrave the invitations yet, didja?"

Oh, great, thought Reeve. Career or wedding. Love when that happens. "Let me talk to Janie real fast."

He went out of Bick's office. Out of the whole building. Into the shade of an overhang. Good thing there were cell phones. He was pretty sure Janie was in New Jersey for Jodie's welcome home party, but a person could get confused following Janie's family schedule.

"Janie? Problems. They don't want to give me July eighth after all. How do you feel about either June third, or else September?"

They both burst into crazed laughter.

"That's it? Those are our choices?" said Janie.

"Yup."

"If we wait until September, I'll be a crazy woman all summer. But there's no way to put a wedding together in—oh, wow—that's ten days!"

"Aren't we just serving sandwiches out in the backyard, though?" asked Reeve. "And aren't you getting a dress off the rack at the bridal mall?"

"Ten days," Janie repeated.

"Come on, woman," said Reeve. "I've crammed all my studying for entire semesters into ten hours. We can figure out how to say I do in ten days."

"Except guess what—the actual wording is 'I will.'"

"Will what?"

"I *will* take this man to be my wedded husband, to love and to cherish from this time forth. I love that word, 'cherish.'"

"And will you want to cherish me in ten days or in four months?"

"I'll call you back in a few minutes, Reeve." Janie flew downstairs to find her mother. "We have to change the wedding date. How does June third sound?"

"Insane," said her mother.

"True, but will you and Dad be here?" Janie giggled. "I know my other parents don't have any trips abroad planned."

"Let's think. Brendan and Brian aren't a problem. They'll be home from college by then anyway, and all we have to do is button them into their wedding clothes. I'll call Stephen immediately. He'll be irritated, but he always is. Let me check with Father John and make sure we can get the church. It'll be very exciting. There will be so much to do, nobody can sleep from now on."

"It's only ten days," said Janie. "Who needs sleep?" She stood close to her mother's cell phone to hear the conversation with the priest. Father John just laughed. Yes, they could get married on June 3.

Janie called Reeve back. "June third is on. Are your parents okay with that? What about your brother, Todd? What about Lizzie?"

"Oh, yeah, I forgot all of them. Can you text me a list?"

"How about I just handle them?"

"Wow," said Reeve. "My bride isn't just beautiful. She's willing to be slaughtered on my behalf."

Dozens of people had only one thing to say on Facebook: *Ten days?*

Mrs. Shields telephoned her son. "Ten days?" she said fiercely.

"I know. Even for me, it's a little speedy."

"Ten days is impossible, Reeve."

"All you have to do is show up, Mom. You're only a few hours from New Jersey. We've scheduled the wedding for two o'clock in the afternoon, so no matter how bad the traffic is, you'll make it. Ideally, though, you'll come Friday and we'll have a wedding rehearsal and a dinner. Mrs. Spring is working on hotel rooms."

"The Friday rehearsal dinner is our responsibility," said his mother grimly. "I'll call Mrs. Spring right now and she'll have to make the reservations. What's her first name again?"

"Donna. You'll like her, Mom."

His mother said nothing.

Reeve said, "Or could you pretend to, Mom? Please?"

"The third of June?" repeated Stephen Spring. "Are you serious? You expect me there in ten days?"

"Actually, I need you in seven days," said his mother. "We

212

have to get you fitted for a tuxedo and you have to help with a million details."

"Has there ever been a time when Janie wasn't a pain?" he asked.

"Jennie," she reminded him. "And I think it's Reeve being the pain this time. And so what? We get to put on a wedding. Now don't dillydally. Get your plane tickets." His mother hung up.

Kathleen was laughing. "When I get married," she said, "it's going to be a lot more organized."

Stephen didn't ask who she planned to marry. He didn't ask her to come to his sister's wedding either. He said, "Let's get our bikes. We need to track down those other two Hannahs."

THE TENTH PIECE OF THE KIDNAPPER'S PUZZLE

The final check was big. Hannah spent it on three things.

First, a dentist. The man had some nerve to charge that much for one silly tooth. But Hannah had known how to handle people from the day she got Tiffany Spratt a post office box. The dentist agreed to be paid in installments. She proved how reliable and honest she was by making payments each month for four months when he hadn't even done anything yet. He was impressed and agreed to fix the tooth while she would keep paying him.

What an idiot. Like she would keep paying after her mouth looked good.

Second, she got her own cell phone. She'd been stealing them, and enjoyed playing the games and exploring the apps, but the phones were quickly canceled. And once everybody in the world got a cell phone, public phones vanished. Her own cell phone was a necessity.

Third, a computer.

She no longer needed the library; instead she needed the

phone company and the Internet supplier. They were harder to scam than the dentist. You had to pay them. And Frank's money was now gone.

She had to work two lousy jobs instead of just one lousy job.

She always disguised herself. When she was a maid at motels, she wore street clothes under her uniform so she'd look fat. But it was just habit. She no longer really believed anybody was after Hannah Javensen. She was old news.

Also, they were stupid. She was smart.

Sometimes she liked to read through her collection of old Jennie/Janie articles, where they said they were going to bring the kidnapper to justice. "Justice" sounded like a town, with streets and sidewalks and a courtroom. Well, they couldn't bring her to the town of Justice. She had vanished better than anybody.

That year, Hannah had her forty-sixth birthday. She could hardly imagine being that old. But she was. She thought sometimes about turning fifty. Or sixty. It was terrifying.

They couldn't expect her to scrub toilets and vacuum hotel rooms when she got old. Already her knees hurt and her back hurt.

The coffee shop was hard. She bussed tables, loaded dishwashers, and put away the mugs when they were still so hot they burned her.

The customers were always clean and chipper and chatty and young. They loved their little mugs. When she returned a mug to the display wall, she had to hang it with the customer's name visible.

They all got to use their real names. It was so unfair!

She kept track of names of people she hated. There was the woman who got hired in Hannah's place when a motel canned her. There was the woman who told on her when she was sneaking the waitresses' tips out of the jar. The woman who ratted when she smuggled meat from the restaurant refrigerator. People had no sense of kinship.

Sixteen years after that day in New Jersey, Hannah was watching TV in a sports bar. The bar was a rough place, but that was not a problem, because Hannah was a rough person. She did not have the cash to pay for her drink and was more focused on that than some college ball game. She pondered how to get money out of Frank and Miranda.

Supposedly, knowledge was money. But Hannah had acquired a lot of knowledge and it hadn't brought money.

On wide screens in front of her, to her left, to her right, and behind, the announcers fumbled their patter. They ended up laughing. Those guys were probably paid a million dollars and when they made a mistake, everybody just laughed. When *she* made a mistake, they fired her.

"We've just been saved!" said the commentator. "Our terrific researcher produced the facts."

"Let's give credit where credit is due," said the second guy. "Don't we have a camera near that kid? Reeve Shields, take a bow."

Reeve Shields? It was not an ordinary name. Could it be the boy next door to the Jennie/Janie? The one who wouldn't friend her on Facebook? The one who came here with the Jennie/Janie to visit the Stephen?

For two seconds, the television showed this person Reeve

in a cubicle somewhere. He was very young and very handsome, with moppy hair and a long narrow face split by a huge happy grin. He got to be on television and he was cute and people loved him and they remembered his name!

Hannah had put up with a lot in this world. She was not putting up with this. That Jennie/Janie not only got two families—including Hannah's own—but also this cute guy?

That girl deserved nothing! That girl had just gone along for the ride.

And that girl even had Hannah's money! They probably had written their wills, those slimy parents of hers, and cut out their real true daughter in favor of this girl Hannah herself had given to them!

Out of her rage burst a brilliant idea.

It was an idea so amazing that it glittered, a jewel resting on velvet in a store window.

After a while she could touch the idea and glow in its light. The idea solved everything. She would have money.

And the Jennie/Janie would be very sorry.

CHAPTER TEN

Nicole gave Jodie a welcome-home party.

Nicole's house was a split-level, with the rec room on the lower floor opening to a big screened porch and a big untended yard. Kids poured in and out of the house, music reverberated, and neighbors looked tense.

"Your welcome-home party is like a preview of Janie's wedding," Nicole told Jodie. "You weren't due home till the end of the summer and that's when I expected to give a party. My mother said just have the party in August anyway, but I said you can't welcome somebody home three months after she gets here. So I slapped this together. You get what you get."

Nicole was serving giant subs, plus those round plastic trays from the supermarket filled with vegetables or fruit and dip. Nobody had touched them yet, even the vegetarians. A stack of paper napkins, a thousand cans of soda, and a cooler of ice wrapped up party preparations.

How awed and excited the little kids in Haiti would be by such a party. But Jodie skipped the Haiti comparison.

"Nicole, this is perfect. I'm thrilled to see everybody. Especially you. Thank you so much. And we have so much to talk about."

Nicole nodded. "Real quick, while everybody is popping open a soda can, I'll start on my cousin Vic. You'll be so disappointed. That post office box where Frank sent the checks? It was closed two years ago. Nobody remembers a single thing about the woman who rented it. Her name was Tiffany Spratt. The police found a Tiffany Spratt who went to college there ages ago, but she never had a post office box and she is who she is, and she's not Hannah. Her backpack was stolen once, when she was a freshman, and it had her wallet in it, and it was a real pain getting another driver's license and canceling her credit card and her debit card. They're guessing Hannah used Tiffany Spratt's ID to rent the post office box, but the real Tiffany Spratt never got billed for a charge that wasn't hers, and so she had no idea that anybody had used her driver's license. It's a dead end."

It wouldn't have been a dead end if Janie had told the authorities about the box. Don't go that way, Jodie told herself. Remember the plan: to love Janie. ,

Okay, in a little dark corner of her heart, Jodie could still be furious that Janie had put comatose Frank and pathetic Miranda first. Jodie spent a few minutes in the little dark corner and then she joined the party.

Stephen Spring not only wanted to be in the wedding party, he wanted it to *be* a party, with noise and dancing and toasts and tears. He was going to need a party after chasing three

Hannahs. He wanted to locate the woman, or rule her out, and be done with it.

He and Kathleen found the second possible Hannah slumped on a chair in a tiny side yard by a tiny garage apartment. She was very thin. Her old sweat suit had once been peach or pink. Now it had bleach stains. A cigarette hung from her lips. Her lips were thin, as was her hair. If "down and out" was your criterion, she fit. If thin and formerly blond were the criteria, she fit.

Stephen thought, She really is possible.

He had not expected Hannah to pull herself together in middle age. Hannah would not have become a good woman with a decent life. He had pictured her melting into her own evil, like the wicked witch in *The Wizard of Oz.*

Now, at the realization that the possible Hannah was possible, Stephen had trouble filling his lungs. He did not want to be near the woman. He wanted to have bullet- and fist-proof glass between him and her, because if she was Hannah, he did not want to damage her. He wanted a trial. He wanted the whole thing—exposure of every ugly vicious act of her ugly vicious life.

No, he reminded himself. What I want is for my sister to have a life without that book title around. "Ma'am?" he said.

The woman took the cigarette out of her mouth. She stabbed it into a metal coffee can at her door filled with sand and butts. "I'm not buying anything. Don't think you can rip me off either."

She had a heavy Brooklyn accent.

Hannah had grown up in Connecticut. Frank and Miranda

had excellent diction, to the point of sounding pseudo-British.

The aura of Hannah fell away and Stephen saw only a weary old woman, much too old to be Hannah Javensen. Although life could have aged her an extra decade or two.

"We're not selling anything," he said. "We're sorry to bother you. We're trying to find a cheap place to rent."

"Ain't nothin' cheap in this town."

"We're finding that out. Sounds as if you moved here from New York. Me too," he fibbed. "What part of New York?"

She softened. "Fort Greene, honey."

"You miss it?"

"Sure. This dump? Compared to home? But I like the mountains."

There were beautiful mountains outside Boulder. But the view this woman had was peeling paint and a row of garbage cans.

Stephen was suddenly deeply sorry for her. "Have you ever run into a woman named Tiffany Spratt? She was looking for apartments around here."

The woman shook her head and lit another cigarette.

We're not going to find Hannah, thought Stephen. These three names really are just bait, designed by Calvin Vinesett. No point rearranging my workweek to find the third name.

Janie did not think of Facebook when she thought of spreading the news, because she never posted. But Sarah-Charlotte, Reeve, Adair, Eve, Reeve's sister Lizzie, and everybody else posted the new wedding date: June 3.

Sarah-Charlotte telephoned everybody who had planned to fly in so they could change their tickets. She reported back to Janie. "Some people can't come after all, and they're sad—but other people *can* come after all, and they're tickled. So it's going to work out fine. We had eleven people for our van and we still do, it's just a different eleven. Plus several people are driving separately and a few are flying straight into Newark. I'm still working on a bridal shower. What day can you be up here?"

"I don't think there's any day," said Janie regretfully.

"How about a shower down there? Maybe Jodie and I can cohost."

"But already there isn't time. You're arriving here that Friday for the rehearsal, Sarah-Charlotte. You don't want to haul back and forth for a shower too."

"Of course I do. But tell me about the reception. How many people are coming?"

"We're not going to know till they get here. Dad says he's buying enough hamburger patties and hot dogs for a couple hundred and he can just freeze them if we only have twenty-five. And Mom and two of her neighbors are going to make vats of potato salad and macaroni salad and my aunt and uncle are going to buy a ton of shrimp and then we'll pack the freezer with ice cream to go with the cake. It'll be your basic picnic, only with a bride."

Sarah-Charlotte did not approve. A wedding should be your basic formal sit-down dinner at a country club, with linens, silver, flowers, favors, and dinner-jacket-clad waiters. But she wouldn't let her best friend down. "I like the theme," she said. "A wedding that starts by leaping over security-line ropes should be frantic, with people bringing their own bags of chips and lugging their own folding chairs."

Janie giggled. "It won't be that crazy. But just picking people up at the airport on that Friday is going to take the whole family and half the neighbors."

Back home in New Jersey, Brendan was in a terrible mood. His mother had just told him about that guy Michael Hastings, and how he stalked Janie and tried to use her. Brendan wanted to chain the guy to the bumper of a truck and drive down the thruway for a hundred miles. He couldn't believe his family wasn't going after this Michael creep. "No," said his mother, "I want to leave it alone."

That's the trouble with this world, thought Brendan. We leave things alone.

He called Stephen, who was excellent at getting mad and would share his mood to perfection. "When are you getting here anyway?" Brendan demanded. "It's very tiring being surrounded by wedding planners."

"I'm flying in Friday night. I actually won't get there till after the rehearsal. My flight doesn't even land until eleven p.m. Mom wanted me earlier but I couldn't pull it off."

"You don't have to try on a tux?"

"Nope. I emailed the rental store. They have my size on file from my senior prom. Remember I went without a date and it was the worst evening of my life?"

Brendan did not remember. He had spent his life thinking solely of himself.

"Bren," said Stephen, "I talked to the researcher. Not the

same one you talked to. Calvin Vinesett has at least three researchers. The one who lied to Janie, the one you met, and the one out here. I agreed to meet the guy because he had a list of three possible Hannahs in Boulder."

What was a possible Hannah? wondered Brendan.

"Kathleen stole the list," said Stephen.

"She stole it? I like that in a person," said Brendan. "Is she coming to the wedding too?"

"Don't change the subject. The researcher insisted that the three names were just bait to get me to talk. 'Bait' is a strange word, Bren. I keep asking myself, what fish does Calvin Vinesett expect to catch?"

"A bestseller," said Brendan.

"Yeah, but I'm wondering if somebody else is behind the whole project. One of us."

"I'm wondering the same thing. Can't be Janie. All she wants is to marry Reeve and live happily ever after. Can't be Jodie. All she wants is to save the world. Can't be you. All you want is to drill down inside the earth."

"And it can't be the Johnsons. Mr. Johnson can't even steer a pencil and Mrs. Johnson would be the worst hurt in a story about the criminal her daughter became. But Brendan, could it be Brian? Brian's a wonderful writer. He can't even choose a major at college, he's so eager to study everything and write about everything and learn everything. He's your twin. You know him. You think Brian could have something to do with this?"

Now Brendan wanted to chain Stephen to the truck as well. The methods behind this book were slimy and underhanded.

"Brian is a good person," said Brendan stiffly. "Listen, I have to go."

"Okay, but one last thought," said Stephen. "Could it be Mom or Dad behind this? They want Hannah to get hers."

Brendan remembered something Stephen had probably never known, because Stephen had not been back East in a few years. Brendan wouldn't have known either, except her schedule had forced him to hang around waiting to be picked up after practice. Their mother had taken a creative writing class last year.

Brendan couldn't say it out loud. "See you Friday at the airport," he said to his brother. Then he checked Calvin Vinesett's website.

Contact the author! read a little smile button. Brendan clicked. It gave an email address and a publisher's street address. Brendan was not a great communicator. It made him tired to think of composing a message for email or paper. He clicked on *Books* and read some jacket copy. Under the author photo on one of the book jackets was a single line informing him that Calvin Vinesett lived in New York City and Deer Isle, Maine.

Brendan loved to time himself using the Web. Sixteen seconds to find Calvin Vinesett listed in the Manhattan white pages.

In the morning, all the girls were going wedding gown shopping.

Brendan had not known there was such a thing, but now that he did, he planned to be far away and safe. He told his mother he was going into the city for the day to meet friends.

But Brendan was not meeting anybody he expected to like.

He had phoned his own researcher, thinking maybe he could learn something about Michael/Mick, but the guy hadn't even known there were other researchers. "I bought you three expensive dinners!" he yelled at Brendan. "And Calvin Vinesett won't even pay me. He won't even answer my emails!"

Nothing about this book made sense. Not the frightening chapter about Frank and Miranda. Not the stalking of Janie. Not the title. And certainly not refusing to answer emails from your own researcher.

Brendan yelled, "Jodie! You know how to reach Janie's roommate?"

"Eve?"

This research stuff was a snap. He hadn't known the girl's name and Jodie gave it to him right off. "Yup. Eve. You got her phone number?"

"What do you want to call Eve for?" Jodie yelled back.

"Ideas for wedding gifts," yelled Brendan, who had not previously considered the possibility of getting his sister a present.

"My cell phone's on the kitchen table!" yelled Jodie. "She's on my contact list."

"What's her last name?"

"Janie says she doesn't use it. She's just Eve."

Okay, just Eve, thought Brendan. Let's talk.

He used his own cell. "Is this Eve? This is Janie's brother Brendan."

"Oh, hi, Brendan! I can't wait to meet you and everybody else and see Reeve. I've never even met Reeve! It's such a kick!

Janie says at the bridal mall she's just going to pick up dresses for all the bridesmaids at one time, right off the rack, and the day of the wedding we just hope for the best! I know it will be the best. We're all so excited!"

"Yeah, me too. Listen. I wanna corner that creep. The Michael guy."

"Good idea. Just remember you can't get in any trouble yourself because the wedding is too soon and you can't be in jail or anything."

"You mean I can't chain him to the bumper of my truck and drag him through the city?"

"What he deserves," agreed Eve. "No. You can only scold him from a distance."

"Where's he live?"

"East Village. Hang on. I'll get the address. I always thought he was shifty. Want me to come along? I have a few things to say to him too."

"No, but if you have a photo, send it to my cell so I can identify him."

"Done," said Eve.

New York City was an easy trip from New Jersey. Before it was light the next morning, Brendan took the earliest available commuter bus. Manhattan never failed to excite him. There just was no place on earth like it. Even at dawn, it was hopping. His heart leapt and he was grinning.

It was seven-thirty when he found Michael Hastings's building on a slightly iffy block. Rents were high, according to the ads in real estate agents' windows, but not killer high.

Eve didn't think Michael was a college student. She thought he had a job somewhere and had lied about that, too. Jobs usually involved leaving your apartment in the morning. Brendan hoped that a man who lived in Manhattan also worked in Manhattan, and did not need to leave home before seven-thirty. A guess based on nothing, since Michael could work nights, or not at all, or be back home in Iowa or wherever he came from. Eve had forwarded the photograph Janie had sent to Sarah-Charlotte, and which Sarah-Charlotte sent on to Eve. It turned out that Sarah-Charlotte and Eve had had several Janie conferences over the last two years, which Brendan thought was a little iffy, girlfriend-wise, but then who understood girls?

Michael/Mick looked like the kind of guy they cast in movies as the thin thoughtful type. No muscle, no brawn, no guts. But sensitive.

Brendan despised that in a person.

One hour and eighteen minutes later, Michael/Mick walked out of his building.

Brendan fell into step. Brendan was gratifyingly taller and stronger. The guy moved away from him. Brendan side-stepped right along. The guy glared. Brendan glared back. "So I'm Janie Johnson's brother," he said. "You and I need to have a talk."

Michael brushed his pretty dark hair off his pretty forehead. "I'm busy. I have to go to work."

Brendan shouldered him against a building. "You're going to be late."

"You can't stop me from going to work!"

"I'd love to stop you. Or we could get a cup of coffee and you can talk." The roughness in Brendan's voice was no act. His smile began to shiver and he could feel himself losing control. He reminded himself of Eve's warning.

"Fine," said Michael nervously. "Whatever." New York was packed with diners and coffee shops. Michael darted into one. He perched on the outer edge of a booth and Brendan sat opposite him.

Brendan ordered bacon, three eggs over easy, rye toast, and potatoes.

Michael ordered coffee. He added sweetener. His hand shook.

"You stalked my sister," said Brendan. He had not expected to feel such anger that somebody had hurt his sister. Especially this sister. "Start with your reasons. How did you hook up with Calvin Vinesett? Did Calvin Vinesett tell you to stalk my sister?"

"Look," said Michael. "Calvin Vinesett just told me that Jane never gave interviews and I had to think of some other way to get information."

Never, not once, had Brendan heard anybody call his sister Jane. It was creepy, as if they were talking about somebody else. "He told you this by phone?" asked Brendan.

New York diners had the fastest service in the world. The waitress put his plate in front of him. Brendan dug in.

"We've never talked," said Michael. "Just emailed. He's reclusive."

"The guy lives right here. How come you didn't just get together?"

"He's got a lot of health problems and doesn't get out much and that's why he hires researchers. He doesn't want that known because his readers expect him to be on site."

Brendan had leafed through, but not read, one of Calvin Vinesett's bestsellers. The guy used the first person a lot ("I met her a total of seventeen times at the jail"). That was all lies too? "I need to know about every email Calvin Vinesett sent you and every email you sent him."

"That's private."

Brendan saved the part about the truck and the chains for later. He leaned across the table, pointing with the tines of his fork. "My family plans to charge you with criminal actions. Stalking, to be precise. If you can prove you were an employee doing a paid job, that might help you." This was nonsense and he hoped Michael was too nervous to notice.

"Nothing I did was criminal!" protested Michael. "It was just fun. We had a good time. Jane can't pretend she didn't have a good time. I'm the one who's hurt. She was two-timing me! She decided to marry somebody else one weekend after we broke up!"

"How do you know that?"

"Facebook, how do you think?"

"Who on Facebook?" demanded Brendan.

Michael grinned in a snarky way. "Eve posts everything and I still have access to her."

Brendan texted Eve to unfriend Michael Hastings. "What did Calvin Vinesett think of the information you sent?"

"I didn't have much to give. Jane wouldn't talk about her

past. But he was very interested that the money Jane inherited from her grandmother was paying for college. He wanted to know the details."

"You and I are going back to your apartment," said Brendan. "You're going to print it all out for me." He took money out of his wallet. He ate three huge mouthfuls and then wrapped the last piece of toast around the last strips of bacon to take along.

"I don't have time for that," said Michael.

"Michael, you're obviously very proud of your nice little suit and your smooth skin and your cute hair. You won't be when I'm done."

"I'll call the police!"

"Go for it. How do you think they'll react to your stalking?"

"You can't prove anything."

"I'm also going to call your employer and explain why you're late. Because you've been arrested for stalking."

"You can't do that! Anyway, you don't know where I work."

Brendan was on a roll. "You think you're the only person who can follow somebody, Michael?"

"All right, all right. There isn't anything worth looking at. I didn't find out anything. He only paid me once. He said nothing else was worth payment. I spent six weeks on your sister for nothing!"

"I'm just flying down for the day, Reeve," his father had said. "The flight from here to Charlotte is only an hour and a half. I'll rent a car at the airport and drive to your office. You and

I will have lunch, that's all. I won't interfere with your work-day. No tours of Charlotte. Just lunch."

"But Dad—"

"My flight lands at ten-thirty-one. I'll get a taxi and I'm guessing I'll be at ESPNU around eleven-thirty."

Reeve was crazy about his father. He wanted to be just like his father, except different. But he knew why his father was coming down with such urgency. Dad wanted Reeve to be strong and loyal and steady and kind and generous, just like Dad himself—and a bachelor.

Dad was coming to talk Reeve out of it. He might even be coming with a bribe.

Reeve dreaded this.

On the phone, it was easy to be flippant with Lizzie or sweet but stern with his mother. In person, facing his father, he was going to have trouble.

He did not want a confrontation, especially over Janie, whose company he wanted so much. The wedding was for her. Living together was for him. He pictured driving home after work, running up the stairs to his second-floor apart-ment. Opening the door. And Janie would be standing there, smiling at him.

What could be more wonderful than somebody glad to see you?

He told everybody in the office that his dad was coming for lunch, and everybody wanted to meet him and had restau-rant suggestions. His dad was a handsome, fit former athlete, and when he arrived, it went perfectly, because he was a peo-ple person and knew his sports and said all the right things.

Reeve was proud of his father, and of his colleagues, and then they got in Reeve's car and Reeve looked straight ahead, careful to have no eye contact.

He drove to the restaurant he'd chosen and parked in the shade, so the car wouldn't be so stifling when they came out. He didn't think he could eat, which would be a new experience. His dad touched his shoulder. "Let's just sit here and talk before we go in, son."

Reeve nodded. He didn't want to let his father down. But Janie came first.

"I'm here on assignment," said his father quietly.

Reeve stared through the windshield at fat green mounds of tropical grasses.

"I didn't accept the assignment," said his dad.

Reeve risked a glance. His father looked very emotional. Reeve couldn't tell what the emotion was.

Dad handed him a check. "This is what we spent on Lizzie's wedding, and it's what we gave Todd when he got married, and it's what we will give Megan when she gets married."

Reeve stared at the check. *"You spent that much money on Lizzie's wedding?"*

"Yup. Tough old attorney Liz wanted the splashiest, most expensive wedding on earth."

"I guess so! Dad, I know Mom wants you to bribe me out of marrying Janie, and this is more money than I could ever save up. But——"

"It's not a bribe to stop you, Reeve. It's a boost to start you. I've always been impressed by Janie, but now I'm really impressed. She's not getting married to have a wedding gown and a reception. She's getting married to have you. My son. No, this is a precelebration check. For you to spend as you choose."

Reeve mentally divided it up. I can buy Janie a ring! She can pick out furniture. I can pay off my car! And even take a honeymoon. Well, if we ever find a weekend I'm not working. "Dad," he said.

"Yeah, don't get mushy on me. I hope this is the kind of place that serves bacon burgers and onion rings. Your mother doesn't let me have grease or salt. I'm counting on you to give me a one-meal vacation from the rules."

Janie had taken the train up to Connecticut and spent the night, sleeping on the foldout sofa at the Harbor. Miranda did not want to come wedding gown shopping. Her excuse was, she couldn't leave Frank for so much time. "Mom, the whole point of assisted living is that they assist. The Harbor is packed with aides who will make sure Frank is fine."

"I don't feel up to it, honey."

"Oh, Mom, I know it's hard to share being mother of the bride, but you are the mother of the bride, and the bride wants you to have some of the fun! This will be fun. You need fun! How much fun are you having here at the Harbor?"

Miranda ended up laughing.

But the next day, Janie had to deal with Reeve's mother. Mrs. Shields picked up Janie and Miranda early in the morning and the three of them set out for New Jersey. Mrs. Shields had had two weddings in her family—Lizzie's earthshaking production and Todd's wedding out West, in which Mrs.

Shields's only participation had been to show up. Happily, her fourth child, Megan, was also making wedding noises. And none too soon, Mrs. Shields felt, since Megan was well into her thirties. Megan, of course, had allotted a year for planning.

Mrs. Shields listed ways in which Janie and Reeve might rethink their own plans.

"What about your college degree?" cried Mrs. Shields. "What about money?"

"I think we can be proud of how mature and sensible our children are," said Miranda. "Reeve and Janie will make a fine couple and if they struggle financially, didn't we all, when we were young? As for college, Janie has promised that she will transfer to a college in Charlotte. There seem to be several in the area."

"But if Janie doesn't work," cried Mrs. Shields, "how will they live? Reeve hardly earns a thing!"

"That's their problem, though," said Miranda. "Our problem is to decide what we wear to the wedding."

"And Charlotte!" said Mrs. Shields in tones of disgust. "Who even knew there *was* a town called Charlotte? When Reeve settles down, I'm sure it will be near home."

Janie began to see why Reeve liked Charlotte as much as he did. It was definitely a test of her own maturity to drive with her future mother-in-law.

They crossed the George Washington Bridge. Janie texted her sister. **Long drive.**

Traffic? Jodie wrote back.

No, texted Janie. **The company.**

Kathleen had called her a "kidnapette," which sounded like a variety of cheerleader.

The kidnapette grows up, thought Janie, and she giggled to herself.

Jodie could not comprehend the choices Janie made.

Janie actually wanted two mothers, one future mother-in-law, and a sister to go with her to the bridal mall to choose her wedding gown.

When it was time for Jodie to choose a gown, she'd go alone. Nobody was horning in on her decisions.

The Shields and Johnson families had lived next door to each other for years, and whenever Jodie visited the Johnsons, Reeve came over. But Jodie had never met Mrs. Shields.

Three more exits, Janie texted. **I'm going crazy.**

Just wait till you're in some shiny little dressing room where four women want you to pick a different gown. See how sane you'll be at the end of that, thought Jodie.

Miranda Johnson had been a wonderful hostess whenever the Spring kids visited. It was the most awkward possible situation, and yet it hadn't been awkward. Mr. Johnson had been a doll. Whenever Jodie caught herself having a great time up there, she used to pout a little and stomp off.

Her brother Brian never exhibited the ambivalence that swept Jodie whenever she was at the Johnsons'. He just enjoyed himself. Brendan had only gone once or twice, having zero interest in missing sisters. Stephen went, but always remained careful and contained.

Inside a family of seven, thought Jodie, are seven completely different lives. You would expect more overlap.

"Are you ready?" yelled her mother, who had been pacing all morning.

"I'm ready!" Jodie yelled back.

They drove to the bridal mall.

Jodie had never been in such a place. An amazing number of wedding gowns were packed in, row after row, aisle after aisle. One side of the immense display room had bridesmaids' gowns in a remarkable variety of colors, styles, and necklines.

Jodie had just come from a place where there were no choices. If there were stores in Haiti packed full, Jodie had not found them. If there were closets jammed with stuff, Jodie had not seen them. She had been embarrassed by the excess in her two suitcases.

She walked slowly along the rainbow of bridesmaid dresses. Salmon pink, lime green, turquoise, neon yellow. Good colors for beach towels. But a wedding?

Janie sent her a final text. They were in the parking lot.

Three women came through big glass doors and onto the soft pale carpeting. The stout, heavily made-up woman wearing a flower-splashed sweater had to be Reeve's mother. But who was the small, bent, frail creature on Janie's arm? Was there some great-great-grandmother Jodie hadn't even heard of?

No.

That old person was elegant Miranda Johnson.

Life could do this to a person's body?

What, then, could life do to a soul?

● ● ●

The onion rings were perfect. The Shields men were into their second pile of napkins and feeling good. Since none of their women were around, they exchanged pleasing belches.

"Dad?" said Reeve. "Instead of showing you around before you catch your plane home, can you go shopping with me?"

"You know how to shop?"

"No, and I plan on Janie doing all shopping necessary for our entire lives. But one thing I have to buy on my own. Rings. Which I can afford now, thanks to you. But how do I know what to get? I drive past a jewelry store on the way to work. I would never go in without an escort. Help me pick out an engagement ring and a wedding ring."

"What do I know? Wait till you get to New Jersey, take Janie to a jewelry store there, and she'll pick them out."

"No, she's into romance. She'll want me to kneel down and surprise her and all."

"Okay, I'll come. Might as well spread the blame for the wrong choice in rings."

Kathleen could not believe it. "You don't want to bother with the third Hannah? You're giving up? That's like climbing a mountain and stopping below the peak."

"Okay, okay," said Stephen.

They got on their bikes.

The third possible was tougher to locate. They couldn't find the house number. They finally discovered a tiny alley where one house opened sideways, so its address was for a road it didn't face.

It was a funny little place, shadowed and ugly. A porch without a rail tilted ominously. You couldn't put a chair there; you'd slide off. But trash—you could put that on the porch just fine.

Stephen wove through the trash bags and then had to talk through the door because the woman wouldn't open it.

Kathleen didn't think anybody around here ought to open a door to strangers. Didn't mean the occupant was Hannah and worried about the police.

"We're looking for somebody," Stephen called. "She might be you. Can I show you a photograph?"

"No," said the woman.

The crack under the front door was large enough to admit major insects. Stephen slid his little wallet picture of Hannah under the door.

Well, that was stupid, thought Kathleen. If she is Hannah, Stephen just screwed up. She'll never answer the door, and furthermore, she'll leave town the split second we walk away.

But they heard the sound of locks being undone and a chain being loosened, and there stood a woman, grinning. She was not Caucasian.

If Stephen and Kathleen needed proof that all the research had been done via computer, here it was.

"Siddown," said the woman. "I'm bored. Sicka TV. Tell me what's up."

They sat on the sagging top step, their backs to the row of bulging plastic bags. Kathleen, who always wore her backpack, took out energy bars to share while Stephen gave the woman the short version of his little sister's kidnapping.

"Funny thing," said the woman. "I remember that milk carton story. It was—what? Five, six years ago? The girl recognized her own picture? They don't do that anymore—put pictures of missing kids on milk cartons. I'm not sure kids still drink milk. They're all about juice boxes these days."

They nibbled their energy bars.

"Now what you gonna do?" asked the woman.

Stephen shook his head. "I don't know. But thanks for your time." He stood up, ready to leave. Kathleen tucked the energy bar wrappers in her pack. Stephen, assuming she was at his heels, rode off.

Kathleen was confused and defeated. What was going on, anyway? No researcher would make up three possible Hannahs on the off chance that it would get a fourth person to talk. Especially when the fourth person—Stephen—didn't know anything. None of the Springs knew anything.

Kathleen sat there, too tired out by useless thinking to move.

"Tell me," said the woman to Kathleen. "After all these years, why do you care?"

"I guess we feel as if the kidnapper is still out there," said Kathleen finally. "As if she'd love to do even more."

"I got a clue for you, honey. A kidnapper wouldn't do nothing for love. She'd only do something for hate."

THE ELEVENTH PIECE OF THE KIDNAPPER'S PUZZLE

For the first time in years, the woman formerly known as Hannah had energy.

She lost weight from all the excitement. At the drugstore, she bought hair dye and a pair of glasses. The sparkling blue frames matched her eyes and now her hair had a beautiful sheen.

She even took a class, using her Jill Williams persona.

It was one of those free evening classes and she didn't expect much; this was just to get her started. But the teacher loved handouts. Each week there was a new list of links and blogs and websites. In class, she kept a low profile, although it was difficult, because a person named Jill Williams felt loud and assertive.

Excitement kept her going during the long hours of scrubbing dishes or toilets. The plan was complex, but brilliant. This year was not going to be so awful after all. This was the year she would whip these people.

There was a difficulty. Much could be done without

money, but in the end, Hannah needed plenty of it. Ideas for getting big money came to her, because she was very bright, and could always think of things. But every plan had to be adjusted to the threat of police. It was maddening. But she would solve it. Then she would fix that Jennie/Janie for good. And Frank, too. He'd be sorry he stopped giving her money.

At the coffee shop, she wore all her layers of clothing so they would not notice how slim and shapely she had become. She worked weekends, which were brutal. At top speed, she had to load and unload the dishwasher, scrub the pots, and hang the stupid mugs back up in the right direction.

By chance, she heard that a really nice hotel was short on help. The jobs she usually held, showing up was good enough. But at this hotel, she had to schedule an interview! She made a good impression with her beautiful hair and sparkly glasses. They hired her.

She learned how to fold a hand towel into a rose and tuck little bottles of shampoo into it. But it was no easier to work in a ritzy hotel than a slummy one. Monday through Friday she worked at the hotel. She had sixteen rooms to do and it took about thirty minutes to clean a room. And people checked! The housekeeper actually went into each room after Hannah was done and checked! Every single day, Hannah had to go back and redo something. She added that woman's name to her list of people she was going to get someday.

It was more than sixteen years after the day in New Jersey when Hannah Javensen knocked, waited, knocked again, and entered a hotel room.

The guy was a pig.

He'd used most of the towels. His junk was all over the bathroom counter. The bed covers were on the floor, along with the decorative pillows. He'd been eating crackers, and the empty box lay on the carpet, while cracker crumbs littered the sheets, the carpet, and a chair.

Guys were more likely to tip than women, but messy guys didn't tip. Only neat ones. She wouldn't even get a dollar here.

A box of disposable plastic gloves was fastened to her cart, supplied because the maids had to clean the toilet. But Hannah wore them for another reason. Fingerprints.

As always, before she started cleaning, she checked the room safe to see if they'd put anything in it and forgotten to close the little door, but they hadn't. She felt inside the open suitcases and under the clothing tossed into the top dresser drawer. Nothing. As she stripped the bed, she lifted the mattress. Nothing.

She fingered the pockets of hanging clothes. The guy might be a slob but he wore a nice suit.

Hundreds of times, Hannah had searched and found nothing. Today made it all worthwhile. The inside pockets of the man's suit had little sheaves of hundred-dollar bills.

Nobody used cash anymore. They used their debit cards and their credit cards.

When she took this, he couldn't report it, because only criminals carried this kind of cash.

It was meant.

She was destined to be here, on this day, in this room.

Hannah had never chatted with the rest of housekeeping,

because they were Hispanic. They couldn't talk to her and she couldn't talk to them. She bet they wouldn't recognize her out of uniform either, but it didn't matter. This hotel guest couldn't report the theft and when she never came back, nobody would look for Jill Williams. The hotel was used to unreliable help. In fact, the head housekeeper, who didn't trust her, would be happy that Jill Williams was gone. And since she wasn't Jill Williams, they couldn't find her if they did look.

Under her uniform, Hannah was wearing her street clothes. In the stairwell, she slid out of the uniform, folded it into a neat bundle, went out a side door, and walked away.

She loved walking away from things.

It was such a good feeling to evaporate. And this time, the woman who evaporated had money. And they could never catch her, because she was smart and they were stupid.

At home, she concentrated on the plan.

The Internet was wonderful. Every day she had another brilliant idea. She felt like the leader of that group, so many years ago. She was in charge, and people looked up to her and aligned their hopes with hers.

The project was so absorbing that she did not keep up with Facebook the way she used to. Adair's little posts were juvenile and silly. All those high school children, now college children, could waste their lives with pointless chitter-chatter, but Hannah had work to do.

She frequently skipped sleep. She worked around the clock.

It was May when she checked back in to Facebook to see what the Jennie/Janie and all her fake friends were doing.

Whatever it was, they'd be bragging. That's what Facebook was for them: brag space.

But they weren't bragging.

They were watching a video.

Hannah was as stunned as Adair and all 476 of her friends.

The Jennie/Janie and the boy next door, cute Reeve from ESPN, were kissing, laughing, hugging, and saying *yes* in an airport.

Where Hannah could never even *go* because of security checks. Which was all that Jennie/Janie's fault to begin with!

The crowd was sighing and whistling and smiling. Even the security guard smiled.

What was the matter with the universe?

Janie did not deserve all that love. She was already getting Hannah's share!

And then Hannah remembered her project.

Her laughter began low and quiet then rose in pitch and flickered all over the room, like blood splatter.

CHAPTER ELEVEN

The saleslady was short and slim, her hair a distinguished gray. "Have we all arrived?" she cried. She beamed at Janie. "I hear you're marrying the boy next door."

"I am," agreed Janie happily. "And here is the mother of the boy next door."

Everybody laughed and air-kissed Mrs. Shields.

"And this is also my mother," said Janie, moving Miranda forward a step.

"How delightful!" said the saleslady, bustling over. She offered one arm to Miranda and the other to Mrs. Shields, as if the three ladies were proceeding down an aisle. Which they were. An aisle packed with gowns, tiaras, veils, and slippers. "Blended families are such an example to us all," said the saleslady.

Janie took her real mother's hand. "Hi, Mom," she whispered, tasting the wonderfulness of knowing that Donna Spring was her mom.

They entered a mirror-wrapped pavilion, with a little

platform on which the bride could twirl. The three mothers and Jodie found places to sit.

"I don't know where to start," said Janie, suddenly nervous.

"Let's not even look in the direction of all those gowns. You close your eyes, dear, and describe for me the dress of your dreams."

Janie closed her eyes. She concentrated. She said, "White."

"Excellent start," cried the saleslady. "That lets out cream, champagne, and ecru! We've narrowed it down! Now! Shall we start with a traditional full long skirt that puffs out grandly?"

Janie thought again. "Um. I don't know."

"We'll try on all varieties! I'll bring the gowns. Each will be quite different. As you give me your opinion, we'll narrow our choices! It'll be such fun!"

She started with six gowns. They were all beautiful and perfect. Janie could hardly wait to try them on.

The first was so poufy she felt like a clothespin doll inside it. The second was so low cut Janie would have been embarrassed on the beach, never mind in church. The third, breathtaking when the saleslady held it up, was so heavily sequined that Janie was all glitter and no Janie. The fourth was short, tight, and sexy, as if weddings were nightclub acts.

As the saleslady unbuttoned her, Janie said, "Mom? What was your gown like?"

Both mothers began to answer.

Both stumbled to a stop.

Her Connecticut mother said, "She's your mom, Janie. I'm just Miranda now." And burst into tears.

Janie flung her arms around Miranda. How thin she was. Even her bones seemed thinner. She's literally breakable, thought Janie. Everything I say and do can break her.

The saleslady stepped in, thinking she understood. "We have many brides with divorced parents. How lovely that you are so close to your stepmother."

My parents didn't divorce, thought Janie. All my parents stayed together. That's what I want most in life. For my marriage to be as good as theirs.

At yesterday's conference, with Reeve on Skype and Janie sitting in his office, Father John had discussed the Ten Commandments. He spent some time on "Honor thy father and mother." It was a commandment that had ruled her life. But she had never known how to make it work. When she honored one set, she dishonored the other.

But what Father had read out loud was slightly different. It turned out that the commandments were not simply a list. They included details. *Honor thy father and mother, that it may go well with you.*

It will go well with me, Janie thought. It will go well with Donna and Jonathan Spring. But how can it go well with Miranda? I may be entering Happily Ever After, but Miranda will never see Happily Ever After again.

And I am abandoning her.

Kathleen caught up to Stephen and they walked their bikes.

They were approaching the Pearl Street Mall. It was a popular place, although Stephen never knew why. A lot of boutiquey stores with stuff nobody wanted or could afford. But he felt the need to rest. There was something about this book project that made him feel dense.

Kathleen walked by his side. Did he love or detest the fact that Kathleen liked to literally keep step with him? His cell rang. "Hey, Mom," he said.

"Darling!" She sounded breathless. "I'm sending bridal mall photos."

"Hey, great." Stephen would never even look at anything so boring.

"Now, I'm just checking that you have your plane tickets, Stephen. I don't want to pry into your financial situation, honey. Can you afford the tickets or shall your father and I get them for you?"

"I'm fine." Kathleen could not hear his mother's voice, but Stephen felt her hovering, wanting all information. Reeve planned to have somebody lean over his shoulder for the rest of his life. What if Reeve lived to be ninety? Had Reeve considered this? Seven decades of the same woman leaning over his shoulder?

"Are you bringing Kathleen?" asked his mother. "I don't want her to feel left out, but of course it's your decision, since we don't even have a guest list. Which is ridiculous. A normal wedding, the hostess at least knows who was asked. Anyway, we'd love to have Kathleen."

"I'm still thinking," said Stephen.

"Honey bunch," said his mother, as if he were a very little boy, "you have to get on the plane in about a minute. Time to decide."

"I'll get on it," said Stephen. He thought of Calvin Vinesett instead. What kind of twisted person spent his life dipping into crime, tasting every drop of blood and capturing every broken hope?

Every time Stephen remembered their own true crime, he felt as if he'd just run a marathon.

And he had. Janie had given the Spring family a run that lasted a decade and a half.

And now she was going to be herself. Get married as a daughter of Donna and Jonathan Spring. But what she really was, was what Kathleen liked to call her. The kidnapette.

The streets of Boulder converged on Stephen, whispering, *Hannah's here.*

Jodie's heart turned over, watching her sister comfort a wasted, pale, exhausted old woman.

Right now, if I had to pick the person I admire most, it's my sister, thought Jodie. Janie passed through the valley of the shadow of death. She suffered, everybody around her suffered, she caused suffering. She decided that the most important thing was love, and she loved the other parents. And now she's decided she has enough love to go around after all, and she's loving all of us, both her families, the ones who sinned against her and the ones who didn't.

No wonder Reeve wants to marry her. He wants to snag her now, before a hundred other guys line up.

"You start, Mom," said Jodie, so that Miranda would have another minute to pull herself together. "Tell us about *your* wedding gown." Her parents' wedding portrait hung in the master bedroom. Dad looked like somebody else—big and tall and very young with almost gaudy red hair. Painfully awkward in his rented tuxedo. And Mom was definitely somebody else—petite and girlish, with the kind of hairstyle women had had thirty years ago, which luckily nobody had anymore.

And the dress! Wrong, wrong, wrong. Wrong length, wrong style, wrong neckline.

"I loved my bridal gown," said Donna, blushing and biting her lip like a young girl. "I was so proud of it. We had so little money, but I was just desperate to have a pretty dress. I saved and saved to buy it. It's been in a special box all these years."

The box was the size of a crib mattress. Through its clear plastic window you could see a square of white satin and a spattering of tiny spangles.

Jodie made a diplomatic move. "Mrs. Shields, I'm dying to hear about your gown."

And Mrs. Shields was dying to tell. She started with Alençon lace and elbow-length white gloves, moved on to the veil and the train, and spoke fondly of the little crown of lilies of the valley. "The gown," she added proudly, "was specially designed to show off my tiny waist."

Jodie tried to imagine Mrs. Shields with a tiny waist.

The saleslady brought six more gowns for Janie, and again Jodie took pictures and sent them to Brian and Stephen. She briefly considered being fair and sending them to Brendan, too, but it was difficult to imagine Brendan caring.

That's Brendan's problem, she thought. He doesn't care about anything right now.

$$\bullet \ \bullet \ \bullet$$

At Pearl Street Mall, Kathleen and Stephen were sitting together on a bench, but he was not communicating with her. He was staring at his cell phone.

Okay, fine, she'd stare at hers. She had downloaded Calvin Vinesett's biggest seller and was trying to get interested. But for Kathleen, reading was a big deal. She didn't choose a book easily. She needed lots of recommendations before she embarked on a project like a book. She disliked fiction. If forced to read, she chose outdoor stuff—books about people who trained sled dogs for the Iditarod or hiked across Africa and waded past crocodiles.

Stephen offered her his phone. "I've been holding out on you. Jodie sent me a slew of photographs from the bridal mall."

In her previous life, Kathleen would have looked at each photo and screamed, "Oh! My! God!" But the Springs did not swear. Therefore, she was on a swear diet. She had read a million times that you could not make your boyfriend into something else, so fine—Kathleen would make *herself* into something else. "Janie is beautiful," Kathleen pronounced. "This gown is perfect. This is the most romantic thing I have ever seen."

"Janie is beautiful," he agreed. "I mean, Jennie."

It struck Kathleen forcibly that even Janie's birth family did not know who this girl was. Even her brother couldn't remember her real name. It was not a joke that the groom planned to have the best man hold up a sign so he could read off the name of his bride. "Jodie, Janie, Jennie," she said. "I hope you're giving the guests scorecards."

"Luckily, I have no function in this wedding except to show up."

And me? asked Kathleen silently. Do I have a function? Do I get to show up? Out loud she said, "Every dress is gorgeous!" Her throat filled. What if I never get married? thought Kathleen. What if nobody really truly ever loves me that much?

She had never suffered. It was one of the gulfs between her and Stephen: the Spring children had suffered.

She had never lacked love or safety. Never been hungry, never been scared, never fended for herself.

There was only one thing Kathleen had not gotten in life: Stephen's affection. He half loved her. Half wanted her.

In her heart and mind, she replayed the amazing video of Reeve and Janie, who fully loved and fully wanted each other.

"I think I'm going to Mass," said Stephen casually.

Kathleen could not have been more amazed if he had said he was going to Russia. She herself was a lapsed Catholic, and Stephen, who had rarely missed church during his childhood, had been on break since the first week of freshman year at college. "May I come?" she asked.

Clearly he was trying to think of a way to refuse permission for her to go to church. There wasn't one. "Okay," he said gloomily.

"We could light a candle for Janie."

"We could," said Stephen. "But Janie will be okay. It's Miranda who is doomed."

The gown Janie chose was shimmery, with small cap sleeves and a double row of ribbon roses along the neckline. A hundred tiny silk-covered buttons ran down her back. The dress fit tightly and then flared below her waist into a tulip of satin. The skirt was very long in back, making its own train.

She looked so fragile and romantic that Jodie wanted to cry. She remembered the ghastly day more than five years ago when Janie had been forced to live with them and the FBI came to the house to interrogate her. Janie had been like a cornered animal. Dad had ordered the FBI to leave. "But the girl may have crucial information!" they protested.

"She was three," said their father roughly. "She doesn't have information."

"She was living with the parents of her kidnapper!"

Janie had been trying to turn into upholstery.

Their father escorted the FBI to the door. It had felt right when he did, and it had felt right all these years, because the most important thing was to prove to Janie that she was back inside her loving family.

But it had been the wrong thing to do. If the FBI had gotten any clues from Janie, if they had kept at Frank, they could have caught Hannah back then and closed the book on it all.

Jodie thought of the book to come.

Impossible to consider a silly interview when she was in Haiti, surrounded by desperate children, starving mothers, ruined tent cities, cholera and filth. And yet the church and its work had been filled with good cheer. Sometimes she even wanted to be one of the nuns, her life's purpose so clear: help the poor; worship God.

Other times she couldn't even look at the nuns, and would tally up all they had missed in life—love and men and children and careers and competition and travel.

She hoped she was marked by her months in Haiti as deeply as Janie was marked by the kidnapping. Jodie wanted knowledge of that little country's suffering to stay in her soul and guide her.

The saleslady cried, "Perfect perfect perfect for you, Jennie! A little loose in the shoulders. We'll alter it immediately, and you can pick it up day after tomorrow. And how many bridesmaids do we have, dear?"

Jodie was sick of this saleslady.

Reeve's mother was still discussing her wedding. "I had seven bridesmaids. Two flower girls. A maid of honor and a matron of honor. Of course, I spent a long time planning."

Jodie was sick of Mrs. Shields, too. But then it occurred to her that the poor woman would never be very important to Janie. Janie had two mothers in line ahead of a mere mother-in-law. And Reeve didn't strike Jodie as the type to put mommy first.

Janie said, "The maid of honor is my sister, Jodie." She waved Jodie forward. "Whatever Jodie picks, we'll get for the bridesmaids, too. So it has to be a style we can take away. We'll have to phone everybody for dress sizes. Sarah-Charlotte. Eve. Reeve's sister Megan can't come. Lizzie will be here, but I don't know whether Lindsay can come or not."

Jodie had never heard of a girl named Lindsay.

"Reeve's brother Todd's wife," explained Janie.

"Of course Todd and Lindsay are coming," said Mrs. Shields. "After all, Todd is the best man. He's so pleased that Reeve asked him, since Reeve has about two hundred best friends he could have chosen from. Todd is very emotional about being best man. I don't know Lindsay's dress size. She's gained weight. She's self-conscious. We'll have to be delicate when we ask. As for Lizzie," she went on, "she's an eight. But she would never wear the kind of thing hanging on these racks. She has a very individual style."

Whoo, boy, thought Jodie. Reeve, honey, stay in Charlotte. "Lizzie always looks smashing," agreed Jodie, who had met the woman exactly once. "But in weddings, only the bride is an individual. The rest of us have to look alike. Janie, there are some just-above-the-knee sky blue dresses over there. See them? Simple, sophisticated lines. They'd look good on any figure."

"Okay," said Janie.

"And the gentlemen?" asked the saleslady. "Sky blue cummerbunds and so forth?"

"Gentlemen!" said Jodie, snorting. "They're my brothers. They're not gentlemen."

"Ah, but they will be gentlemen during the wedding," said the saleslady. "That's what the clothing is for."

Brendan followed Michael Hastings to his apartment. It was a fifth-floor walk-up and very tiny. That was the New York conundrum: pay a fortune and get practically nothing in return but the privilege of living in the city.

Brendan would do it in a heartbeat.

In the miniature living room was a futon bed that was supposed to double as a sofa, but Michael had not folded it up. The little dining table was also his desk. From the look of the kitchen—not a room, but a niche in the wall—Michael did not dine in.

That was another of New York's virtues.

Restaurants.

Brendan was suddenly at peace with his failure in sports. There were other things in life. There was New York.

Michael was using a laptop computer in desktop fashion. He went to his emails and began printing. Brendan read each brief message as it printed out.

Calvin Vinesett's messages were the introductory one; the one congratulating Michael on meeting Janie; the one promising to send five hundred dollars; and the one fascinated by the trust fund story. Calvin Vinesett sounded like a creep. He and Michael had been a good match.

As for Michael's messages, Michael had been a failure as a researcher or Janie had been brilliant as a protector. The only faintly interesting information he had passed on was the name of the grandmother who set up Janie's college funds. Other than that, the best Michael could do was the layout of Frank's rest home.

Like a reader of a true crime book cared about slow elevators.

"Calvin Vinesett wrote you a check for five hundred dollars for this?" said Brendan. It looked like fifty cents' worth of information to him.

"He paid cash."

"So you got together with him?"

"No, I told you. We've never met. He sent cash in the mail. It was weird. But writers are eccentric."

"Did he tell you to interview Mr. and Mrs. Johnson?"

"No. My job was Jane."

Brendan walked down the stairs after Michael Hastings. He was thinking of that shivery chapter where somebody had followed Miranda Johnson around. Those pages had included Miranda's thoughts. To know a person's thoughts, you'd have to interview that person, and she'd have to tell you. Otherwise, you'd have to make it up.

Were Calvin Vinesett's books made up?

Brendan thought about his mother's creative writing class. Would Mom ask Calvin Vinesett to write a book? Or help her write one? If it was Mom, she was filled to the brim with wrath, and Brendan had never noticed.

But how much *have* I noticed in my family? he asked himself. I always figured it was their job to notice *me*. I wasn't supposed to notice *them*.

He so didn't want his mother to be the employer of a man who said, "My job was Jane."

First, rule out Brian, he told himself.

Back on the sidewalk, Michael Hastings flagged a cab. Thoughtfully, Brendan watched him disappear. Then he called his twin. They were not the kind of twins who were on the same wavelength. In fact, Brian sounded astonished to hear from him. "Hey, Bren! What's up? I'm getting wedding gown photographs from Jodie on my cell phone, in case I want to vote. You into that puffy one?"

"She isn't sending me photos," said Brendan, and realized that he was hurt.

His twin said, "Wait a sec. I'll forward them."

"No, this isn't about dresses. Bri, you talking to this researcher?"

"No. Are you?"

Brendan skipped over that. "What's that writer want, do you think?"

"A bestseller, I guess. Money. Fame. TV interviews."

"It's you, isn't it?" said Brendan.

"Me what?"

"I'm your twin, Bri. You can't fool me. You're behind this. You've always wanted to be a writer. You're exactly like Reeve at that radio station in Boston. You've got a story you can tell forever. And you've hired guys to get material for you."

"Brendan, if I wanted to write our story, I've got all the material I could possibly need. The exact same material you've got. But why would I want to? Nobody in our family needs more of this nightmare. We need less of it. Anyway, Calvin Vinesett is writing it."

"You're supposedly going to summer classes, Brian. But I bet instead you're writing your novel."

"Calvin Vinesett doesn't write novels, Brendan. He does true crime. It's fact."

"It's fiction. It's stuff. It's people's thoughts. Nobody can know what anybody else is actually thinking. So it's made up, and you made it up, Brian."

His twin sighed. "Bren, let's not fight."

"Let's not sell out, either," snapped Brendan, fully aware that he had sold out more than anybody during his three interviews.

"I'm not the writer," said Brian. "I'm the fellow sufferer. But I'm in favor of a book. Might turn up Hannah. I just wish the timing weren't so tricky. I want Janie and Reeve to have a safe wedding."

People never wish a bride and groom a safe wedding, Brendan thought. Except in my family. "Safe" is our big word. He said, "We're groomsmen."

"Yup. Gotta wear tuxedos. I'm kind of excited. I didn't ever go to a prom. So I've never worn one."

"What's our job? Seating the guests?"

"Yes. Plus lining up at the altar behind Reeve. We catch him if he faints."

"I'd sure faint if I found myself at the altar," said Brendan. Then he added, hoping his twin would talk about it, "Mom seems really happy."

"She is. Which is a relief," said Brian Spring. "You know, Bren, I kept having this weird feeling that Mom was somehow behind the book."

Brendan remembered that they were twins. That they did sometimes think alike.

"I read some of Calvin Vinesett's stuff," said his twin. "He does gruesome mass murders and analyzes the victims and how they happened to be there and how they contributed to their own death, and he analyzes the killer and how the killer turned out to be what he is, and then he starts in on the police and where they failed and how they succeeded, and the personalities of the attorneys. Our story is so gentle in comparison. Nobody shed blood. And shedding tears isn't exciting. Calvin Vinesett is mainly fascinated by the bad guy, but our bad guy is offstage. This book will be a real departure for him."

"You think the book will hurt Janie?"

"Nah," said Brian. "Janie's too busy with the wedding. I think if Hannah got caught this afternoon, Janie would say 'Oh, good' and keep juggling her two sets of parents, which in a few days will be *three* sets, and going to the mall to choose china."

Brendan thought, Let Janie have her wedding. Let Mom be the mother of the bride. Let all of us be together and let Reeve keep Janie safe.

He realized that he was praying.

Stephen and Kathleen walked to St. Thomas Aquinas. He did not explain why he suddenly wanted God.

Kathleen's parents had a list of reasons for her not to stay with Stephen, and his failure to communicate was high on the list. "You need somebody you can discuss everything with," her father said.

"I love Stephen, though."

"I'm not sure he loves you," her mother said.

Kathleen wasn't sure either. On the other hand, he didn't date anybody else and he always seemed glad to see her.

They entered the church. At home, weekday Mass was very early. It was thoughtful of St. Thomas to have theirs at five p.m. Kathleen imagined being a bride here. Being a bride anywhere.

She and Stephen slid into a pew. He put down the kneeler, got to his knees, closed his eyes, and bowed his head.

Wow. He's serious. Are my parents right? Is there too much space between what I believe and want and what Stephen believes and wants?

The Mass began and she could feel the intensity of Stephen's participation.

The reading was the familiar parable of the Good Samaritan. A man walking down the road was attacked by thieves who left him for dead by the side of the road. Two respectable well-to-do people walked on past, not wanting to get involved. The third person, a person nobody respected, stopped, and when he realized the victim was still alive, he got the man to an inn and paid for his care. So no matter how respectable you were, you weren't the good guy unless you stopped to help.

Jesus did not address the problem of the robbers, who would shortly run out of money and want another victim. The next person who got attacked might be too old or too young to survive. The next one might die. Your truly good guy, in Kathleen's opinion, would also have done something about the robbers.

"The Mass is over," said the priest. "Go in peace."

Kathleen was full of questions for Stephen, but she saw that he was going in peace. He had come here for something and he had found it.

Kathleen had silenced her cell phone when she entered, and now, with relief, turned it back on, as did everybody else coming out of the church.

Your truly good guy, she thought, would stop our criminal. Hannah. "Stephen, why don't I call my father? I don't think the three possible Hannahs mean anything, but they might, and my father——"

"*What?*" Stephen swung around hard and glared. "Your

father? Meaning the FBI? Is that what you mean? You're so greedy for details you'd go that far? Throw the FBI back into this when Janie's wedding is almost here?"

When the surprise call from his twin ended, Brian Spring called Jodie. "So we're closing in on gown number seven?"

"Yes."

"And the reception is definitely in our backyard? That's no fun," said Brian. "When I get married, we are so not serving hot dogs in the backyard. We are reserving the country club, we are getting a great band, we will have a theme, there will be ice sculptures, we will dance till dawn, and people will get fabulous favors they cherish forever."

"You have a candidate?" asked Jodie.

"No. Do you?"

"No, but Reeve is inviting every single boy he ever went to school with, was on a team with, or sat in the bleachers next to. I figure a great guy like Reeve has great friends, and my plan is that one of them will fall in love with me across the room and follow me around the nation."

"You're moving away already?" asked Brian. "You just got home. I haven't even seen you yet."

"I'm being romantic. Have you ever heard of romance?"

"It's all I'm thinking about," said Brian. "Reeve set the bar awfully high for the rest of us."

"Mainly it's insane," said Jodie. "She's twenty, they have no money, she's dropping out of college, Reeve can take only three days off, there's no honeymoon, and he can't afford a ring, so he wants to tattoo one on her finger."

Brian was laughing. "Mom around? Lemme say hello."

Jodie handed their mother the phone.

Brian let his mother talk wedding talk. He had his own tuxedo from when he sang tenor in the high school concert choir, so he would not have to get there early to rent one.

"I can't talk long," said his mother. "We're working on bridesmaid dress sizes. We're going to have emergency alterations. Heard from Brendan lately?"

"We're doing better," said Brian cheerfully. "By the time we're thirty, we might behave like twins again. Or bond at the wedding. Listen," he said. "I don't have any money to contribute, but I just want you and Dad to know that hot dogs on the grill won't cut it. Janie needs more of a party."

"I totally agree. Janie doesn't know, and I'm not sure she cares, but we've found the only caterer in New Jersey willing to take on a wedding where nobody knows how many people will show up. The food will be fabulous."

Conversation swirled around Miranda Johnson. Reeve's mother, who for years had been Miranda's dearest friend, babbled on and on. "Reeve is practicing using the name Jennie," she said. "He hasn't quite mastered it."

Miranda hadn't quite mastered it either.

She sat on her little tufted velvet bench and watched her daughter step out of gown number seven. Not my daughter, she reminded herself. Donna's daughter.

Way back, in a misty past Miranda rarely allowed to surface, there had been another daughter. How thrilled she and Frank had been with their pretty little Hannah.

Their beloved daughter. Difficult from the day she was born. Nothing came easily to Hannah. Not sleep, not eating, not potty training. Not school, not friends, not piano, not softball.

The pediatricians had been comforting. "Every child goes at her own pace" was a favorite remark.

But Hannah did not have a pace. She just stood there while life flowed around her.

What hadn't they tried? From horseback riding to tennis, slumber parties to Girl Scouts, public school to private school.

"She'll come into her own" was another pediatrician's piece of nonsense.

There were all these new syndromes today, like Asperger's, that you never heard about decades ago when Hannah was growing up. Miranda had read extensively about these and their symptoms did not match hers. But if Hannah were a teenager today, Miranda thought some psychiatrist somewhere would be able to name her condition.

"It's fine for a child to daydream," the pediatricians would say.

Indeed, Hannah had loved to sit in a daze and tell her mother she was planning to be a yacht captain or a film-maker or a spy or a poet. But she never did anything about a goal. She just sat.

If only they had known enough to bypass the pediatricians and go straight to a psychiatrist. But when a child is pretty and smiling and cooperative, what does a parent say? "There's something wrong" was all she and Frank could come up with, and every doctor dismissed it, laughing.

Janie stroked the fabric of the seventh wedding gown, smiling as if she and the gown were friends.

Miranda had known that a wedding was not a likely outcome for Hannah. But she never dreamed that Hannah would drop out of college—a huge choice; a choice that seemed way beyond Hannah's capacity to make—to join some quasi-spiritual group that hid her away for a few years and then sold her body on the streets for a few more. Miranda and Frank had fought in court for the right just to visit Hannah, who didn't want to see them. They won. Hannah hated them for it. Her return home lasted less than a week.

Hate was not an emotion Miranda had ever felt, and to see it possess her daughter like the devil in some terrifying story could still reduce her to trembling.

When Hannah showed up all those empty years later with that lovely, sweet, chatty toddler, asking her parents to bring up her baby for her, Miranda had known that it was the one good act of Hannah's adult life: saving her child from the life Hannah was leading.

Miranda also knew that when Hannah was back in her group, the group would want that baby again. So she and Frank changed their names and hid themselves and Hannah's lovely child.

When the truth came out, Miranda was stunned.

Hannah had never had a good moment after all.

She had had only evil moments.

My daughter, Miranda would think, unable to fathom how this could be.

In the last few months, sitting in the parlor downstairs at

the Harbor, often the only available activity, Miranda some-times wondered if she and Hannah led the same life—just sitting, dreaming of things that could not be, pretending the past had a different shape.

When Miranda looked into the future now, there were only shadows. Frank was no longer a companion but a re-sponsibility. She still loved him. But the man who had been her rock and her joy had mostly departed.

And now Janie had turned into Jennie and was moving a thousand miles away, and Miranda might see her once a year for a few days. And Donna would be kind, and the Spring family would be courteous, and life was over, really.

"Reeve keeps repeating his vows," Janie was saying. " 'I, Reeve, take thee, *Jennie*'—as if some other bride might leap into my dress and take over."

An inexplicable sense of horror paralyzed Miranda.

Brendan took the subway to the Upper East Side and the ad-dress he had found online. It was a big white-glove building whose large tasteful awning extended from the front door to the curb, so that residents getting in and out of limos or taxis would not have to deal with the weather. The two uniformed doormen, very spiffy-looking, were never going to let him in.

Nevertheless, Brendan walked right up.

"May I help you, sir?" asked one doorman.

"Sure. I'm here to be interviewed by Calvin Vinesett."

They held the door for him.

Brendan grinned.

And the moment they opened the real door, Brendan

knew that the next door would open too. After all, the man was writing a book about Brendan's family. Calvin Vinesett had the notes from Brendan's three interviews. Calvin Vinesett would explain everything and Brendan would feel at ease and the author would agree to let it drift until Janie was safely married.

The foyer was small and elegant. Mirrors and black marble, leather benches and immense green ferns. Smiling people at the desk also wanted to help him.

"I have an interview with Calvin Vinesett," said Brendan. "Could you let him know Brendan Spring is here?"

"Of course." The concierge picked up her house phone, called the apartment, and then frowned slightly. "He doesn't remember scheduling anything," she said.

"Tell him I'm Janie Johnson's brother Brendan."

"It's Janie Johnson's brother Brendan," repeated the concierge. Then she handed the phone to Brendan.

"I'm sorry," said a deep voice. "I don't know the name."

The author of the book did not know the name of his subject? "The kidnap book you're writing?" said Brendan. "Janie Johnson? The face on the milk carton?"

There was a long silence.

The deep voice said, "I'll be right down."

THE TWELFTH PIECE OF THE KIDNAPPER'S PUZZLE

Every day, sometimes ten times a day, Hannah checked Facebook. Everybody else out there had a life. Success. Friends.

Every day, sometimes ten times a day, Hannah counted her money. Every day it dwindled. The day came when there was none left.

She lay down in the nest of old coats she kept on the floor, when it seemed easier to be a cat or a dog instead of a person. She did not awaken until morning, when her alarm rang. She had to work at the Mug.

The Jennie/Janie would never have to bus tables.

Hannah struggled to her feet. She wanted to curl back up in the nest. But without money, she could not keep even this miserable excuse for a home.

She could take no comfort in her brilliant plan. Without money, it could not proceed.

She took a quick peek at Facebook before she left for the

Mug. Adair really did have 476 friends and they all had posted. They all had something to say about the wedding.

What wedding?

Hannah scanned the material.

That parent thief was getting married in July!

She remembered her very first plan, when she had been sitting on a stool at an ice cream counter. When she decided to show a stupid smiling three-year-old that not everybody was a friend.

The plan had not worked.

Everybody *was* the Jennie/Janie's friend.

Except me, thought Hannah Javensen.

She thought of a white gown spattered with red blood.

The alarm rang a second time, the way she had programmed it to do. She had to run all the way to the Mug, and when she got there, the owner was very rude, lying that Hannah was not clean and she smelled. They wouldn't let her bus tables because they pretended she would upset the customers. But they would let her do the dishes, because they had nobody else.

She hated that word, "let."

Customers came in and out of the Mug at warp speed, throwing coffee down their throats. The owner kept snapping at Hannah to work harder. Nobody cared how difficult her life was. In the tiny kitchen, next to the huge sink, Hannah opened the dishwasher to load it with juice glasses and mugs and oatmeal bowls. Each glass was slippery. Each plate was heavy.

The owner was yelling now.

Hannah was already going as fast as she could.

Mug after mug had to be turned upside down, and the silly handles jiggered so they fit against each other. She repositioned a dark red mug with navy blue writing.

Stephen Spring

One of those red rabbits had been here? In her space? In her life?

She flung the Stephen Spring mug against the tiles of the floor. It shattered into sharp nasty triangles, long and thin, that you could cut a person with.

Yes! She would! She would show them!

She took a second mug and threw it harder, and then a glass. Shards flew around the floor and sparkled on the tiles. She emptied the dishwasher, throwing, throwing, throwing. It was wonderful. Sound and glitter and smash!

The owner and the prep cook walked her out the back door, their shoes crunching on the glass and china. They deposited her in the alley among the trash cans. "Don't come back, Jill," said the owner. From her voluminous apron pocket, the owner pulled out cash, paying Hannah what she was owed and not one dime more. That woman didn't even care that Hannah had to face next week and the week after that!

The cook usually left the back door open to get fresh air into the tiny kitchen. But they closed it this time, and she heard it lock, and she was alone with the garbage.

She opened her hand.

The longest, thinnest, sharpest piece of Stephen Spring's mug lay in her palm.

CHAPTER TWELVE

Kathleen hadn't finished her explanation for wanting to talk to her father about the three possibles, and Stephen was on his bike. He left Kathleen without a glance and without a word.

Her parents were right. The distance between Stephen and her hopes was too great. She was always putting a foot wrong, and it was always over Janie, whose history was an octopus—sticky horrid tentacles. "I was trying to help," she said to the person who was no longer there.

"Some wounds don't heal," her father had said once, and Stephen Spring might never heal from the blows dealt his family.

Kathleen clung to her cell phone. Surely Stephen would call her back and tell her he was sorry and had acted thoughtlessly and would she please forgive him?

But he didn't.

This was going to be his way out. He could extricate himself from his tiresome girlfriend and feel good about it—she would have been a traitor anyway. Nosing around in private family problems—bringing in the FBI—ruining Janie's wedding!

Even if I do call my father, she thought, I don't have anything to tell him. And what would Dad do next? There aren't any next steps.

In her smartphone she had the Evernote photos of the preface and the Hannah list.

The other night, killing time, she had gone online, trying to find the same public records the researcher had used. But phone bills, water bills, electricity bills, cable TV bills—any bills she could think of—were not public.

Only property tax was public.

Kathleen easily figured out how to research the owners of buildings. Combining that with people searches, she had quickly established that the first possible Hannah did not own the building in which she lived, but she had been at that same address for twenty-two years. Before Janie had been born! Back then, Hannah would have been with the group. Even if she had resembled Hannah in any way, that woman couldn't have been a possible.

How could the researcher have put her on a list, then?

The other two names didn't show up on anything. Kathleen figured that if you were a renter and you moved a lot and you had a cell phone, not a landline, and you've never had a car loan, say, you wouldn't show up. That fit with the marginal existence they figured Hannah would have, but it did not fit with Calvin Vinesett's list. How did he get the names if the names weren't anywhere?

She could think of one thing she'd like to do. But if she and

Stephen were no longer a couple, who cared whether those women were Hannah? Who cared about anything?

The good person, she remembered from Mass, is a person who does not walk by. The good person gets involved and helps strangers.

But it didn't help *me*! she shouted silently at God. When I tried to get involved, it wrecked everything.

Donna and Jonathan Spring's house was only ten minutes from the bridal mall.

They all drove back to inspect the yard and discuss the reception. It was a big yard—the kind the kids would have enjoyed so much when they were little. But by the time the Springs had moved there, only Brian and Brendan were young enough to play in a yard. Brian never went outdoors if he could help it, and Brendan was so busy with organized sports at school that he rarely noticed the space behind his own house.

Huge maples and oaks towered in the neighbors' property, giving wonderful shade and greenery to the Springs' yard. The back-to-back neighbors had edged their property in yellow and gold daylilies. The neighbors on the left had a rose garden and the neighbors on the right had planted a row of weeping cherry trees. The Springs had grass.

"This will be lovely," said Reeve's mother, obviously surprised that anything in this wedding was working out to her satisfaction. "Don't you think so, Miranda?"

"I do," said Miranda obediently.

Jodie fixed a tray of lemonade and iced tea, cookies,

chocolates, and fruit and brought it out to the deck. Miranda and Mrs. Shields sat on big comfy chairs. Mrs. Shields filled her chair. Miranda hardly made a dent in her cushion.

"Be right back!" trilled Jodie, making her getaway.

Janie was whipped. She had not expected the dress event to be so emotional. She had not expected to worry so much about Miranda. When she saw her dad, she summoned the energy to beam at him and he gave her the usual bear hug. "How's my little girl?"

He always said that, as if he still thought of her as her missing three-year-old self.

"I'm good, Daddy. Mom is getting her bridal gown out to show me."

He laughed. "You haven't had enough gowns? You tried on so many! My personal fave was eight."

"Jodie sent you photographs of each one?"

"Yup. Brian liked eight too. Stephen said he would settle for whatever you settled for, but that Kathleen liked nine."

"Nine was gorgeous," called Jodie, as if she and gown number nine had a long acquaintance. "Kathleen has good taste."

"Is Stephen bringing Kathleen?" asked their father. "If he loves this girl, and she's our next bride, we want her. Maybe Stephen can't afford the airfare."

"I think it's more likely he can't afford the implication," said Jodie. "Bringing your girlfriend to your sister's wedding is a statement."

"Talk to him," their father ordered her. "Tell him Mom and I will get Kathleen a ticket if he wants her to come."

"You talk to him," protested Jodie.

"He'd argue with me. He'd say he wants to be independent. Oh, and Janie, by the way, you have mail."

Except for letters from Calvin Vinesett, Janie didn't get mail. It was probably more of the book stuff.

Or maybe not! Maybe she was about to get her first wedding present!

But it was not either of these. It was a business envelope with the ESPN logo and a Charlotte return address.

It was not like Reeve to use the U.S. mail. He had gone through a greeting-card stage a few years ago, trying to convince Janie that he wasn't so bad after all. He didn't know what to say, so he let greeting-card poets try. Janie had not been impressed and told him so. Since then, all communication had been electronic.

Jodie and Dad were waiting for her to open the letter.

She felt a shiver of worry. No greeting cards existed for guys who wanted to back out. This very day, Mr. Shields had flown down to Charlotte. Janie knew what Reeve's dad would be saying: that Reeve was too young. She knew what Lizzie had been saying: Janie was not stable. She had read all the posts on his wall. *Marriage is for old guys. Your life is over, Reeve.* She knew what his boss was saying: he still had to work sixty-hour weeks.

And his heart?

What would Reeve's heart be telling him, now that reality was sinking in?

Was he saying, "Uh-oh. I actually asked a girl to enter my life for good. To live in my tiny apartment and share my toothpaste and credit card. Maybe I'll just scribble a note, so I don't have to say it out loud."

He wouldn't write *Let's not get married.*

But he might write *Let's wait.*

Please, no. I'm the one who can't wait now.

She tore the flap on the long white envelope.

Brendan and Calvin Vinesett were in a narrow hall, behind the greenery at the back of the elegant foyer. Brendan could see the package room and the mailroom. He and the author sat on a narrow bench. In spite of its thick leather cushion, it was not soft.

Brendan's brain was soft. For the third time Brendan said, "You're telling me that you are not writing any such book?"

"Correct. And you're telling me that at least three men have been interviewing your family and using my name," said Calvin Vinesett. "I write about murders. They have to be complex and the killer has to be in prison. I deal with the drama that brought the victims and the killer together. I write about the lives of the survivors and how that played out during and after the trial. Of course I followed the Janie Johnson case. Who didn't? But even if that kidnapper were caught, her story isn't what my readers expect from me. I'm furious that some writer is hiding under my name. I'm even more upset that it worked. May I read the emails that this Michael/Mick gave you? Supposedly from me?"

Brendan handed them over. "I have a chapter too."

Calvin Vinesett read the pages carefully, slipping each page under the other until he was back at the beginning. "Whoever wrote these, Brendan, is not much of a writer. Poor phrasing. Odd choice of words. A lot of repetition. This person gets a thought and sticks with it. I'm going to guess this person is a beginner who hasn't published a thing."

It's Mom, thought Brendan, absolutely sick. I so don't want Mom to be the one doing this. But why would Mom call her book *The Happy Kidnap*? Is it Janie she's been mad at all these years? We've all been mad at Janie some of the time. But I thought we loved her too.

"And why," Calvin Vinesett continued, "would any author tell a researcher to use a fake name and lie to the person he's interviewing? You can't use information obtained like that. It's just gossip."

If only his twin were here. Brian was so quick. Brian would figure this out; find the clues in the writing and the title.

"And finally," said Calvin Vinesett, "this chapter? It's practically hate mail. There's something radically wrong here. I'm going to follow up. It is unacceptable that some third-rate writer is using my name."

"How will you follow up?" asked Brendan.

"First, we want to find the computer where these emails originated. We need a subpoena to do that. But I'm not sure that a few pages of lousy writing will impress a judge. I have contacts with the FBI. This situation is distantly related to an unsolved kidnapping, so they might look into it. But it wouldn't be high on their list."

Brendan remembered suddenly that he had his own contact with the FBI.

When each of their children first got a cell phone, Mom and Dad had already filled the contact list: relatives, neighbors, and the three officials who had dealt with the kidnapping—the local police, the state trooper, and the FBI agent.

The Spring kids detested those entries, living inside their precious phones as if they might need the police again. Brendan knew that Stephen had deleted them all the minute he moved to Colorado.

But even though Brendan was on his fourth cell phone, having updated whenever he had the money, he always kept the numbers. Not because he cared, but because he and Brian were the youngest, and Mom, who paid their bills, kept tabs on their cell phone use, and that included knowing the contact list.

Brendan was reeling. If it really is my mother writing it, or Brian, I don't want a judge or the FBI talking to her about her bad writing, or anything else. "Mr. Vinesett, wait a week, okay? Janie's wedding is Saturday. In fact, I have to get home for all this stuff that my mother wants me to get done. I don't want anything to hurt Janie's wedding."

"I couldn't get anything done that fast anyway," said Calvin Vinesett. He was grinning. "That is so great. After all that poor child suffered, she's grown up and getting married? I wouldn't have said she was old enough. I've lost track of the story, I guess."

"She's twenty. My parents don't think she's old enough either," confided Brendan.

• • •

From the ESPN envelope, Janie Johnson drew out a single sheet of plain white paper, folded crisply in thirds. She unfolded it.

Out fell a single green maple leaf.

Reeve's bad handwriting spread messily over the page. *Remember the year we raked that huge pile of leaves? Remember how you fell down into the leaves and I fell down on top of you? Remember our first kiss?*

Remember!

That year, the sugar maples lining their street in Connecticut had been a symphony of color. Yellow and red leaves had covered every blade of grass. She and Reeve had tumbled into the pile they had raked and, in the shelter of crispy color, had their first kiss.

She kissed the handwriting.

Jodie said, "Oh, blecch. You are so far gone, Janie!"

Their father was laughing. "Reeve is pretty far gone too," said Jonathan Spring. "It's summer, so no leaves are falling. He had to rip that leaf off some innocent tree. In a million years, I would never have thought of doing that."

"Come in here!" yelled their mother. "I got the box out of the attic!"

"You better come too, Daddy," said Jodie. "This is your bride we're talking about."

His face went all soft. "She was so beautiful," he said.

"Don't say it as if her beauty is in the past," Jodie warned.

"Be right with you," Janie told them, going into her bedroom.

The bedroom was stuffed with boxes from college and

boxes from the Connecticut house from when Janie finished moving her parents to the Harbor and herself down here. It looked like the room of an organized hoarder. She was glad she'd never unpacked. Now they could just ship the stuff on to Charlotte. She hadn't even labeled the boxes, thinking she would open them immediately. She had no idea what was in anything or whether she wanted it.

Most of the Johnsons' books had been sold at the yard sale. There had been a huge old Webster's dictionary that Frank had loved. For some craft project, Janie had once dried flowers between the pages of that dictionary. She mainly used an e-reader now.

She spotted a paperback, set the leaf carefully in the middle of the book, and balanced a heavy cardboard box on top of it. Pressure was supposed to draw the moisture out of the leaf and into the pages.

Maybe the leaf would dry out and she could frame it.

"Janie!" her sister yelled. "We're ready!"

Jonathan Spring watched his girls. Such a treat to have all three of them together.

He had gotten used to missing Janie, but Jodie's absence had been hard. He had not had a moment to talk to Jodie and find out about Haiti. Jodie was his scrappy one, quick to anger. There was a difference in her now. She seemed easier, somehow.

And Janie——he was at a loss to understand how Janie could have gone in literally two or three hours from that Michael guy to Reeve. Women were amazing. Michael turned out to be a sleaze, so Janie hopped a plane and took the old boyfriend back.

Sealed the deal too. No more dating.

Nope.

Marriage.

Jonathan Spring had studied that video. Reeve was the one who proposed. So there was no understanding men, either.

Basically, love was insane.

His eyes turned to his wife.

How tenderly, how carefully Donna lifted the long pink cardboard box that held her wedding gown, as if her life would break if she dropped it.

How anxiously and eagerly she peeled back the seal. Holding her breath, she eased the thirty-year-old gown out of its box.

Jonathan remembered how in love he had been then. Not the soft old love of thirty years. But the pulsing, breath-stealing love when every glimpse of your bride was treasure.

He had been praying that Janie would have the love he and Donna had.

Now he changed his mind.

He wanted the love Janie and Reeve had.

To Janie's eye, the gown was a little tacky. It had too much tulle and too much sash. Too much ruffle around the neckline. But her mother was misty, soothing its lines with her fingers and caressing its satin with her palm.

Carefully they unfolded the gown, shaking it gently. It didn't even need to be pressed.

We're the same size, thought Janie. Because she really is my mother. I really did get my bones and my shoulders and my complexion and my hair from her. "May I try it on?" she asked.

"For sure *I* can't wear it anymore," said her mother. "I'm back in shape, but I'm not *that* back in shape!"

Janie slid into the gown.

Her father gasped. "Oh, Donna! I'm gonna break down. She's you."

Her mother did break down. "I was so happy that day. When I walked into the church and I saw your father wearing a tuxedo for the first time in his life, so nervous and standing so straight and swallowing so hard—oh, Janie! I wanted to fly down the aisle and hold him tight. It was all I could do to walk the way we did then. Hesitation step, it was called. I've always wondered about that. If you hesitate to walk down the church aisle, you better not go."

"My name is Jennie," she said, "and I don't hesitate."

Jodie wanted to laugh. The wedding gown was so dated. It was a dress an unsophisticated teenage girl would pick if she wanted to look like Cinderella. It fit Janie perfectly, and of course Janie would be cute in anything, but the dress was hopeless.

Next, their mother lifted from the box a circlet of gold leaves and beaded flowers from which a vast puff of tulle sprang out. It looked like a halo imploding.

Lovingly, she tucked Janie's hair back, and adjusted the tulle around Janie's head and shoulders. Donna Spring was weeping.

Jonathan Spring was wiping his eyes.

Jodie rolled her own eyes.

"I'm going to wear this instead," said Janie.

"When?" said Donna. "Instead of what?"

"For my wedding. I'm going to wear your gown."

Jodie was appalled. "But you chose such a lovely gown! Number seven was perfect. We pick it up tomorrow!"

"I can cancel that. I want my marriage to last. Mom and Dad's marriage lasted. I'm going to wear the dress that started the good marriage."

Stephen was dumbfounded by Jodie's most recent message and photograph. Janie was going to wear their mother's old gown?

Even to him—and his knowledge of fashion hovered around zero—that gown was from some other century.

But then, everything about a wedding was from some other century. Stephen tried to think only of weddings and flight plans. He might have just taken the biggest flight of his life, riding away from Kathleen.

He felt sick and shaky.

He thought of going to the Mug, because it was nearby and because coffee always settled him down. But he and Kathleen usually went together. The waitress would bring Kathleen's mug to the table along with his, expecting them to meet.

He headed to Starbucks, feeling like a traitor.

Two times in an hour: traitor to Kathleen, traitor to the Mug.

Kathleen wandered in various boutiques. Considered various kinds of food. She couldn't go home. She couldn't face the photos of Stephen and the silly sweet souvenirs of dating.

After a while, she returned to the home of the second Hannah, the one thin enough to seem right, with the New York accent that seemed wrong. Stephen had not shown this woman the photographs. He had just asked if she knew Tiffany Spratt.

This time, the woman was standing in her doorway. She was very tall. She could not be Hannah, who was five foot five.

I am so stupid, thought Kathleen. The list of possibles really was just bait. There's no link anywhere to anything.

She felt sick and embarrassed. She couldn't think of a thing to say.

"You back?" said the woman. "What kind of scam you trying to pull?"

"*Somebody* is trying to pull off a scam," said Kathleen. "I just don't know who or why. I need your help."

"I don't know nothing."

"But somehow, I think you are connected. May I show you a few photographs? Could you tell me if you've ever seen these people?"

The woman lit a cigarette. She barely glanced at the two photos.

Kathleen said timidly, "Could you really study them? In case maybe you worked with one of these women once, or lived nearby, or—I don't know—were in a club with her or something?"

"A club?" repeated the woman contemptuously. "I never been in any club." But she did take the photographs and she did study them.

Time passed.

The woman stood staring at Hannah young and Hannah old. Her cigarette burned by itself and the ash fell. Slowly she raised her eyes and stared at Kathleen.

The woman didn't blink, didn't even seem to breathe.

The glittering eyes looked crazy.

"I'll keep these," said the woman.

Kathleen was suddenly aware that it was late, and dark, and she was in a bad neighborhood. "Thanks for your help," she said, and leapt onto her bicycle and fled.

Reeve was at home, sprawled in front of his television. He had muted the game and dozed through the wedding gown discussion, barely managing to match each photo on his cell with Janie's verdict.

"Jennie," she reminded him. "This is the third time tonight you forgot."

Reeve clicked the TV off. Even mute, it was sucking up too much attention. "Listen, Janie," he said. "I've loved you a long time, and the girl I love is Janie. I was with Janie when she went to New Jersey for the first time and saw her real family. I drove Janie there. I knew the same minute Janie did that her true name was Jennie. And I was there when she fled being Jennie, and turned away from the fact and the family of Jennie. She came home Janie still. It tore her heart in half." He paused for breath. "As for my heart, maybe someday in my heart you'll be Jennie, but if I could engrave a name on my wedding rings, it would be Janie, cut deep into the gold so I could trace it with my finger. So if I get the name wrong, and sometimes I still say Janie instead of Jennie, it's because I love Janie. I love everything about her. Including the fact that her name isn't Janie."

When she and Reeve were finally off the phone, Janie repeated her names to herself: Janie Johnson. Jennie Spring.

In that old horror of finding that she was a kidnap victim— She! Janie! Child of Frank and Miranda Johnson!—she had clung to her Janie name as if to a life raft.

Slippage into the Spring family began the very first weekend she was there, and from the first she stomped it out, as if it were a spreading fire.

The Springs had surrendered on the name front, and they too called her Janie. When she left them, they wrote to her and telephoned her as Janie Johnson. How glad they would be when Janie Johnson no longer existed.

Perhaps there are actually two Janie Johnsons, she thought. There's the creation of Hannah, a fiction born of crime. I never want to be that Janie again. But there's another Janie Johnson. The happy girl who really was the daughter of Frank and Miranda. The good daughter. A person I'm proud of.

And now, for a few days, I am Jennie Spring. A name like ice on a hot day. A name that will melt and be gone. I will have been my real self for less than two weeks when I become a third person.

Jennie Shields.

A stranger. We haven't met yet, because she won't exist until I'm married. Jennie Shields. Even if my husband calls me Janie.

Janie found herself laughing and dancing.

Husband, she thought. Such a beautiful word.

Miranda Johnson and Mrs. Shields had left for Connecticut. Jodie and her mother were cleaning up the kitchen. "I'm afraid," said Donna Spring.

Although their lives had been ruled by fear, Jodie had never heard her mother say such a thing out loud. "Afraid the flowers won't come?" she said flippantly. "Afraid the weather will be bad?"

"Afraid for Janie. The theory is that a true crime book will shake loose information about the Javensen woman, but what if it actually shakes Janie loose?"

"She's not hanging on by a thread, Mom. And Reeve is one of those protective types. Janie will be fine."

"You know what amazes me?" said her mother. "Janie, with her tragic history, is not considering for one moment that tragedy could lie ahead. She sees nothing but joy ahead. It's as if she didn't learn anything from the past."

"She learned everything from the past," said Jodie. "She learned to put it behind her. She's rejoicing in the moment. It's what I learned in Haiti, Mom. The children and the nuns were so wise. They could rejoice in any tiny thing—the joy of seeing a friend approaching eclipsed the tragedy around them."

Her mother was staring at her.

"What's wrong?" said Jodie.

"Nothing's wrong. You grew up, didn't you? Haiti matured you."

"I wasn't immature before," said Jodie irritably.

"Let's not bicker."

"I love to bicker," said Jodie. "It's why marriage is going to be a problem for me. Janie will agree with everything Reeve says and go along with everything Reeve wants, but I'd be bickering the whole time." She giggled. "Still, I'm hoping to meet Mr. Right at the wedding. I'm looking for a guy who is adorable, strong, smart, launching an interesting career, and never bickers, because bickering will be my job."

On his way home, Brendan drank in the city.

The rush of people, the cacophony of voices and horns and engines and construction and music, was strengthening.

He loved New York.

He strode down the sidewalks the way everybody else did: going fast, with a plan. His only plan was to get the express bus to New Jersey while everybody else was probably planning to conquer the world, but still. However minor it might be, he too had a plan.

It made him grin, and suddenly he was happy.

Once he was back in New Jersey, he dutifully looked at Janie in some puffy dress and said hi to Nicole and ate leftover pizza. He retreated to his room when the girls began a lengthy gown recap, and watched a game on his iPad on MLB.com.

I guess I'm going to be a spectator, not a pro, he thought. I think I can still be happy.

The word "happy" buzzed in his brain. *The Happy Kidnap.*

Brendan's hair prickled.

His mouth dried out.

His heart raced.

From the very first reading, the writing had seemed female.

There were a lot of women to consider. His mother. Janie. Jodie. Miranda. Sarah-Charlotte. Lizzie. Kathleen.

None of them felt right.

But there was one other woman.

Hannah.

THE THIRTEENTH PIECE OF THE KIDNAPPER'S PUZZLE

All conditions were right. Witnesses, darkness, weakness—these tilted in Hannah's favor. An older man, definitely not one of Boulder's athletes, trudged up to the ATM Hannah was watching. He inserted his card, entered his numbers as if it took the last of his strength, took his card back, and counted the stack of bills.

He was afraid of Hannah's knife. She was disappointed when he just gave her the wallet. He left the way he had come and she went the other way, peeling off her outer layer of clothing and her enveloping scarf. In a moment she was slim and beautiful and young again. Nobody could ever recognize her as the person at the ATM.

She was invincible.

Why had it taken so long to assert herself? Once she jettisoned that silly thing called caution, it was easy. She just had to act casual, as if she belonged, and of course, now that she was slim and beautiful and young again, she did belong.

When she got home, she counted the money.

She was beside herself. All that risk! All that planning! And the bills were just twenties. They hardly added up to anything!

She would have to do this over and over.

Which had a certain appeal.

She was not a person who wasted time. When she had a brilliant idea, she ran with it. By noon the next day, she had pulled off three more ATM events. People saw her knife and they gave her everything.

Safely back home, she counted her twenties again and again.

There were so many possibilities for this money. Yes, the original plan. But she was getting tired of the original plan. It was actually very hard to write all those pages. Each page seemed to say the same things she had said on the previous page. It wasn't her fault. She hadn't had the advantages other writers had. It was so unfair. But now she had new plans. She tried to sort out her plans, but they meshed and separated and wriggled around in her brain.

Somebody knocked.

Hannah froze. She had never had a visitor.

She picked up her knife. She picked up her shard of china.

"Jill?"

Somebody from one of her jobs was standing at her door?

Impossible. They didn't have this address. She always gave a false address. She didn't rent this place as Jill Williams, either.

Who could it be?

The FBI?

The police?

Hannah stood motionless, listening hard.

Eventually she heard the person leave. She crept out to see who it was. Some woman. Unidentifiable from the back.

Hannah Javensen followed.

When Hannah got home, she was so excited she couldn't sleep. She couldn't reread her pages and polish them. She twirled in giddy circles, admiring her knife.

Several hours passed before she checked in with Adair. Everybody was going to the wedding. It was going to be super fun. They would meet at Adair's and, in rented vans, drive to New Jersey in groups.

Wait!

It wasn't in July anymore!

Those people had changed the date!

That Jennie/Janie was probably laughing at Hannah! *Ha-ha! I got you! You thought you had until July.*

Adair thoughtfully provided a map to the church.

Hannah read everything.

One post was particularly interesting.

—*They're not sure Janie's dad can go,* wrote somebody. *He might not be well enough and have to stay in the nursing home and miss the wedding.*

It wasn't a nursing home. They didn't have nurses at the Harbor. They had aides. Stupid Michael had told her every-thing about the Harbor. She even knew which elevator to take.

The word "harbor" was meant to imply that the institu-tion created a safe harbor for its residents.

No, Frank, she said across the years and miles. It doesn't.

She giggled, caressing a new plan. She was experienced now, because of that woman who tried to blackmail her. Using a knife was easy and fun.

And she had money. Where to drive? The wedding? Or the Harbor?

Choices, choices.

CHAPTER THIRTEEN

Jodie and Sarah-Charlotte were on the phone, putting together a Friday morning shower for Janie.

"Reeve doesn't fly in until Friday afternoon," said Jodie. "He has to see Father John one more time, plus get his tuxedo and shoes and see his parents and make it to the rehearsal on time. Janie has nothing to do on Friday morning."

"Who's coming?" asked Sarah-Charlotte. "Adair's group is driving down Saturday morning."

"My group's here, though. And Reeve's family is showing up Thursday at the hotel so they can have a family reunion at the same time. They'll come. You drive down Thursday night, Sarah-Charlotte, and stay with us. I wanted to ask you something else. You met that guy Michael, didn't you? The one pretending to be a researcher?"

"He was pretending to be a boyfriend," Sarah-Charlotte corrected. And then she thought, Jodie's right. It was *all* pretend. He wasn't even a researcher. That was pretend too. Why? And why follow me in Boston?

"Nicole's cousin Vic is on the local police force, the one that originally handled the kidnapping. Calvin Vinesett hasn't even talked to them yet. If you haven't talked to the original police on the scene, who have you talked to?"

It was a good question, thought Sarah-Charlotte. Why have Michael/Mick try to interview me when I know nothing? The only thing I can talk about is Janie herself.

Because the book isn't about Hannah, she thought suddenly. It's about Janie.

She remembered the weird thought of a few days ago.

It was no longer weird.

It was possible and it was terrifying.

"Jodie, I have to go," said Sarah-Charlotte. "See you Thursday." She stared down at her cell phone.

Janie had received her first cell phone from her New Jersey parents. The Springs had entered Agent Mollison's number into Janie's contact list. Janie was grumpy and didn't want it there. Sarah-Charlotte's mother had said, "You never know, Janie," and to Sarah-Charlotte's shock and excitement, entered that same number into Sarah-Charlotte's cell.

"Mom, what are you picturing?" Sarah-Charlotte had demanded. "That the kidnapper will rise to life again? Corner us in the high school parking lot? We'll need to summon the cavalry?"

"You never know," said her mother again.

It was fun to have that contact in her phone, as if she really did lead the kind of life where a person needed her own FBI contact.

I really do, she thought.

She called.

An unidentified voice asked her to leave a message.

It's probably not even him anymore, she thought. Whoever hears this message probably won't have any idea what I'm talking about.

She said, "Okay, I'm hoping this will reach Agent Mollison. This is Janie Johnson's best friend from high school. Sarah-Charlotte Sherwood. Remember Janie? The face on the milk carton? Janie is being stalked. She knows about it. She thinks she solved it. But who would want that stalking to happen? I think it has to do with Hannah. I think we're in trouble."

Stephen Spring spent a sleepless night. A miserable day. A second bad night.

If only he could see Kathleen as clearly as Reeve saw Janie.

Like Reeve, Stephen saw his career with clarity. But unlike Reeve, he was lost when it came to girls.

He gave up on sleep. He went and opened the window that faced the distant mountains. The night was clear. On his cell phone he had a star app. He turned it on, and up came the shivery music and the wonderful strange map of the sky. He leaned way out the window and rotated, and the star map on his phone shifted to match what was above him. Too much ambient light here to see much.

He and Kathleen had once slept out under the stars, up in the mountains, and used this app in the pitch-darkness, identifying the tiny twinkles of light.

At four in the morning, when the sky was darkest, Stephen texted Kathleen.

R u up? can I come over?

In spite of the fact that Kathleen had thought of nothing but Stephen, she did not know what to do. She lay in bed, staring at the glowing little message on the glowing little phone. Finally, she called back. "Stephen?"

"Kathleen, I'm sorry. I apologize for losing my temper and stomping off. I——I'm very sorry. Can we talk?"

"It's too late, Stephen. I made a decision you will not like."

"I think I still love you," he said fearfully, although he had never said that he loved her in the first place.

Kathleen tightened a blanket around herself. Timing is everything, she thought. Neither one of us has good timing. "I definitely still love you," she told Stephen. "But I did call my father. And I did call him as an FBI agent, not as a parent. Because I think the situation is bad. I told him everything."

She had called her father while she was still hurrying away from the spooky eyes of the possible Hannah. Her father was on the phone to his colleagues in a minute, and the New York office called Calvin Vinesett. They were going to trace the source of the emails sent to Michael Hastings. Brendan Spring had turned over the book chapter. Experts would peruse the "preface" Kathleen had photographed.

"Would you like an update?" she asked Stephen.

Her father's report had been shocking. He told her, "Our expert had a lot to say about the writing. There was no reason to send Brendan's or Stephen's interviewers any chapters or paragraphs. That was done from pride. *Look at what I've written* pride. The chapter on Miranda Johnson is not simply filled with hate, but with inaccuracies, repetitions, and threats. The real thrust of that chapter was to excuse the author from any responsibility in life and place it all on a three-year-old or a parent she herself chose never to communicate with. The author is almost certainly Hannah Javensen."

"Dad, that's crazy," Kathleen had said.

"You were thinking that Hannah Javensen was sane?"

"But why would Hannah expose herself through a book?"

"Criminals are cocky," her father had said. "They believe they're smarter than the law. And she has been. Seventeen years of not being found is long enough for anybody to feel smarter than us. The Javensen woman probably looks back on that day in New Jersey with excitement. What better way to showcase her brilliance than a book?"

"But—wouldn't she be caught?"

"Obviously she didn't think so. Whatever her plan was, she expected to pull it off. And she might have. Luckily you and Brendan Spring and Sarah-Charlotte all knew enough to call the FBI. Three friends or relatives of Janie Johnson, scared enough to call? After all these years? That got attention. As for the three possible Hannahs—that list is in an email to your researcher. So Hannah chose those names. You ascertained that these women exist. We now assume that Hannah knew or knows those women. I cannot believe you and Stephen were stupid enough to interview them yourselves."

"Stephen is not stupid!" Kathleen had cried.

"Stephen is a jerk," said her father. "I'm glad you've broken up with him."

Now, on the phone, she listened to Stephen's voice. It was rougher and quicker than usual. "I don't care about any news on Hannah. She is what she is. I'm thinking of us. Kathleen, it's Friday. Or it will be when the sun comes up. I checked the flight. I can still get you a plane ticket. Will you come to the wedding? Will you fly to New Jersey with me today? I—I want you to meet my family."

My family has just decided you are a jerk and I'm better off without you, and I don't own a dress, and now you're not leaving me time to buy one. "Have you thought this through, Stephen?"

"I haven't thought of anything else since I stormed away from you. I didn't ask you to come to the wedding earlier because just thinking about my sister getting married gave me the hives. We've gotten close, you and I, and I didn't plan on closeness in my life, and I'm still not that sure of it. But I want to show you off to my family." He paused. "And I'm sorry. I was wrong to run."

He may be a jerk now and then, Kathleen told her father silently, but he can say the right words in the end. "When's our flight? Do I have time to go shopping first?"

Brendan had a lot to tell his parents.

They were the ones putting on the wedding. They had to be told about Hannah.

They also had to know about some seriously unpleasant

paperwork that had just arrived from college. No surprise, since he had blown off an entire semester, but seeing it in writing made him feel sick.

He could discuss how he had learned a lot this year about life and effort and family and loss and Calvin Vinesett. But he didn't see his parents falling for that.

He wondered if the school would take him back next September. Or if he should live at home and commute to classes. He'd rather join the army.

Actually, he *would* rather join the army. Which maybe he wouldn't discuss with his parents, who were knee-deep in houseguests and flower arrangements. Rental vans were dropping off tables and chairs for the reception. Everybody was either back from an airport run or setting out.

Brendan kept trying to corner his father but in the end, his father cornered him. "Hey, kid. You and I better talk." Dad swept Brendan away from everybody and everything. His father was a big man, but Brendan was bigger. It was odd to be shifted around as if he were still a little guy. It was kind of touching.

"You got a letter from the college?" Brendan asked nervously.

"College is not our main worry right now," said his father. "First of all, I'm proud of you, cornering Michael Hastings and finding Calvin Vinesett. Brilliant work."

"You know about that?"

"I've been talking to Agent Mollison all along. I wanted him at the wedding. From the minute it hit Facebook, I knew anybody anywhere could find out every detail of this wedding. We can't find Hannah, but she can always find us."

Brendan's thoughts had not gone that far. He had been thinking books, not a physical invasion.

"I haven't read that material you got hold of," said his dad, "but I understand that this crazy woman holds a three-year-old or her poor mother responsible for her decisions. I want the church secure."

Brendan was horrified. "We should move the wedding someplace else."

"No. My daughter is getting the wedding she wants with the boy she loves and neither she nor Reeve is going to be aware of this. Your mother isn't going to know either. She's too happy. We're not slapping her with this. Father John is okay with it."

Brendan was reeling. "What's my job, Dad?"

"I don't know. But I have to get a daughter and a wheelchair to get down the aisle, so I need somebody in the family who knows about the threat and can jump in."

He trusts me, thought Brendan.

Kathleen and Mandy hit the department store the minute it opened. They galloped into Better Dresses and told the saleswoman they had exactly thirty minutes to find clothes for a rehearsal dinner and a wedding, size 10, shoes 7B. Mandy handled shoes, racing back and forth with matches.

Kathleen kept saying, "It can't be a cocktail dress, it has to look right in a church, that's too short, I'm five nine, that's too frumpy!"

"Stop being picky!" yelled Mandy. "You're down to twelve minutes and you still have to swipe your credit card!"

"I found just the right thing!" shouted the saleswoman. "Here! Perfect for you! Sleek and stylish in a good color."

They dashed into the dressing room.

Kathleen stared at the reflection in the mirror. She was no longer a leggy hiker or a camo-clad college student with a torn sweatshirt. She was a woman with style. And the shoes didn't even hurt. And she did have the best ankles in the world.

She even had time to text Brendan. **Stephen didn't want an update. He doesn't know anything. It's you, me, and S-C.**

On the plane, Stephen and Kathleen could not get seats next to each other. He was two rows down, across the aisle, and in the middle. He would never have bought a middle seat for himself. So he was in the last-minute seat and he'd given the good one to her.

See, Daddy? she said silently. He isn't a jerk.

She yearned to communicate with Stephen. But all cell phones had to be off. The woman next to her was doing a crossword puzzle with a pencil. Kathleen didn't carry pencil or paper. She opened the flight magazine, ripped out an advertising card, and said to her seatmate, "May I borrow your pencil for one second?"

She wrote Stephen a note and passengers passed it on.

He wrote back. Soon the narrow white margin of the card was full.

She started a second advertising card.

Then she found a receipt in her purse with a blank back.

She had never passed notes before. It was so much fun. And what a way to get Stephen to commit: he had to write it all down!

She was actually sorry when the woman next to her offered to switch seats with Stephen.

Reeve had to work a half day Friday.

When he left the office, Bick said, "But you'll be back here Monday afternoon, right?"

"Yes, sir."

"Good. You'll be going to South Carolina for the USC-Clemson game. It's not much of a drive. You're going with Josh and Al, they've done it before, you'll learn a lot. Right?"

"Right," said Reeve, glowing.

It wasn't until he was parking at the airport—short-term—that he realized he and Janie would fly down here after one night of married life, get in the door of his apartment—and he'd leave.

Lizzie called.

"Lizzie," he said, racing into the terminal where twelve days ago he had proposed marriage, "no more opinions. Please?"

"This isn't an opinion. This is a fact."

"Am I ready for it?"

"We're all at the hotel in New Jersey. Twenty-three relatives. Eager to get the groom at the airport and welcome the bride into our family." Lizzie burst into tears.

Reeve made a mental note that he was definitely getting

married only once. This wedding stuff was seriously emotional.

He got on the plane, fastened his seat belt, and fell sound asleep.

Friday morning in Boston, Brian Spring finished packing, slung his bag over his shoulder, and set out for the railroad station. He liked everything about trains. He had his e-reader loaded with good stuff, his cell phone, and his summer semester textbook, and was early enough to get a window seat. He never chose the quiet car. He loved the racket and chaos of a dorm, and a packed train was similar.

His phone rang; of course it was his mother. Brian's guilt over his mother was huge. He had been the attentive son, the domestic son, the reliable easy one. And the moment he set foot on his college campus, he had forgotten his parents completely.

They didn't forget him, and emailed or texted or phoned all the time, and this was good, because he would answer immediately, whether he was in class or at a meal or wandering around Boston. A great town for wandering. But he never thought of his parents first.

He almost hesitated to return to New Jersey. Would he become the old quiet Brian who shadowed his twin? And now that his twin had collapsed in school, how would they get along? How could Brendan possibly think that he, Brian, was writing a true crime book? "Hi, Mom," he said cheerfully. "I'm almost at South Station."

"I'm so glad I caught you. I need you to do a huge wedding favor."

"Of course."

"Reeve's parents were going to pick up Mrs. Johnson and bring her down for the wedding. But they packed so much household stuff to give to Reeve and Janie that they don't have room for Miranda in the car."

"Household stuff matters more than Miranda?"

"You and I are not dealing with that issue. We are also not dealing with the fact that Reeve doesn't know about any of these household hand-me-downs and Janie doesn't want any and they don't have a vehicle to drive anything back in anyway, since they're flying. Our consideration is getting Miranda here. She has a car but she's afraid to drive in the city. You'll get off the train in Stamford, take a taxi to the Harbor, and drive Miranda's car the rest of the way."

Brian wasn't keen on New York traffic either, and as a matter of fact had never driven through the city. He was intensely pleased that his mother didn't realize this or didn't think it mattered. "What about Mr. Johnson?"

"He's not well enough, apparently. Janie will be upset," said his mother. "Now I'll call Miranda and tell her when your train is arriving."

"I'll call," said Brian. "I like Miranda. She and I always get along. And I still shiver every time I think that Mr. Johnson is ruined. He was totally a good guy."

"With lapses," said Brian's mother tartly.

"If you mean supporting his daughter, I'm not sure that was a lapse, Mom. He went on loving his little girl. Maybe that's to his credit. I like to think you would go on loving me, no matter what."

"Yes, but you're not a deranged vicious amoral kidnapper."

They laughed. Brian thought, Wow. After all these years, we can laugh about Hannah. "Give me Mrs. Johnson's phone number," he said. "We'll see you this afternoon."

Janie didn't feel secure driving alone to that huge airport, managing the traffic, the interstates, the tolls, the exits, finding the cell phone lot, picking Reeve up, and doing it all in reverse. So her New Jersey father drove while she fidgeted in the passenger seat.

She had not seen Reeve since the last airport. They talked on the phone—texted—chatted—posted—but they had not touched. "I'm nervous, Daddy," she said.

He'd spent his life driving in this kind of traffic and never gave it a thought. He took her hand. His grip was strong and warm. "It's all coming together," he said comfortingly. "We're going to have a great weekend. And then you're going to start a great life."

"I don't know that I want a great life. I want a nice life. A nice ordinary loving life. A life like yours. Without the kidnap."

They laughed.

Janie thought, Wow. It took a decade and a half. But we can actually laugh about the kidnapping. "I love you, Daddy."

He squeezed her hand. In the dark, catching the light of oncoming headlights, she saw a tear on his cheek. "Gonna be hard giving you away at the altar," he said. "I only just got you back."

Reeve texted. **My plane landed.**

"Daddy! They landed! Skip the cell phone lot!"

"We weren't going there anyway," said her father. "He has a ton of luggage. We're parking in short-term and meeting him at baggage claim."

Reeve had a ton of luggage? What was he bringing to New Jersey? All their stuff needed to go the other direction. Not that they had figured out how to transport it. She didn't own a car and he didn't have time to drive up.

Reeve texted, **Off the plane.**

Slow down, she texted back. **We'll be a minute.**

The minute lasted forever.

Her father drove up and down car aisles, looking for a good slot. Who cared about a good slot? Just park the car already!

Finally, he parked. She leapt out. He got out in a middle-aged kind of way, locked the car, and ambled along.

At last they were on the right sidewalk, going through the right doors, coming up to the right luggage carousel.

Reeve texted again. **I see you.**

She turned twice and then she saw him.

Oh, yes.

Reeve did not normally check luggage, because he did not normally bring anything. One change of clothing always seemed like enough, and he was already wearing shoes, and if he brought work, it was on his iPad, and how much room could a toothbrush take?

But Reeve's mother had had to yield on many points. She was not yielding on clothing. She dictated exactly what he was to have on his body for every meal and event until he and Janie left Sunday evening for Charlotte. She even ordered him to bring shoe polish. Like he owned any. He had to go out and buy shoes that even needed polish so he could fulfill that one. By the time he checked off all her instructions, he had two suitcases.

It was a small price to pay to get his mother on the wedding team.

He saw Janie twirl around, trying to spot him in the heavy crowds.

He watched her twirl a second time. Then he waved both arms.

She ran toward him and he swallowed hard, thinking of every time to come when they would run toward each other and be happy.

He flung his arms around her. Every time he let go, he had to hug her again. Every time he looked at her beautiful face, he had to kiss her again.

I'm getting married tomorrow, he thought. Wise plan.

He shook hands with Mr. Spring. He couldn't say Jonathan yet. He couldn't imagine saying Dad, either. That word applied so completely to his own father. How had Janie done it—making two men Dad?

The little siren at the luggage carousel began wailing.

Reeve and Mr. Spring and Janie were quite far away. Other passengers crowded forward, trying to see their bags.

Reeve didn't care about his bags.

He cared about Janie. She was aware only of Reeve. He liked that in a person.

Even for Janie, they had hugged enough. She wanted to get the suitcases and go. She released Reeve, straightened up, and fixed her hair. Were they at the wrong carousel or something? Why wasn't he over there grabbing his suitcases?

A dark crisp uniform inserted itself between her and Reeve. She had to take a step back. Reeve took two steps back.

It was a pilot. Glaring at Reeve. "Excuse me, sir," said the captain, his voice loud and slightly hostile.

No, thought Janie. Enough has gone wrong in my life. I don't want a glitch now.

The pilot paid no attention to her. He frowned at Reeve. "There are certain protocols in airports. They must be followed."

Oh, great. Reeve had made some stupid joke about terrorism or bombs. Not now! We can't have anything go wrong *now*! Janie was ready to yell at him, but she caught herself. She didn't want to be the kind of wife who yelled at her husband in public. The kind of wife who didn't even ask for her husband's side of the story first.

"I believe you forgot something, Mr. Shields," said the pilot sternly.

Her Reeve was a Mr. Shields. She was about to turn into somebody named Mrs. Shields. Well, assuming they didn't arrest the groom.

And suddenly there was also a flight attendant there, her cute pert features arranged in a cool stare. "We are all disappointed, Mr. Shields."

How did you disappoint a flight attendant?

"You're right," said Reeve. "I left something out."

He sank to his knees.

Janie looked down at the floor, unable to imagine what Reeve could have dropped.

The captain handed Reeve a small box.

The flight attendant handed Janie a small bouquet.

Reeve opened the box.

A diamond glittered on velvet.

Janie was laughing and crying and down on her knees too, and Reeve took the diamond ring out of the little white box and slipped it on her finger. "I will," she said. "I will marry you, I will be Mrs. Reeve Shields, I will love you in every airport."

They kissed, kneeling.

Jonathan Spring filmed it on his camera.

The pilot took Janie's arm to help her up and the flight attendant said, "We recognized him from the video. Everybody totally loves that video. And we said to Reeve, airport proposals have to have airport engagement rings."

"You bought me an engagement ring at the newsstand?" said Janie.

"No, I bought the engagement ring at a jeweler in Charlotte. My dad helped me pick it out. I was going to give it to you tonight. But these guys had a better idea."

"It was a better idea," said Janie, kissing him again. "Everything about you is a better idea, Reeve."

• • •

The Harbor was a plain brick building, undistinguished and solid. The taxi pulled into a covered drop-off area. At the far side of the building, a similar drop-off had a larger roof and wider doors. Big letters proclaimed AMBULANCES AND VANS.

Every time you drove in, you knew where you'd leave in the end.

Brian paid the driver (a lot) and went inside, pulling his own two bags on their little wheels. A woman at the desk had him sign a register and told him where the Johnsons' apartment was. "My name is Grace," she said. "We just love your sister Janie."

"Me too," said Brian. "Thanks, Grace."

Mrs. Johnson answered the door. She was beautifully dressed, as always. The lace of a white blouse showed at the cuffs of a bright pink suit, and the scarf and pin around her throat were stylish and cheerful. But under her makeup, she looked trembly and exhausted.

Brian hugged her. "Pink is your color!" he said. "I'm so glad to see you! And I love how you're doing your hair!"

She tried to beam.

The living area of the apartment was so tiny he was shocked. Bland walls held a few of Mrs. Johnson's fine paintings, but they hung in a stranded sad way. Furniture meant for a larger place crowded the floor. A folded wheelchair sat by the door. Mr. Johnson sat in a recliner of the clinical type that could pop him upward and help him to his feet.

Brian picked up Mr. Johnson's slack hand and shook it. "Hi, Mr. Johnson," he said. "It's me, Brian. Janie's little brother."

Mr. Johnson's hand tightened on Brian's. The pressure was

surprising. Mr. Johnson's expression was as intense as his grip. He did not let up the pressure but struggled to speak. The sounds were a meaningless jumble. He seemed desperate to talk.

It broke Brian's heart. "I'm listening," said Brian, pulling a footstool over and sitting on it. "Take your time. Tell me."

Mr. Johnson could not utter one clear syllable.

"I had to make a difficult decision," said Miranda, trying not to cry. "Frank is going to stay here. An aide will sleep in the room for the nights I'm gone."

"It's Janie's wedding!" protested Brian. "He has to come! Don't worry about the drive. If we need to make stops for men's rooms, and stuff, I'll handle it."

"It's not that," said Mrs. Johnson. "It's that I don't want him talking in front of everybody the way he is."

Mr. Johnson was squeezing Brian's hand on and off, as if sending messages by Morse code.

"I think it's okay if he mumbles," said Brian. "Janie wants all her parents at her wedding."

"No," said Miranda. "He thinks he's spoken to Hannah. He thinks she called him on the phone. Over and over again, he keeps calling for Hannah. I can't let him cry out to Hannah during Janie's wedding."

Brian squatted down. Now he was eye level with Mr. Johnson. "Did she call?"

Frank nodded. The grip on Brian's hand lessened, but the eyes grew more intense.

Frank Johnson was afraid.

Brian raged at Hannah with a ferocity he had thought long

gone. Trying not to let it show, he took out his cell phone and opened the photographs within it. He held one up for Mr. Johnson to see. "This is Janie in her wedding gown. Isn't she beautiful?"

With less difficulty than Brian had expected, Mr. Johnson took the phone in his good hand. "Werring."

"Right. Wedding. And you're the father of the bride. Actually, she's got a pair of fathers, and she wants them both at her wedding."

"But what if he talks about Janie's kidnapper during Janie's wedding?" cried Miranda.

"Nobody will know," said Brian brutally. "Nobody will understand what he tries to say. The good news is, Frank knows his daughter Janie is getting married to the boy next door. Frank needs to be there. Go pack Frank's bag."

Miranda Johnson went into the bedroom and began opening drawers. Brian Spring took his cell phone back. "Everything's okay, Mr. Johnson," he said. "I got your message about Hannah."

Brian went out into the hall, shut the apartment door behind him, and opened the contact list on his phone. All these years, he had kept Agent Mollison's number. Just in case, his parents used to say.

For all he knew, the man had changed his phone number years ago. Retired. Died, even. Nobody answered. Eventually a machine requested a message.

Brian identified himself. "Frank Johnson believes that his daughter, Hannah, telephoned him and he's afraid."

THE FOURTEENTH PIECE OF THE KIDNAPPER'S PUZZLE

People were so stupid and Hannah was so smart.

She headed to the nearest post office branch. Lazy customers ignored the designated parking, parked where they felt like it, blocked everybody else, left their cars running, and slouched in to get their mail.

It was a terrible world when people wouldn't follow simple basic rules that allowed everyone to get along in harmony.

Maybe the car she found would have GPS, which she had heard about but never seen. She was panting with excitement. Oh, there were so many cars to choose from! Now, *there* was a handsome car! A mysterious gray-brown, meant to vanish in a thick fog.

Its driver was fat and slow and deeply concerned with a little package. Letting his engine idle, the man waddled into the post office, face down and frowning. Hannah waited for the big glass doors to close behind him and then she slid into his seat.

The police would not bother to look for this car, because

finding one stolen car was hopeless, and because they had better things to do.

Me too, thought Hannah, giggling. I have really good things to do.

She eased into traffic, tuned the radio to a better station, and set out for Interstate 80.

Two thousand miles, more or less. A lot of hours.

But that's okay, she thought. I'm so excited. I don't need to stop for sleep or food.

Traffic was heavy but I-80 was straight. Hannah could watch stuff on her cell phone at the same time she drove. She was a very clever person and could always multitask in ways that defeated other people.

She had been driving only an hour when the car started to beep.

She checked her seat belt. Looked around to see if it was some other car beside her, honking. Checked the dashboard for the glow of warning signs.

She was practically out of gas.

The needle shivered below E.

She'd have to take the next exit and find a gas station.

Of course when you needed to get off an interstate, they didn't have an exit. They conspired against you!

She drove slower and slower, hoping to use less fuel. People honked and gave her the finger. At last she was going down an exit ramp, a stupidly long curve of concrete, leading to yet another highway, but also a whole bunch of gas stations. She made it to the first one and pulled up exactly right, the little flap of the gas tank positioned perfectly by the pump.

She was amused that she had had even the slightest worry. She didn't make errors and she had not made one this time.

If you paid cash at this gas station, you had to go inside first and give them the cash before they would turn the pump on. Nobody trusted people anymore! It was terrible.

She was sick when the cashier said how much money it would probably take to fill the tank of her big car. She was sure the man was trying to rip her off. But he turned out to be right.

A large fraction of her cash was already gone.

The moment she was back on the road, she forgot about cash. Driving so fast was so exciting. She would drive through the night. Her timing, of course, was superb. She would arrive with an hour or two to spare.

The miles flew by. Each mile lifted her pulse. The hours passed like minutes.

And soon, way too soon, the tank was empty again.

She had always been good at math. She could divide the miles she had left to drive into the money she had left to spend. She would barely make it.

Money!

It always came down to money!

How Hannah hated this society, so focused on money. As if money mattered, compared to the depth of your heart and spirit.

That parent thief wanted all of Hannah's money. Well, it wasn't going to happen!

Hannah was getting it! So there!

CHAPTER FOURTEEN

Janie had crammed a year's worth of bride activity into Friday.

The morning had begun with Jodie and Sarah-Charlotte's crazy bridal shower. Nobody had had time to buy anything, so there were no gifts; there was just discussion of what people would have bought if they'd had time. Jodie kept a careful list of each nonexistent present so Janie could write a prompt thank-you note.

Next, Janie, Sarah-Charlotte, and Jodie had sped to the motel to greet all the Shields family. "Our job, Janie, is to get you in and out in one sane piece," explained Jodie. "When people mention carloads of household hand-me-downs for you and Reeve, pretend you don't hear."

That was easy. Janie didn't hear a thing. She was deaf from the shouts and cries and laughter of this new family. So much family, multiplying, increasing, filling rooms and hearts. She could not believe how lucky she was. All these families! All hers!

But no Reeve. The day was so strange without Reeve. She

ached for him to come, to be here. All these nice people, and who cared? She wanted Reeve.

"Time to go!" Jodie shouted finally. "Janie has a plane to meet! See you at the rehearsal tonight!"

And then, the joy of another airport. The man she loved. And a diamond ring.

Now on the drive home from Kennedy, her father at the wheel, Reeve sat as close to her in the backseat as the shoulder strap of their seat belts would allow. Janie kept touching the tiny glittering stone of her engagement ring, turning it inside to hug it in her palm, and turning it back out to watch it twinkle, and turning to give Reeve another kiss.

Reeve was falling asleep.

"Daddy?" she said.

"Nice ring, huh?"

"Did you know?"

"Yup. Had to coordinate everything. Didn't know about the pilot, though. That was a nice touch. I almost fell for it myself."

"Reeve is asleep."

"Wake him up. We're at the church."

The minute she saw the church, Janie remembered music. She who loved music had not the slightest idea what, if any, music was planned for the church or the reception. She didn't want silence! Could they still get somebody? Who?

What a relief when a man walked up and announced that he was the organist and would run the rehearsal.

He gathered the wedding party at the back of the church to do a walk-through without music.

"We have three mothers," said the organist. "Ushers will stop seating guests at two p.m. At that time, the mother of the groom will be escorted to her seat by a son. Son?"

"Me," yelled Todd. "I multitask. Best man, cue card holder, and mom escort."

"Lower your voice, Todd," said Mrs. Shields. "We are in church."

"After that, one mother of the bride will be seated by a designated usher," said the organist.

"Me!" called Brian. "I seat Miranda."

How marvelous that people knew what they were doing.

"Last person seated before the ceremony is the mother of the bride, escorted by a son."

"It'll be Stephen," said Brian, "but he isn't here yet. Their plane lands around eleven."

"Brendan, you don't get to seat anybody?" whispered Janie.

"Everything's cool," he said. "I'm getting Stephen and Kathleen at the airport."

"That's tonight. I was thinking of the ceremony. I wanted you to have somebody special to escort."

Brendan grinned and shook his head. "I'm the bouncer."

"Oh, you'll be a fabulous bouncer. If the media shows up, they'll regret it," she said, hugging him. She was surprised by the emotion on his face. Weddings took it out of the most unexpected people.

"With all mothers seated," said the organist, "the ushers regroup in a room off the front of the church, which I will show you in a minute, and then the wedding march begins.

The ushers, best man, and groom enter from the right to stand in a row by the altar. Let's practice that much."

Mothers were escorted and seated. Ushers regrouped.

"Next come the bridesmaids, one by one," said the organist. "Then the maid of honor. You will line up at the opposite side of the altar from the men."

The bridesmaids argued about what order to march in. "I'm the maid of honor," said Jodie. "I'll decide. We're going by height. Lindsay, you're short, you're first. Lizzie is last. How tall is Eve, Janie? And why isn't she here?"

"Eve will be here tomorrow. She's just your average height, I think." I knew two weeks ago, thought Janie. This is why brides hold their father's arm. So they don't tip over from too much detail.

"Don't walk so quickly, Lindsay!" cried Mrs. Shields. "Lizzie, slow down. Be dignified."

Down by the altar, Reeve's brother and brother-in-law shoved and hooted as they took their places, holding up one sick and twisted cue card after another. Janie couldn't help laughing. From her spot in the front pew, Mrs. Shields snapped, "This is a church! Not a bachelor party."

The organist hustled down the aisle to arrange all the participants in their proper spots.

Father John appeared at Janie's side. He said softly, "Don't worry about a thing, Jennie. They'll be on their best behavior at the wedding. But just to be sure, I will confiscate all cue cards."

She had forgotten she was Jennie.

For a moment, in the midst of a noisy crazy crush of people who loved her, she was afraid. Who in the world was Jennie?

She almost said to Father John, "Forget it. Skip the Jennie thing. I don't even know a girl named Jennie."

"Bride!" yelled the organist.

How long had she been standing there, wondering who Jennie was? How long had her father Jonathan been grinning at her, and waiting, while her father Frank sat smiling to himself in his wheelchair?

Reeve was laughing, jumping up and down semaphore-style, signaling where she should land.

"Reeve!" said his mother. "Behave yourself!"

When the rehearsal ended, they had the rehearsal dinner. It was chaotic and crazy, like everything else. And like everything else, somebody other than Janie had planned it. Or not planned it, in Mrs. Shields's view.

Reeve was awake through the entrée and then he crashed. His brother, friends, and brother-in-law hauled him off to the hotel, where Janie hoped he would be allowed to sleep, while the girls hauled Janie back to the Springs' house, where nobody had the slightest intention of sleeping.

The slumber party lasted most of the night. Kathleen didn't even get introduced until after midnight. Somewhere around one or two, Janie fell asleep on an air mattress. She woke up to find sunlight streaming through the window. Sheets and pillows covered the floor, but she was the only person in the room. She grabbed her cell phone to check the time. It was eleven in the morning! Her wedding was only three hours away!

She should have been up at dawn!

She raced down the stairs and found all the girls in the family room in various stages of undress. "What were you going to do?" she shrieked. "Have the wedding without me?"

"Good morning, darling," said her mother, giving her a hug and a kiss. "There's plenty of time and you needed the rest."

"But Mom, I have only one wedding day, and I lost hours of it!"

"Those early hours don't count." Her mother hugged her again, and Janie was stabbed through the heart. What about her other mother? Miranda was sitting in a hotel, staring at furniture or a ruined husband, waiting in silence and sorrow.

Oh, Mom! thought Janie. Oh, my poor mother. I should be with you. Or you should be here.

But no. Her real mother was the mother of the bride.

I still don't know, thought Janie. After all this time, I still don't know who my real mother is. How can Miranda know?

Janie had a horrifying icy thought that she had not had in all these years. She and Hannah had had the same parents. That made them sisters.

No, she told herself. I will not think about Hannah today.

Jodie, hair wrapped in a towel turban, smiled at her. "Don't worry, Janie. Everything's falling into place. Go shower and then we'll get your hair done."

"We're going to a salon?"

"No, the salon came here. Lizzie and Lindsay have already had their hair done. Sarah-Charlotte is next. We don't know what to do about Eve. She hasn't called and isn't here."

Janie could not worry about Eve, who would do the best she could. Janie asked the only really important thing. "Has Reeve called?"

"A hundred times. He's already dressed and ready to go to the church and his brother is tying him to a chair because they can't leave for two and a half hours."

Janie lifted her cell phone.

Everybody gave Janie a threatening look. "You can't talk to him!" yelled Jodie. "The bride doesn't talk to the groom or see him on her wedding day until she starts down the aisle!"

"Oh," she said. "Then I'll take my shower and get in line for hair." She ran back upstairs and texted Reeve instead.

Hi. You ready?

Beyond ready. You?

Beyond ready too.

At one o'clock, Brendan and Brian went to get Mr. and Mrs. Johnson at the hotel where they were staying.

Brendan was surprised to see Nicole's cousin Vic hanging out with the Johnsons, laughing and telling stories. He had known Vic slightly when Vic was a tough teenager who wore grunge clothes. He'd seen Vic a few times in his army uniform and later his police uniform. He had certainly never seen Vic in a suit and tie. "Hey, Vic. What are you doing here?"

"Just pitching in. Your mom called for reinforcements

from every corner of New Jersey to achieve wedding perfection in ten days."

Brendan and Brian had just been killing time, trying to avoid or admire a bevy of half-dressed girls who had taken over the house. How come Mom hadn't asked them to pitch in? Especially Brian, who loved Frank and Miranda? "You coming to the wedding, Vic?" asked Brendan.

"Yup. You got room for me in the car?"

"It'll be tight," said Brendan. Why was Vic, as remote an acquaintance as the family had, invited to the wedding? He and Brian tucked Mrs. Johnson in front, got Mr. Johnson into the van, and then the wheelchair, and Brian and Vic wedged themselves in back while Brendan drove.

At the church, Brian took charge of Frank, handling him as well as any medic, keeping the extra parents of the bride happy.

Brendan said to Vic, "And? You're here because?"

"Everything kind of moved up a level last night," said Vic. "A few days ago, a woman in Boulder, Colorado, gets knifed several times. At the hospital, she keeps losing consciousness. She finally tells a cop that a woman she knew as Jill Williams stabbed her, but that Jill Williams's real name is Hannah Javensen. The cop has never heard of Hannah Javensen and doesn't react. The police go to the address of the Jill Williams person. Place isn't rented in that name and nobody's home. They get fingerprints, though, and catch on to the big picture. But Hannah Javensen doesn't come back to her apartment. They get into the apartment. Last thing the Javensen woman does on her computer is print out a map to this church. They figure Hannah Javensen, now wanted for attempted murder as well as kidnapping, is on her way here."

At one-twenty, at the Springs' house, everybody piled into cars, vans, and limousines. Everybody was on the phone. Everybody who wasn't coming—and everybody who was— wanted constant updates and videos and photographs. Friends all over the country were texting.

The second limousine held Janie, Jodie, Sarah-Charlotte, and Lizzie. It was just leaving the driveway when a little red car came skidding in, and Eve leapt out. "Bad traffic!" she yelled.

"I've got your dress!" yelled Jodie. "Just get in the limo with us!"

"I'm wearing shorts!" yelled Eve. "I need to clean up. I need makeup. I need a hairdresser. I want my nails done."

"This is what happens when you have a wedding without a plan," said Lizzie severely.

"No," said Eve, scrunching in. "This is what happens when you have the wedding in New Jersey and there's an accident on the turnpike. Hi, Jane. Happy wedding day, you beautiful bride you. Whoa, this is a big vehicle. There's enough room in this thing for me to use it as a dressing room. Hi, Jodie."

"Peel off the shirt, Eve. I've got wipeys, you can scrub yourself one square at a time."

"Makeup?" asked Eve.

"Makeup," agreed Sarah-Charlotte, waving an Estée Lauder bag.

"Shoes?" asked Eve.

"You were supposed to bring your own!"

"I was teasing. I have my shoes. We're all wearing white satin slippers, right?"

One bride, one maid of honor, and two bridesmaids stuck out their feet.

White satin slippers.

Jennie, Janie said to herself. My name is Jennie. I, Jennie, take thee, Reeve.

Brendan and Vic stood on the grass between the church and the parking lot.

A stream of wedding guests stopped to tell Brendan how terrific he looked in his tuxedo.

"Thanks," he repeated over and over. "Great to see you. Welcome." To Vic he said, "Who else knows?"

"Your father and Father John. Plenty of police here. They are extra guests, parking lot attendants, and even a priest."

Brendan had never thought of his sister's kidnapping as a violent crime. No blood had been spilled. There had not even been a bruise. But of course kidnapping was violent. A kidnapper was a raptor, a predator.

"Is it in the news yet?"

"No, but reporters in Boulder will figure it out soon."

"My sister, my mother, and Miranda Johnson need to have this wedding. It has to be safe and happy. It can't have Hannah in it. It can't have arrests and chases and guns and media."

Vic nodded. "We'll prevent that part. As for people finding out and spreading the news, see Father John greeting everybody at the door? He's requiring everybody to turn their cells off the minute they step inside the church. People are a little irked, especially the ones who wanted to take photos and videos, but he's a priest and they're doing it. So far, anyway. If people turn on their cells later, it'll probably be for photos. The wedding should be okay. Reception, maybe not."

Todd opened the limousine door and helped Janie out. Sarah-Charlotte fluffed Janie's skirt and Jodie adjusted Janie's tulle and Eve said, "Don't get grass stains on your slippers!"

"Is Reeve here yet?" Janie asked Todd.

"You kidding me? We got here before the priest. You have the most eager groom in history. Me—I was scared to come to my wedding. I cut it pretty fine." He grinned at Lindsay and tenderly helped his wife out of the limo, and Janie suddenly realized that although Lindsay had gained weight, it wasn't fat. Lindsay and Todd were going to have a baby.

Life was so wonderful.

Janie was beyond happy.

Next, Lizzie's husband, whom Janie barely knew, helped her out. Marriage to Lizzie would be demanding. Janie wondered if marriage to *her* would be demanding. She thought of herself as so reasonable and pleasant. But she hadn't been easy for the Springs. And she had abandoned her mother, her other mother, for the whole weekend.

A wide portico with slender columns marked the front entrance to the church. On either side were fat holly bushes, green and prickly, rimmed with hundreds of daylilies in buttery yellow. Sarah-Charlotte gathered the bridal party and photographed them against the green and gold.

The vans from Connecticut had been here for hours. The guys were mostly hanging out with Reeve in some back room in the church. The girls stood on the portico with Janie and Sarah-Charlotte, introducing themselves to the other bridesmaids. Everybody talked as if they'd known each other for years.

The ushers were seating the ladies while the husbands walked slowly in their wake. The ushers weren't bothering with groom's side or bride's side. They were just packing them in. There was going to be a serious crowd.

There were ushers Janie didn't even know! It struck her as wildly funny.

And then she did know one of them.

Agent Mollison.

Whom she had seen once, when she was fifteen; when she was first reunited with her family. From whom Janie had hidden her face. And then her dad had thrown him out.

She had known from the moment Reeve put everything on Facebook that there was risk. She had never displayed herself anywhere; never gave the girl named Janie Johnson a stage or a page. The sense of her kidnapper hovering in the wings, waiting for another chance to enter Janie's life, had never entirely left Janie. Reeve and Adair and Sarah-Charlotte and all the others exhibited their hundreds of friends and photographs and posts, but not Janie. She saw that as a threat, a door to her past creaking open, beckoning to Hannah.

Apparently, the FBI agreed.

Father John had not managed to confiscate every cue card. Todd was waving his sign around. It was white poster board, with scalloped edges. It must have been Lindsay's creation, because Todd wouldn't know a decorative edge if it cut him. In fat bright blue marker, it said J E N N I E.

Sarah-Charlotte poked the bride. "Janie Johnson, aka Jennie Spring, will exist for eleven more minutes."

She meant eleven more minutes until she had another name.

But it sounded as if Janie had eleven more minutes to live.

CHAPTER FIFTEEN

Kathleen had expected to be the outsider among the bridesmaids. But they drew her in, and made sure she was part of
everything. She didn't want to break away, it was such fun,
but she said softly to Stephen, "I should be seated before the
mothers, because they're always last. Do you want to take me
to my pew?"

He held out his elbow.

She took it.

The formal gesture and the stately pace brought her close
to weeping.

She genuflected before she slid into her pew, lowered the
kneeler, and sank down.

Take care of Janie and Reeve, she prayed. Take care of all
this family. Bring them joy instead of sorrow. And if You have
extra time, make Stephen realize that I would be a fine member of the same family.

She tilted the kneeler under the pew and sat back.

I'm not going to end up going to church again, she told

herself. I'm done with all that. It's just that weddings are sentimental. I got carried away.

The bridesmaids lined up.

Jodie had chosen their gowns well. They all looked lovely in the short crisp blue dresses, everyone pencil-thin except Lindsay. The cut of that dress would make its own announcement. Janie hoped Mrs. Shields would be thrilled when she saw Lindsay, so thrilled that she would transfer her energy from Reeve and Janie to being a grandmother.

The florist passed out bouquets. Hers was beautiful. Just what Janie would have chosen if she had chosen.

"Zhany," said her father.

She knelt beside Frank. "Daddy, you look so handsome in your tuxedo and your sky-blue tie. You're a perfect father of the bride."

"I uv you," he said.

She dried her eyes on his tie, leaving little mascara tracks in the blue silk.

Her cell phone rang.

"Turn that off!" said Jodie, laughing. "I'm the maid of honor, and I say no more phones!"

"It isn't bride and groom anymore," observed her New Jersey dad. "It's bride and phone." He looked fabulous in black and white. Janie thought of the wonderful photos they would have.

The phone call was from the Harbor. Why would they call? Her parents were here.

"We should have put a teeny little cell phone in the hands of the little sugar couple on top of the cake," said Lizzie.

"Hello?" said Janie into the phone.

"Janie?" It was Grace. The front-desk lady. Janie was touched that Grace would call to give best wishes on her wedding day.

The wedding march began.

Lindsay was shortest and first. "I'm off!" she whispered, giggling. "See you down there!"

"Janie," said Grace urgently, "a woman just arrived who says she is Frank's daughter."

Frank's daughter, thought Janie Johnson. Her body seemed to lose shape. She became remarkably solid.

"She knew where their room was and everything, so I let her go up, but I'm sort of frightened. I didn't know Frank and Miranda had a child from a previous marriage or whatever. She's certainly never visited before. And since your wedding's been all over Facebook and since thieves can be so clever, I thought I'd check."

Eve followed Lindsay down the aisle.

"Janie!" whispered Jodie. "Get off the phone!"

Janie pasted a smile on her face and waved Jodie away.

"A minute ago she wanted to fly down the aisle," said Sarah-Charlotte to Jodie. "Now she wants to stay on the phone."

"Can't be Reeve," said Lizzie. "Todd confiscated his cell."

"Janie, I took her picture on my cell," said Grace. "I'll send it to you."

Jodie tried to exchange Janie's phone for the bridal bouquet. Janie held up one finger to mean "Hang on a minute."

"Give me a break," said Jodie. "And give me the phone. You can have your bouquet in exchange."

Her New Jersey dad was laughing silently. All his kids were

deeply attached to their cell phones, but he hadn't known it went this far. He maneuvered the wheelchair closer to the door and now his back was to Janie.

"Jodie," breathed the bride, "make them walk very slowly down the aisle. I need time." She backed up as far as she could without falling into the shrubbery.

The photograph from Grace showed a fat seedy-looking woman with lanky hair, which was dyed as yellow as a daffodil. The woman's posture was tilted forward, as if she were catapulting away from the reception desk. Away from anything normal.

Away from us, thought Janie, which is good. Everybody I love is safe, here, in another place. Whatever Hannah is doing, she is doing it alone in an empty space.

Her soul flooded with grief for Miranda. What she was going to have to face! The person she would have to see! The past hurtling into the present, about to slap her down!

Mom, I love you, thought Janie. I'm going to do it right this time, but it won't make anything right for you.

Lizzie held up two hands in a sharp, irritated "What in the world?" gesture.

"Walk slow, Lizzie," Janie stage-whispered. She cupped her hand over her mouth. "Call nine-one-one, Grace. The woman is known to me. She is a criminal. Her name is Hannah Javensen. If there is a way for maintenance to lock her in the room until the police get there, do it. Whatever you do, don't get near her. She is dangerous."

Jodie was about to take preemptive action and snatch the phone.

"Ten more seconds," Janie told her. "Sarah-Charlotte, go!"

Her New Jersey father said over his shoulder, "Come on, Janie. It won't be any fun without you!"

Janie walked over to the usher she was not supposed to know. "Grace," she said into her phone, "this is a policeman. Tell him what's going on." She handed her cell with its photograph of Hannah Javensen to Agent Mollison.

Jodie gasped. She couldn't see the phone, but she had recognized Mollison.

Janie said softly to the agent, "When the wedding is over, I want a signal. You got her or you didn't."

"Done."

"What's happening?" demanded Jodie. "What's wrong?"

"Everything's all right for a change. You know what, Jodie? I love you." Janie hugged her sister fiercely. The cheap fabric of the old wedding gown made crispy sounds.

The maid of honor fastened the bride's hands around the thick gathered stems of the bridal bouquet. There was a big gap between Sarah-Charlotte and Jodie, but nobody noticed. They didn't mind waiting for the bride who couldn't wait to get married.

The bride knelt beside the wheelchair. "Daddy, remember how we practiced? It's time."

Her real father offered his arm.

Very softly, so her sitting-down father couldn't hear, Janie said to Jonathan Spring, "You are the best father of the bride in the whole world."

She could hardly wait to see Reeve, who would be the best groom in the whole world—so handsome that the boys and men around him would look like cardboard cutouts.

Here comes the bride, said the music.

The entire congregation was standing. Flashes went off. Phones came back on and photos and videos were taken.

Janie couldn't see Reeve yet, because Jodie was still in the aisle, blocking the view, but she saw her Connecticut mother next to Reeve's mother on one side of the aisle, and Donna on the other side. There was a space next to Donna for Jonathan.

Because I will stand alone with Reeve, she thought. But that's the thing about Reeve. Once I'm with him, I won't stand alone.

Jodie turned to the side, taking her place at the front of the line of bridesmaids, and now Janie could see Reeve. He was grinning, the way only Reeve could grin, his entire face split apart.

Now she knew why people wept at weddings.

It was hope.

Let the future be bright. Let catastrophe and pain stay away. Let this bride and this groom love and be joyful.

The wheelchair rolled smoothly. Frank waved to the people he knew, which broke Janie's heart.

But there was one person in this church who might never feel joy again, who had no hope and no future. Miranda.

Lord, help me help her, Janie prayed. I'm the pitcher in the final inning. I have to make the save.

The high ceilings and the gilt paint and the beautiful altar seemed to lean toward her and Janie knew how to save her mother.

I'll move my parents to North Carolina. There's no reason

for Frank and Miranda to be at the Harbor. Day after tomorrow, I'll be in Charlotte, Reeve will be headed out of town, and instead of shopping, I'll find an assisted living facility. Daddy won't know where he lives. And Mom can start a new life.

We all need a new life.

My new life will be as Jennie Shields.

In Connecticut, sirens were screaming and police cars converging.

In New Jersey, Father John asked who gave this woman to be married to this man. Jonathan Spring said, "We do. Her fathers and mothers. All four of us."

The congregation sobbed audibly.

Janie kissed her real father's cheek before he sat down. Think again, Daddy, she said silently. You're not giving *me* away. I've found my families at last and I'm keeping them.

She gave Reeve her best smile.

It's over, she thought. Hannah is a predator, but the leopard does not always catch its prey.

It was time for the vows.

Reeve Shields looked at the face of his beautiful bride and really and truly couldn't remember her name. It wasn't Janie anymore. What was it?

Father John had rounded up every last cue card. Reeve cast a desperate look at his brother, who extended the back of his hand. Written in black marker was the word *Jennie*.

"I, Reeve . . . ," he said, so emotional he made no sound. He had to start over with more air in his chest. "I, Reeve, take thee, Jennie, to be my wedded wife."

In Connecticut, the police entered Frank and Miranda's apartment. The woman had emptied every drawer, turned over every chest, and flung open the door of every cabinet. The floor was covered with papers and books and broken dishes. "I'm busy," she said sharply, emptying a file. "I'm a writer. I'm getting material. And they owe me money anyway. Everything here is mine. It's always been mine. That girl stole it."

In New Jersey, Father John said, "Heavenly Father, we ask your blessing upon all four of Jennie's parents. Upon Donna and Jonathan, who gave Jennie life and suffered her loss. Upon Miranda and Frank, who brought Jennie up and also suffered her loss. We ask your blessing on all parents everywhere, and upon this new family, the family of Jennie and Reeve Shields." He laid his hands on their heads. "I pronounce you husband and wife."

The younger guests leapt to their feet, applauding, whistling, laughing, and stomping.

Jodie handed the bridal bouquet back to Janie. When Janie wrapped her fingers around the flowers, she felt the two rings on her finger, the diamond from the airport and the gold circle from the vows they had just taken.

Reeve kissed her again. They turned away from the altar to walk back down the aisle and into their new lives.

The organ was playing an exit march, but it could barely be heard. The friends and family of the new Mr. and Mrs. Reeve Shields were making too much racket.

Donna Spring thought the shouting was the most beautiful music she had ever heard: the music of rejoicing. We passed through horror, she thought, and came out fine. My beautiful daughter has done all the right things. Well, except for dropping out of college. Now I'll pressure her to go back. But I'll wait a week.

Reeve wanted to run out of the church. He wanted to run several miles, he had so much energy. He could have run carrying Janie in his arms. But his bride stopped after two steps, knelt beside her father's wheelchair, and kissed Frank. "Hey, Daddy. I'm a bride!"

"Boo-ful," whispered Frank.

Janie kissed her other three parents and then she kissed Reeve's parents.

Reeve grinned at his dad. He flung an arm around his mother. "Thanks, Mom. Thanks for coming through for me."

The bride and groom moved slowly down the aisle. Their friends had gone to so few weddings they didn't know the usual rule: you wait in your pew until the bride and groom are out of the church. They were leaping forward to hug and take photos; barging around yelling for confetti.

• • •

When at last Janie and Reeve got out on the portico, Agent Mollison was standing to the side. Janie had forgotten him. She had forgotten Hannah. He made a gesture, as if slamming a door and turning a key. But Janie had already done that.

Janie and Reeve were covered in a cloud of rose petals flung by giggling friends.

Reeve tugged her down the steps onto the grass and Janie almost lost hold of her bouquet. Already the fragile roses were starting to fade.

I am no fragile flower, she thought. In fact, if I were a flower, I'd be a tough old dandelion. You can cut me down over and over, but I had four strong parents and I have strong roots. I'll flower again.

"Throw the bouquet!" yelled somebody.

Even the girls who planned never to do anything traditional in their lives raced up, hoping to catch the bouquet. Janie knew who wanted it most.

She flung it to Kathleen.

"Mrs. Shields," said Reeve to his bride, "they want us to pose for a formal photograph."

"That's no surprise. Mrs. Shields is very photogenic," said Janie.

"You bet. Mr. Shields isn't too bad either."

"Mr. Shields is drop-dead gorgeous," said his wife.

And they kissed one more time, the cameras clicked, and Janie Johnson vanished for good.

AUTHOR'S NOTE

Five books about Janie and Reeve! No one is more astonished than I am.

Over twenty years ago, when I was in LaGuardia Airport, I found a concourse plastered with a homemade missing-child poster. Under the photograph of a toddler was a caption stating that she had been missing for fifteen years.

All I could think of was her parents. That mother and father got up that morning with their stack of homemade posters and their roll of Scotch tape and drove to LaGuardia, still hoping, after fifteen years, that as tens of thousands of people passed through this airport, one of them would recognize the photograph and tell the parents where their little girl is now.

But nobody can recognize a kid fifteen years later from a picture of her at age three. I boarded my plane weeping for those parents—and then I thought, Actually, there is one person who might recognize that photo. The little girl herself. What a great idea for a book: You recognize yourself on a missing-child poster.

I knew right away that this little girl would have grown into a terrific teenager who has a good family, whom she loves. When she recognizes herself in a missing-child photo, what should she do? If she tells anybody what she suspects— that her parents are her kidnappers—her family will be destroyed by the courts and the media. She loves her family. She cannot let that happen. But what about that other family, still out there worrying? What does a good person do when there is no good choice?

The Face on the Milk Carton is a book about worry, and I wanted my readers to go on worrying even after they finished the book, just like that real family who put up posters at LaGuardia. So the ending of this book is not tidy.

My readers wrote a lot of letters, wanting to know what happened to Janie. But I had no plans for a sequel, because such a book would resolve Janie's situation, and then my readers could stop worrying.

I was a church organist at the time, and our minister gave a sermon one Sunday about the story of King Solomon. Two women face the king, each claiming to be the mother of the same child. "Oh, just slice the kid in half," says Solomon. Immediately it is clear which woman is the real mother: the one who says, "No, no, I don't want the baby hurt. Let her have the baby."

I knew that was the sequel to *The Face on the Milk Carton*. Who is the real mother? The one who brought Janie up? Or the one who gave birth to her?

This second book had to be called *Whatever Happened to Janie?* because that was the question my readers asked.

I was never going to write a third book about Janie. But in the first two books, an adorable boy, Reeve, lived next door. (You should always have a handsome boy live next door.) Reeve was perfect, because if you're going to have a boy in story, he ought to be perfect.

At that time, my son was in college—he attended for about a minute, but it was enough time for me to get a book out of it. Because my son worked at his college radio station, I decided that Reeve, too, would work at his college radio station, where he dreams of being a brilliant talk show host. But what should he talk about? He decides on the long-fascinating story of Janie, the girl next door. He sells her, and her two families, and their tragedy, night after night, on the air.

There's another character in these books: the kidnapper, Hannah, who is the biological daughter of Mr. and Mrs. Johnson, the couple who then brought Janie up. But Hannah has vanished. Among the many listeners who call in to Reeve's talk show is somebody who just might be Hannah. If Reeve has drawn Hannah out of hiding, there may be a trial, and a kidnapper brought to justice, but Janie will have to relive her nightmare in a media circus.

That became *The Voice on the Radio*.

I knew I would never write another book about Janie and Reeve.

But my readers loved Reeve. He used to be perfect, they wrote, and you have to write a fourth book in which Reeve is perfect again. Furthermore, Reeve and Janie should get married. Most of all, they stressed, the kidnapper should be caught and punished. My editor, Beverly Horowitz, and I often talk of future books, tossing ideas back and forth. Beverly called with what I think of as a postcard idea: a snapshot from the midst of some not-yet-written story. "I see a parent and a teenage child in an attic," she said. "One of them has found something in a box or a trunk. I don't know what it is. But if it is revealed to the other one, their lives will be irrovocably and tragically changed."

Immediately I said, "It's Janie and her kidnap mother, Miranda. Janie has stumbled on old family files. She discovers that her father Frank has always known where their kidnapper daughter, Hannah, is and in fact, he's been sending her support checks all these years." That idea became *What Janie Found.*

I loved writing these books. In spite of the darkness of the central theme—kidnapping—the Janie books provided a lot of fun. I sponsored my son-in-law's race car, and we reproduced the cover of *The Face on the Milk Carton* on the hood of his car. As far as we knew, we had the only book race car out there. One evening, *The Face on the Milk Carton* was a question on *Jeopardy!* That book also became a TV movie starring Kellie Martin. For my movie party, so I would have favors to give out, a middle school in Indiana made dozens of pretend missing-children half-pint milk cartons, using their own school pictures. For Halloween, I used to wear a big puffy milk carton over my head, with a cut-out so that I was the face.

Twenty years after I wrote *The Face on the Milk Carton,* Beverly asked me to write an e-original short story about Janie and Reeve. "Janie has been in high school in all four books," she said. "Reeve has been in college since the second book. But make them adults. I think millions of your fans want to know what happened to them. And it has to be a thriller, as well." What a great idea!

I hurled myself at every character mentioned in all four books. I wrote little tiny stories about what each one would be doing. It was time, I realized, to give my readers the two things they wanted: a wedding and a capture.

I called Beverly. "How about I write a fifth book instead of a short story?"

So now we have both the fifth book—*Janie Face to Face*—and the e-original short story—*What Janie Saw.*

There are still missing-child posters and I still weep for heartbroken parents. But in the Janie books, love and integrity save two families and create a new one. I thank all my readers who fell in love with this story and gave me the privilege of following Janie and Reeve into their new lives.

caroline b. cooney

is the author of the following books for young people: *The Lost Songs; Three Black Swans; They Never Came Back; If the Witness Lied; Diamonds in the Shadow; A Friend at Midnight; Hit the Road; Code Orange; The Girl Who Invented Romance; Family Reunion; Goddess of Yesterday* (an ALA-ALSC Notable Children's Book); *The Ransom of Mercy Carter; Tune In Anytime; Burning Up; The Face on the Milk Carton* (an IRA-CBC Children's Choice) and its companions, *Whatever Happened to Janie?* and *The Voice on the Radio* (each of them an ALA-YALSA Best Book for Young Adults), as well as *What Janie Found, What Janie Saw,* an ebook original short story, and *Janie Face to Face; What Child Is This?* (an ALA-YALSA Best Book for Young Adults); *Driver's Ed* (an ALA-YALSA Best Book for Young Adults and a *Booklist* Editors' Choice); *Among Friends; Twenty Pageants Later;* and the Time Travel Quartet: *Both Sides of Time, Out of Time, Prisoner of Time,* and *For All Time,* which are also available as *The Time Travelers,* Volumes I and II.

Caroline B. Cooney lives in South Carolina.

JANIE JOHNSON has received unwanted attention eve
since she recognized her three-year-old self in a picture on the
back of a milk carton and learned that she was the victim of a
kidnapping. Now she's headed for college to make a fresh start.

Janie's kidnapper has been in hiding all these years and is
just as desperate to become a new person—and more deter
mined than ever to seek revenge.

Will Janie and those closest to her be devastated just as the
might be healing?

You'll want to read more about Janie....

THE FACE ON THE
MILK CARTON

caroline b. cooney

WHATEVER
HAPPENED
TO JANIE?

caroline b. cooney

THE VOICE ON
THE RADIO

caroline b. cooney

WHAT JANIE FOUND

caroline b. cooney

US $7.99 / $8.99 CAN

ISBN 978-0-385-74207-8

5 0 7 9 9

9 780385 742078

randomhouse.com/teens
Also available as an ebook

EMBER

Cover photographs © 2013 by IZO/Shutterstock (frame)
and Giorgio Fochesato/Getty Images (figures)
Cover design by Christian Fuenfhausen